Shadow felt himself waver,

felt some of the anger drain from his face when he certainly couldn't afford the weakness. He was sick of it, he thought suddenly. Sick of playing the role of the cruel, heartless villain. Sick of scaring the proud and beautiful woman in front of him when all he really wanted to do was hold her. He wanted to know if her skin really was that soft, if her hair really did feel like satin. He wanted to taste her lips, to feel her arms around him.

After a year and a half, he wanted to hold someone who was good and warm and wonderful. Someone like her.

And just for a moment, her eyes did meet his. Just for a moment the fear left her eyes and he saw a glimpse of something else....

"Don't," he said, his voice sounding thick even to his own ears. "Don't forget who I am."

Dear Reader,

What a great lineup of books we have to start off your New Year. Take our American Hero, for instance. In *Cuts Both Ways,* award-winning writer Dee Holmes has created one of the most irresistible heroes you'll ever meet. Ashe Seager is a professional tracker, but the case Erin Kenyon brings to him is one he'd rather not take. Solving it will mean solving the mysteries of his own heart, and of his feelings for this woman who has haunted his memory for years.

Our Romantic Traditions miniseries continues with *Finally a Father,* by Marilyn Pappano. This is a terrific "secret baby" book! The rest of the month is equally fabulous, with new offerings from Naomi Horton (who can resist a book called *Born To Be Bad*?), Barbara Faith, Sandy Steen and Alicia Scott. You'll want to spend every evening curled up on the couch with the heroes and heroines who populate our pages this month, and I can't blame you.

So ring in the New Year the romantic way, and then make a resolution to come back next month for another taste of romance—only from Silhouette Intimate Moments.

Enjoy!

Leslie J. Wainger
Senior Editor and Editorial Coordinator

Please address questions and book requests to:
Reader Service
U.S.: P.O. Box 1325, Buffalo, NY 14269
Canadian: P.O. Box 1050, Niagara Falls, Ont. L2E 7G7

SHADOW'S FLAME

Alicia Scott

Published by Silhouette Books
America's Publisher of Contemporary Romance

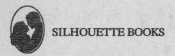 SILHOUETTE BOOKS

ISBN 0-373-07546-4

SHADOW'S FLAME

Copyright © 1994 by Lisa Baumgartner

Printed in U.S.A.

Books by Alicia Scott

Silhouette Intimate Moments

Walking After Midnight #466
Shadow's Flame #546

ALICIA SCOTT

is thrilled that her dream of being published has finally come true. Born in Hawaii, but a native of Oregon, she is now living in Philadelphia and studying at the University of Pennsylvania.

Majoring in International Relations, she has a deep appreciation for different peoples and cultures. And while reading and writing romances is one of her favorite hobbies, she also enjoys traveling and just talking to people—so much so that in her junior year of high school she entered a contest for impromptu speaking and won eighth in the nation!

She's been to exotic locales such as Venezuela, Ecuador and Mexico, and intends on using them all in future books. Alicia brings her natural enthusiam for life to her stories, and believes that the power of love can conquer *anything* as long as one's faith is strong enough.

To my wonderful editor, Mary Osorio, for having the patience and vision to help turn seeds into fruit and buds into blossoms. The effort is greatly appreciated and always welcome.

Special thanks to my uncle and favorite pilot, Gary Holmes, whose expertise and consultation enabled Riley to fly. Thank you very much for all your help.

And, as always, this book is dedicated to my terrific family. I love you all.

Prologue

Dusk settled swift and thick through the old airstrip. Deserted metal buildings loomed dark against the distant mountains while the small, twin-engine planes housed within them sat silent and still.

Until the woman came.

She had brilliant red hair that glowed even in the shadowy dusk, and her eyes were a vivid green that scanned each plane with expert care. She moved with the lean grace of a wildcat down the rows of machines, each step sure and true.

She noted the rust and disuse on the elderly planes. She noted the missing bolts and flat tires. But she didn't give up looking. She'd come much too far for that. With a last critical sweep of her gaze to the metal vehicles, she turned to the owner.

"This one," she told the man who had been following her wordlessly. Having found a plane, at last, that suited her needs, she walked a little straighter, feeling the weight of uncertainty lift from her shoulders. It was all coming together now. It was really about to happen.

Relief and excitement overwhelmed her and she shot the man beside her a dazzling smile. Whatever words he'd been about to say died a dazed death in his throat under the onslaught.

Ahh, the woman was beautiful.

She was smarter, too, than he'd originally thought. These Americans all seemed crazy to him in one way or another. And this woman, who was so extraordinarily beautiful and young—by American standards anyway—hadn't seemed any saner. Why, only a crazy woman would want to rent one of his ancient planes and fly out into the jungle. But she seemed to know a fair amount about his seven 1963 Beachcraft Barons. While once the planes had been shiny and new, glowing a pure white with red and blue detail stripes, the last few years had been far from kind. Glistening hulls were now dark with rust, and he wasn't sure if they would even start. But the woman had looked them over well, and the one she'd selected would have been his choice, too.

She was young, but she obviously knew a thing or two. She supervised the pumping of the gas tank herself, legs apart, hands tucked in the pockets of her leather flight jacket. Once again her green eyes were riveting as she watched him replace the old fluids with the blue-colored aviation fuel.

She didn't speak much, which rather surprised him, for her cheeks were high with color, her dazzling eyes sparkling with barely contained excitement. The old man was used to Americans who went on and on and on until a man could barely think straight. But she kept her thoughts to herself, even as they struggled to burst out.

He found he liked her, but waved the thought from his mind as soon as it appeared. Because the woman didn't have to speak for him to know her secrets. He'd seen her map; he knew where she was going. And there was only one reason any person would head for those coordinates.

He shook his head against the lunacy of it all. It was a shame. Such a beautiful woman, too. She might seem smart, he decided, changing his mind the more he thought about it, but only a fool would head where she was going. Only a fool.

When all the preparations were completed, she climbed into the pilot's seat, confidently checking the dials and switches and spreading out her navigational charts in the right-hand seat next to her. As he watched with expressionless eyes, she familiarized herself with the control panel, tested out the throttle. Then, with a few low words and encouraging whispers, she had the coughing engine reluctantly sputtering to life.

She smiled again, that dazzling smile that seemed to light up the entire night. With quick and expedient movements, she then handed him his payment—in cash—from her duffel bag. Thanking him for his help, she went through the last of the pretakeoff procedures and, the moment he stepped back, headed the wavering plane straight for the runway.

He watched until the very end, for perhaps the plane would be unable to take off. But, with a bit of bumping and bouncing, it at last headed up into the dusky sky.

Alone now in the deserted airfield, he felt a twinge of pride for his plane, which, after five years of disuse, could still fly. And because, even now, he could still smell the light whip of the woman's fragrance in the wind, see the wonderful brilliance of her smile.

He shrugged to himself and went back into one of the hangars. There he picked up the CB and performed the call he knew he had to make. These were not the kinds of things a man liked to do, but these were the times in which he lived.

Riley McDouglas was still smiling as the courageous plane took off, climbing at one-hundred-forty miles per hour. She could hardly believe she'd actually done this, could barely believe that it was all really happening. She could feel her stomach dip and sway as her emotions fluctuated from gleeful exhilaration to pounding dread. But she kept the fear away for now, concentrating instead on flying the plane to her destination.

Only five years ago, she'd been graduating from college with a degree in journalism and a head full of grand intentions. Journalism had been her life—give her a pen and she could do anything. Her parents had never understood it. She'd been raised in a small town in Ohio, and women's lib had definitely passed her mother by. Mrs. McDouglas just wanted her daughter to marry a nice young man—like Mark Stevenson, for instance—and settle down to a nice domestic life. At first she'd considered Riley's "writing thing" a phase. Then, when it had become apparent her daughter wanted to pursue it further, she'd aired concerns. And when, just three years ago, Riley had announced she was breaking off her four-year relationship with that "nice young man" Mark Stevenson and moving to New York, Mrs. McDouglas had collapsed in tears.

It had been hard for Riley. She didn't want to hurt her parents, and more than anything in the world she would have liked to hear them say, just once, "Yes, dear, we understand. And we're proud of you." But over the years she'd come to realize that those were words she would probably never hear. And though that didn't quite stop her from working harder and demanding more from herself—in the faint hope that perhaps one day they *would* say the words—she made do the best she could.

All her life she'd been in love with writing. All her life she'd longed to see the world outside of Ohio. She wanted to travel, she wanted to explore, she wanted to do things. She'd been restless from the day she was born, searching, never quite finding. She loved her parents, and Mark Stevenson *had* been a nice young man, but somehow she needed more.

She just wasn't sure what that was yet.

But she'd gone to New York and, through a bit of luck and lots of persistence, had landed herself a job at the *New York Daily*. Well, so what if she'd been hired as a mail clerk? It had been a foot in the door, at least. It had allowed her to get to know the staff, and it had eventually paid off. She'd submitted enough writing samples and story ideas to the local news editor that he'd finally allowed her to write a small news brief. That had led to additional news briefs, and then, just one year ago, she'd been officially promoted to an entry-level field reporter. She'd also been assigned some small travel pieces, since her writing, she was told, had a lively flare.

The work wasn't glamorous, though, and it was only remotely exciting. It merely whetted her appetite, leaving her hungry for bigger and better things. There were so many great stories out there, people and events just waiting to be found. And she could do it, she was sure of it. She could make a difference.

Then had come the opportunity she'd been waiting for—her first overseas assignment. It was a small travel piece really, kind of a descriptive historical piece on Myanmar, or, as the state was more commonly called by the Western world, Burma.

Originally she was just supposed to land in Thailand, get to Myanmar and look around, take a few tours, interview a few locals for color. And things had begun normally enough. She'd hired a young boy to act as an interpreter for her and gone around to different bazaars, taking pictures, interviewing. By and by, a week had passed and her young interpreter, Khun, had gradually begun to relax around her. One day it had rained, and they had huddled together under a tarp for shelter. To pass the time, she'd asked *him* questions for a change. Simple things. About his family, about Buddhism. Then talk had drifted more to the general history and politics of the turbulent country, and she'd been amazed to discover that Khun had first-hand experiences with some of the events.

There had been other days, he told her, days when he'd been very young and General Saw Maung had cracked down in Rangoon. The streets had been filled with gunfire then, and the soldiers had come to his house with olive uniforms and big guns. They'd pushed his mother down, demanding answers. It wasn't until he was much older that Khun understood the soldiers had been looking for his brother.

But his brother had escaped, Khun told her. Gone back to the hills to enlist with Ko Tan and fight there.

At first Riley had just nodded at the words, captivated by his experiences. She'd researched the volatile history of the country before coming and knew of its violent past, including General Saw Maung's crackdown in 1980. And of course she'd read about Ko Tan. Already the man's reputation was infamous. While he maintained a guerrilla army of over five thousand men supposedly fighting for the independence of the Shan state of Myanmar, his major fund-raiser was heroin. He controlled roughly sixty percent of the world's supply. The United States had already indicted him for drug smuggling, while Thailand had sentenced him to death. He was the ultimate "untouchable," however. No one could get to him. According to rumor, he'd already survived forty-two assassination attempts and was as brutal as he was clever.

She'd heard of Ko Tan, all right.

At the time, however, listening to Khun's stories, she hadn't really paid them much attention beyond that of purely casual interest. Perhaps she'd use one in her article. She hadn't de-

cided. It wasn't until later, lying in bed one night, staring at the
ceiling, that it had come to her. Of course. She already had
more than enough information for a simple travel piece, but as
long as she was here . . . what about an interview with a few of
the guerrillas fighting for independence? What about an in-
depth look into the turbulence and violence that still shook the
country? Surely Khun could set up an interview with his
brother. Then imagine what her editor would say!

Khun, however, had been less than helpful. He didn't keep
in close contact with his brother—it was too dangerous. And
the rebels certainly couldn't just show up in the city for an interview. The soldiers were still looking for them.

Riley had been determined, though. All throughout her
journalism training, anyone who knew anything about reporting had told her that opportunities weren't found, but made.
And this was her opportunity. She would show the other side
of the story, beyond the tourist attractions and government
statements. She would show the lives of the people, the rebels
fighting to make their voices heard.

Finally it had occurred to her that if the guerrillas couldn't
come to her, perhaps she could go to them. Again, Khun had
been hesitant. He wasn't sure of his brother's exact position,
and even if he knew it, he certainly couldn't just give it away.

Once again she'd been at a loss. Until, one afternoon she'd
overheard Khun talking to one of his uncles. Her grasp of the
native language wasn't good enough to catch all of it, but she
had recognized the pseudonym that Khun's brother used. With
a bit of straining, she had gathered that the brother was now in
a settled camp. The family would be sending some money to . . .
She'd caught it. The coordinates of the camp.

It was all she'd needed. She could go in good faith now,
without pressuring Khun to betray his brother. She had a
multiengine-rating pilot's license, as her Uncle Gary had taught
her to fly years ago in the flat expanse of Ohio. All she'd needed
was a plane, and that could be rented.

Even as she'd made inquiries, she knew she couldn't be certain of the reception she would receive, but she counted on her
press credentials to help her. Besides, as a woman, she could
hardly be too threatening. There was also the alternative of in-

troducing herself as Khun's friend, and that, hopefully, would afford her some protection.

Her plans were made. She withdrew a quarter of her savings to rent the plane and prepared her supplies. She was nervous and scared, but she was also exhilarated. This was the start of what she'd spent her whole life saying she wanted to do. This was the start of adventure, exploration, all the things she'd dreamed of. If she could just pull it off....

She *was* pulling it off. Riley laughed to herself quietly as she cleared the first range of green-covered mountains, and then saw jungle spread beneath the plane, flat and smooth as she edged toward the Thai border on the east. Very soon she would come to a large clearing right before the border. Then she could land her plane, and, using the map, hike the rest of the way to the camp.

But just as she was beginning to relax, giving her master plan a final review, the plane began to sputter and cough. One engine paused, resumed, then paused again.

Her blood surged, then settled. And whereas she'd been overwound all day with anticipation, now, in the face of extreme danger, her nerves calmed and her head cleared. Now was not the time for hysteria.

"Come on," she urged softly as she pulled back on the yoke to maintain altitude.

The plane wheezed in response, pulling sharply to the left as the one hundred eighty air speed dropped to one hundred seventy and the engine died completely.

Grim now, she tightened her knuckles on the yoke, pushing both throttles forward, increasing the prop RPMs and the fuel boosts as she began a slow descent of one hundred forty miles per hour. Her face tight but controlled, she countered the strong left pull by pressing on the right rudder-pedal control. "Dead foot, dead engine," came her uncle's words. Since she was pressing her right foot down with her left foot off, the left engine must be dead.

For a moment the thought froze her with fear, but then she shook herself out of it. A plane could be flown on one engine. Her uncle had even done it a few times himself. It was just something she'd always hoped to avoid. Well, it wasn't as if she had many choices.

But no sooner had she calmed herself down than the other ancient engine gave out with a small clink. The plane gave a crazy plunge, and the green jungle rapidly approached.

Reacting on pure instinct now, her right hand came up to the transponder, switching to Emergency as she began broadcasting, "Mayday, Mayday."

Valiantly, she tried to maintain a steady yoke, tried to master the wayward plane into a gentle glide. Up ahead, the green jungle opened into a small clearing, and with determined eyes and a quickly muttered prayer of gratitude, she headed the plane for it.

It wasn't until those very last few seconds, when the green jungle rushed forward even as she frantically pulled the flaps down and flipped all the switches off, that it occurred to her she was definitely going to crash.

"Oh, hell," she said softly, and then destiny rushed in.

From the dark recesses of the jungle, a man watched the iron bird fall from the sky. He watched the trees and leaves catch and break under the plane's metal weight and felt the ground beneath his booted feet tremble at impact. The white-faced monkey on his shoulder squeaked in protest.

But the man did not move right away. Instead he continued to squat, steady and still, even as a thick green snake slithered over his foot. Finally, his dark gray eyes somber and unreadable, he stood and strode lithely forward as the monkey leapt from his shoulder in protest.

He picked his way through the wreckage carefully, climbing up one broken wing to stare down into the cockpit. There he could see the slumped outline of a woman. And even through the dirt and dust of the glass, he could make out unmistakably red hair. It was definitely the woman the hangar owner had radioed in about.

A beautiful, crazy woman, the old man had said.

Looking at her, Shadow could see why. But he wasn't taken in by her beauty as he carefully wrenched the door open. He spared no thought for the purity of her skin or the silkiness of her hair as he ran his hands dispassionately along her limp body, searching for serious injuries.

The only emotion he showed at all flashed across his face in a spurt of impatience: anger.

The woman was definitely alive. And, according to her credentials, definitely American. A member of the press, no less. He felt the anger grow and burn in his gut. What type of fool bumbled her way into such a pit of vipers? Didn't she know the risks? Did she value her life so little?

But then he drew in a deep breath and shut off the emotion completely. He'd come too far to change plans now. He'd already seen too much, done too much, not to withstand a little more. He wouldn't give in now, not even for a beautiful woman.

Bending down, he untangled her lithe form from the wreckage and settled her softly against his chest. She sighed a little, but didn't regain consciousness, her head slumping against his shoulder. He could feel the gentle whisper of her breath against his neck and smell the soft fragrance of her perfume. He began to walk back into the jungle.

The woman was still alive, all right.

He wondered which one of them would regret it first.

Chapter 1

She was truly beautiful.

Lying now in a bamboo hut, her skin looked incredibly pale and translucent against the rough green of the enshrouding army blanket. And her hair tumbled around her like a blazing red cape, silky and shiny even in the dusky light. Her sleeping form was long and graceful beneath the covers. Standing, Shadow imagined she would come close to his chin, and he was six-four himself.

Her eyes were closed now, blond-tipped lashes lying gently against her cheeks. He hadn't seen her eyes yet, but he imagined that they would be green. A vivid, emerald green to go with the deep fire of her hair. He shook his head against the picture.

She shouldn't be here, he thought abruptly. God only knows what fool's mission brought her. She looked young, probably mid-twenties. Well, he hoped the same youth that gave her such rashness also gave her resilience. She was going to need it.

Once again he could feel the anger begin to rise. He stood, and started pacing the narrow confines of the hut. They'd known the woman was coming. Shadow would have blamed the irresponsible plane owner, but after all these years, he understood him. The man had simply done what was necessary to survive in these hills—he'd cooperated with Ko Tan.

Even then, when the message had first arrived that some crazy American journalist was on her way, Shadow had half expected Ko Tan to order him to shoot her from the skies. After all, the only person that knew of her coming was the hangar owner, and he certainly wouldn't tell anyone. So it would be a simple move. One pull of a trigger and that would have been the end of the journalist.

They all would've gone on with their lives.

Except that Ko Tan hadn't ordered her to be shot down. Instead, he'd simply told Shadow to see to it she was captured. That was it—nothing more, nothing less.

And it worried him.

Shadow had been working for Ko Tan for a year and a half now. His own reputation for quiet efficiency had quickly moved him up the ranks. He was now the closest thing to a right-hand man Ko Tan had ever had. It suited Shadow's purposes nicely. But while his status made him privy to many things, in the end, Ko Tan was still a man of secrets.

Most often, those secrets were deadly.

She never should have come, Shadow thought vehemently. Furthermore, whoever was foolish enough to pursue one of the world's most powerful drug lords probably *deserved* to get killed. It wasn't his problem. He shouldn't worry about it.

There'd been the temptation, he acknowledged, when he'd first realized she was still alive, to just leave her. He could tell Ko Tan that the crash had killed her and wash his hands of the whole affair. But Ko Tan didn't like leaving things to chance and would have demanded proof of the woman's demise. Worse, if the woman had regained consciousness and stumbled blindly onto the camp...

Shadow's jaw muscle tightened. He hadn't survived this long just to get himself killed over a woman. Damn her, anyway, he thought. She shouldn't have come. A journalist. A lousy, nosy journalist.

Still, her sleeping form maintained a supple innocence, he supposed. No frowns marred her brow, no hidden worries or fears twisted her face in slumber. She looked like a young child napping with her long hair spread around her like a glorious cape. He had to consciously restrain himself from reaching out and touching it.

His gray eyes darkened again in anger, and he paced a little faster.

He'd been in this hellhole for too long. He'd seen things a man should never have to see. He'd done things a man should never have to do. He tried to rationalize it late at night, tried to tell himself that the end justified the means. But that didn't keep the images from twisting and turning in his mind. That didn't keep the darkness from encroaching ever closer to his soul.

But it was almost over now, he reminded himself. He just had to survive a little longer. And he had to be more careful than he'd ever been in his entire life.

For a brief moment the strain flashed across his face, then he caught and controlled it. For a brief moment more, he allowed himself to wonder how his life had ever come to this. What would Sabrina Duncan say if she knew that the child she'd saved from the evils of the street had grown into a man living in the evils of the jungle?

He hoped she never knew what had become of him. And, deep down inside, in a small part of himself he rarely acknowledged, he hoped that, if she did know, she understood.

Ruthlessly, he pushed the thoughts away. Almost against their will, his eyes drifted to the sleeping form of the beautiful red-haired journalist. For one instant, he almost hated this green-eyed woman who'd fallen from the sky and into his life. Didn't she realize how much it could cost him? Didn't she realize that she'd come to a land where nothing was as it seemed, where everything was fraught with danger? One wrong move, one wrong guess, and that was the end of it.

She stirred slightly now, wincing as she moved. Judging by the knot on her forehead, she would be wincing a lot more before the week was through. Yet the crash had been amazingly kind to her. She would be a bit sore and cramped, and earlier he'd discovered a few dark bruises beneath the cover of her shirt. Her bones remained unbroken, however, and there was no dangerous swelling around her ribs. Most of all, her skin still glowed, pure and unmarred, above the rough green of the blanket.

Damn but she was beautiful.

It tore at him, pulled at his soul, at his desire. He paused in his pacing, his eyes drawn to her form. Even as he wanted to hate her, he still wanted to touch her skin, to see if it really was as soft as it looked. God, it had been so long since he had seen skin so pale and smooth. And her hair. Red, flaming hair. How long had it been since he'd seen any hair other than black? At least a year and a half.

He didn't move as he watched her; his hands never strayed from his sides. He just looked, wondering how there could still be such softness in the world after all these years of violence. He didn't touch her. There was no point to such pursuits.

He shook his head in the silence.

From the edge of the cot, where he'd been sitting patiently for the past few minutes, Nemo cocked his small white face and looked at Shadow with huge brown eyes. Then, without a blink, he bounded up Shadow's form to perch upon the man's shoulder. He chattered lightly, then reached up a swift little hand and tweaked Shadow's nose. Shadow gave the hand a small swat, but without any force.

The monkey's small face swiveled about, and with a nimble leap he flew from Shadow's shoulder back to the sleeping form. Curious and fascinated, and definitely lacking his master's control, Nemo picked up handfuls of the shiny red hair.

Shadow snapped his fingers at the mischievous creature and clearly motioned no. The monkey chattered his disagreement, but finally desisted and returned to his perch.

One last time, Shadow let his gaze return to the woman whose beauty so fascinated him. He couldn't help her. Not now. Not after waiting so long, after finally being so close. He was a man on a mission, and there were others depending upon his success, lives at stake. He'd made it this long, come this far. He couldn't blow things now.

But watching her sleeping form, seeing the pale satin of her skin, the flaming silk of her hair, he found himself wondering how he was going to be able to bear such a burden.

Damn her, he thought once again as he headed for the door. Damn her for coming now.

But even then, he still wanted to touch her.

His eyes were dark and unreadable as he left the hut with Nemo balanced on his shoulder. And his face was the cold passionless face of the man he had become—a man who could kill . . . and had.

Damn, her head *hurt*. She would have groaned, but even in her befuddled state she realized that it would probably hurt even more if she did. Wincing, she rolled over, searching for the pain-free oblivion of sleep.

But then she slowly began to realize that the cot beneath her sagged while the blanket above her itched. Oh, God, she thought. What have I done?

She kept her eyes tightly shut under the impact of consciousness. Maybe if she just fell back asleep, when she woke up, she'd be back in Ohio. But somehow she knew that wasn't going to happen.

She lay there a few minutes more, mustering physical strength and mental endurance. She was going to have to face this strange world sooner or later. And maybe, just maybe, she allowed herself to hope, wherever she'd arrived was a good place.

Riley opened her eyes. Life was definitely blurry, but after a bit of adjusting, she managed to distinguish what looked remarkably like a bamboo hut. She'd crashed her plane and wound up in a hut somewhere in Myanmar. What in the world had she done?

She tried to raise her head, but that definitely hurt too much, so she settled for just lying there, trying to figure out what to do next. Perhaps a villager found her, she thought hesitantly. She knew a few words of the native tongue; she'd be all right.

But then she cocked her head the tiniest bit, listening for the first time to the sounds outside the hut. She could hear rhythmic thumping, marching perhaps, and the quiet buzzing of mingling people.

A feeling of foreboding came to her, and she braced herself as she turned her head until she could see the window she knew was close by. Sure enough, one window . . . complete with bamboo bars.

She sagged back down into the cot. She was someone's prisoner.

When she'd first decided to go on this little venture, she'd known she was taking a risk. But somehow, she'd always imagined being able to at least meet the soldiers and reason with them first. Certainly she hadn't pictured her plane crashing and being discovered while she was still unconscious.

She licked her lips and took a deep, stabilizing breath.

"Whatever you do," she whispered to herself levelly, "don't panic." She was still alive, and she *did* know how to speak a bit of the language. Perhaps these people knew Khun's brother. All she had to do was explain her connection, and surely things would work out.

Trying to keep herself calm, she gritted her teeth and sat up. The world took a sickening lurch, and for a moment, she really thought she was going to pass out. But then things righted enough for her to throw off the army blanket and swing her feet onto the floor. And promptly encounter bare feet.

Her captors had taken her boots and socks. She frowned. Maybe, then, they were only interested in money? Maybe, if all else failed, she could buy her way out of this mess.

She took another calming breath, finding some small reassurance in this last thought, and glanced around. By the looks of things she definitely was in some sort of prison. A faint shudder crept up her spine again, but grimly she pushed it back down. Concentrate, she reminded herself fiercely. Slowly she clenched and unclenched her fists. Panic accomplished nothing. She returned her attention to her surroundings. The hut seemed to be pacing room only. The furniture included a lone cot, which she was sitting on, and in the right-hand corner was a large clay pot that she had the uncomfortable feeling served as a latrine. So much for the comforts of home.

There was the one small window, which perhaps she could fit through, she decided, if it should come to that, but it did have bars on it. Abruptly she frowned. For the life of her, she couldn't find anything that resembled a door. She looked down at the floor. No, she didn't see any sort of entrance there, either. She was like a rat in a trap, she thought faintly.

Her hands began to tremble, and this time it took several deep breaths before she could force the fear down. Don't give in to panic. *Don't give in.*

Really, this may all be much less terrible than it looks.

Yeah, right, whispered a little voice in her mind. She sought to ignore it.

What time was it? she thought suddenly. Automatically she looked down at her wrist, only to discover that her watch was gone, as well. Further investigation revealed that her small earrings and the identification she kept in her pocket were also missing. And she was without her duffel bag, which had contained a fair amount of money.

It appeared that she was bootless and moneyless. But that didn't worry her half as much as the fact that she honestly wasn't sure how much time had passed. How long since the plane had crashed? Hours? Days?

Experimentally, she ran her hand through her hair. She swallowed with grim amusement. Definitely a few days, anyway. The shudder started back up her spine again, and once more she fought to contain it.

Don't panic don't panic don't panic. Please.

Resolutely she got to her feet and took a few experimental steps. As she got closer to the wall, she could make out a faint line of light. She followed it around with her fingertips and realized after a minute that it was the outline of a door. Only it fitted perfectly into the wall, without any handholds for her to grasp. She tried pushing it, but it remained firm.

In a sudden flood of frustration and panic, she smacked her fist against it vehemently. All she managed to do was bruise her hand.

All right, she told herself. The door was definitely out. How about the window? No, the bamboo bars were much too strong. Once again frustration threatened to take over and she was tempted to grab and shake them, like some bad actress in a melodramatic movie. She wanted out. She just wanted *out*.

She swallowed once more and felt the sting of tears welling in her eyes.

She was a prisoner. She was really and truly a prisoner.

The panic soared again. The desire to pound furiously on the walls and beat her way out with physical violence was only countered by the equally strong desire to simply sit down and cry.

What was going to happen to her?

What if she was a hostage? What if she never escaped? What if she was a prisoner for ever and ever? Journalist Terry Waite had been held hostage in the Middle East for seven years. *Seven years*.

Her throat started to burn with the effort of restraining her tears. She took a few deep, steadying breaths. Her eyes were still misty, her hands still shaking, but she fought and won a thin thread of control.

"Okay, McDouglas," she whispered to herself thickly. "It appears that escaping is out. But maybe, after meeting the…people here, you can negotiate your way out. Yes. You're smart, you have access to money, and you're an American. Surely some of that must mean something to someone."

But still the fear remained, dark and tense in the pit of her stomach. Hometown girls that had been raised in Ohio didn't exactly receive much training in how to escape from huts in the jungles of Myanmar. Then again, she reminded herself bitterly, she'd never been a typical girl from Ohio.

Oh no, she'd been the girl-next-door who had always dreamed of moving away. The girl who had started buying copies of *Vogue* and *Cosmopolitan* at twelve just to see all the pictures of the places waiting for her out there. And now? Now what did she think of great adventures?

She shivered slightly and sat back down on the cot, wrapping the rough blanket around herself.

But simply sitting left her mind open to all sorts of horrible imaginings. Different scenarios and outcomes raced through her head, each worse than the last.

She stood up quickly. She needed a distraction. Returning to the window, she looked for something, anything, that might allay her fears. It was late in the day, she observed, probably an hour or two before sunset, judging by the shadows. She could see people moving about on a dirt road not far from her hut. A small herd of ducks waddled along, while a young boy in torn shorts chased after them with a stick. Farther away an older woman looked on, her face impassive.

Directly across from her, Riley could make out another row of bamboo huts, all raised above the grass on small platforms. They each contained bars on the windows, and she began to understand that she was definitely on some sort of prisoners' row. Concentrating, she tested her still-pounding head by counting the buildings.

"One hut, two hut, three hut, four," she intoned softly, "five hu— What the—?"

She stopped suddenly, peering dimly into the shadows between the rows. God, it hurt to focus. But yes, sure enough, there was a man standing there, and not just any man, but a distinctly Caucasian one. Perhaps an American? Feeling a small flicker of hope, she waved her hand frantically at him.

But the man didn't move, and after a moment, her hand slowly fell to her side and the spark of hope died. Whoever they were, he was one of them.

He stood relaxed, so tall and lean he seemed to blend in with the buildings until he could have been just a trick of the light, a figment of her imagination. He wore a dark green military outfit, heavy boots laced tightly around his ankles. His hands were in his pockets, and a cavalry hat was pulled down low over his eyes.

She could make out the lower half of his face, and it was as lean as the rest of him. He looked like a panther—sleek and coiled with whiplash energy.

Once again, she swallowed heavily. Then she realized that the man was watching her.

And she had no sooner digested this fact than he began to walk forward. Straight toward her.

The darkness had completely enshrouded the camp when Shadow finally made his way back to the hut. The air was still warm and humid, sticking his shirt to his back, but not too bad. The real heat and humidity was still a month away in mid-May, when the rainy season would start in earnest.

In the dark, the hills surrounded the camp like an overwhelming fortress, reaching tall and black. Here and there he could see the occasional light of one of the guards dutifully making his rounds. There was no sense of urgency in the patrols tonight compared to nights of not so long ago. There hadn't been any major raids or skirmishes since the establishment of this new camp. But training went diligently on. Soon, once they'd received fresh supplies, the small battles would resume.

The small rebel group was supposedly fighting to secede from the statehood of Myanmar, but they spent most of their time fighting insurgency groups from Laos. Shadow didn't particularly care. The only thing that concerned him was the leader himself, Ko Tan. Even now, after a year and a half in the camp, Shadow knew that Ko Tan didn't fully trust him, still halfway wondered about Shadow's motives, just as Ko Tan would always distrust and wonder about everyone around him.

For that matter, Shadow had never trusted Ko Tan, either. Especially now, especially with the woman. Ko Tan still hadn't said why he wanted to see her. In fact, he refused to talk about her at all, and it was making Shadow nervous. He'd been immersed in a paranoid world for far too long now to keep from being suspicious. Perhaps this was the ultimate test from Ko Tan. When confronted with a choice between helping a woman from his own country versus following Ko Tan's orders, which would Shadow do? With whom did his loyalties ultimately lie?

Damn him, Shadow thought as he strode across the grass. Damn the man for his tests, and damn the woman for entering the picture now, when he could least afford to make a mistake. And damn her for being so beautiful, for looking so soft, for looking so alive.

She was dangerous, he reminded himself again. A journalist, of all things. She'd probably be completely hysterical, or completely enraptured with the foolish notion of interviewing the world's most infamous drug lord. Either way, she could only lead to trouble. He must never forget that. Whatever else happened, he just needed to hang in there a little longer. In a matter of weeks this assignment would finally end and he could return to the sanity of the real world once more. Finally, after all these years, Ko Tan would be brought to justice. Shadow had worked too hard, given up too much, to sacrifice it all now because of a woman. Even a woman with flaming red hair and brilliant green eyes.

Yet he still paused slightly when he reached the final row of prison huts. He found himself standing between the small buildings, hesitating when he shouldn't be hesitant. Dammit, he couldn't help her. He *couldn't.*

And then he saw that she was awake, standing at the window, staring right at him. His jaw tightened and his eyes narrowed. So the journalist was up. The test had begun.

His face harsh, he didn't hesitate. He took the first step forward.

Riley rushed back to the cot. Wildly her eyes searched the room, but there was no means of escape nor anyplace to hide. She would have to face her captor. She had no choice.

Once again her mind replayed the image of his lean, muscle-hardened body standing in the shadows. What was she going to do?

Don't panic, she reminded herself, inwardly wincing at the words that were becoming almost a mantra to her. She sat down hard on the cot, pulling the blanket onto her lap as if it were some meager form of protection. Don't panic don't panic don't pa—

The door swung inward.

He seemed to fill the small room, a tall shadowy man who had to duck his head to avoid hitting the top of the doorframe. Up close, she could make out all of his features—the black hair that waved across his head, the dark stubble that shadowed his cheeks, the long thin scar running down his left cheekbone. His eyes were still hidden by his hat, which was pulled down low over his forehead, but she could feel the power of his gaze boring into her, stripping through her slim defenses with dispassionate expediency. She had to forcibly restrain herself from shivering under the onslaught, consciously concentrate on keeping her head high. He looked powerful; he looked strong. He looked angry.

He didn't move. The moment stretched on in silent strain until she could almost hear her nerve endings scream from the pressure. He did nothing, and she waited. In the end, nearly faint with the tension, she gave in first and broke the silence.

"My name is Riley McDouglas," she managed to whisper, licking her lips to get them to function. "Who...who are you?"

He didn't answer, but raked her up and down with a clearly disdainful gaze. Unconsciously, she clutched the blanket on her lap closer, but she still kept her head up. At this point, she wasn't about to lose her dignity, and was damned if she'd show her fear.

Shadow felt the anger within him rising yet again. Her words only served to make him angrier. He'd thought to find her cowering with fear or rash with foolish bravado. He certainly hadn't planned on this combination of genuine fear and genuine courage. Damn her. He didn't want to respect her; he didn't want to like her. Disdain, contempt, indifference would make his task easier.

"Get up," he informed her curtly. "There are orders that you're to be fed."

She swallowed under the terse command, feeling her fear magnify tenfold at the word he'd used—*orders*. Oh, this was definitely some sort of guerrilla camp and she was in a hell of a bunch of trouble. Why hadn't she just stayed home? For once in her life, why hadn't she just taken the safe route?

But there was no time for regrets now. She had no choice but to go with the grim-faced man with his clipped words and uncaring eyes. What else could she do?

Slowly, she rose to her feet, and after a minute's hesitation, she let the blanket slide back to the cot. Once again she felt the power of his eyes skimming down her body. Whatever he saw, he kept it contained in the tight clenching of his jaw.

She swallowed resolutely and struggled to find words once again.

"My boots?" she asked faintly.

He glanced at her bare feet and negated the request with a single shake of his head.

She could only nod.

He turned then, stepping down out of the hut and presenting his hand to her.

She hesitated slightly, and the next thing she knew, he'd seized her hand and pulled her through the door. She couldn't escape the force, only follow it down off the platform into the wild tangle of the grass.

She felt the slight dampness of dirt beneath her bare feet as well as the satiny smoothness of the grass. But most of all she could feel the blazing strength of the fingers curled so firmly around her own. Callused, hard, demanding, she managed to register, and then her hand was unceremoniously dropped.

He motioned for her to start walking, then fell in beside her, his gaze keen and observant. She had a feeling that if she so much as twitched he wouldn't hesitate to throw her over his shoulder and forcibly carry her to their destination.

Her nerves stretched tighter.

She licked her lips once more, and it seemed his eyes noted that, too.

"What—" she swallowed heavily "—what is your name?"

He didn't answer. He just kept walking.

She let the effort drop, and instead tried to distract herself with the scenery. Working fast now, her mind poured her nervous energy into registering and memorizing everything for escape. Because if this man was any indication, she definitely needed to escape.

With covert glances and anxious darted looks, she sought to internalize the details of her surroundings, from the chirping of the crickets to the dim shadows of unknown buildings. She could see the huge mountains she'd barely topped surrounding the camp on all sides, and she could feel the insistent humidity of the jungle. She saw a distant shadow and judged it to be a barricade of some sort.

It became apparent that the small prisons were actually outside of the heart of the encampment, but the reasoning behind it escaped her. She saw no signs of life at this time of the evening, just long, empty stretches of grass.

She risked a slight glance at the man beside her.

He was still striding purposefully forward, his face giving away nothing. It was a lean face, hard, grim. The scar he had seemed to blaze out in the night, flashing wickedly. Still, something didn't seem quite right. She debated about that for a small moment, stealing more covert glances. And then it came to her. The scar should have made him seem sinister, evil even. But it didn't. It gave him a certain edge, made him striking, to be sure, but it seemed more a mark of character than anything else. In all his face, with its harsh planes and angles, she didn't detect any sign of cruelty. He was a hard man, but not a petty one.

Or so it seemed.

Then again, she reminded herself slightly hysterically, what could she possibly know about a man with no name?

You had to go out and see the world, McDouglas, didn't you? You just had to go after this story. Just had to—

Abruptly she clamped down on the mocking thoughts. She was already stuck in this mess—berating herself wouldn't help. All right, she was a prisoner. But while not friendly, this man hadn't been cruel to her, either. He hadn't hit her, he hadn't . . . well, tried to rape her. And he *was* feeding her.

If she could just stay calm and keep her wits about her, she might get herself out of this yet. She might. She could.

Then she had another thought. Just how did an American fit into all this? A mercenary? Perhaps a military adviser of some sort? He didn't carry any weapon that she could see, but his clothes fit him too well, comfortable and worn. He'd been around for a bit.

And why was he the only one she'd seen, anyway? Surely, if she was a prisoner, it made no sense to have another American, of all people, supervise her. Unless, of course, he was related to the government in some way, and therefore asked to be in charge of her by right.

Then why was he so silent and uncooperative? She risked another glance at him, and felt the small thread of hope die. No, judging from the harshness of his face, he probably was just a mercenary. And why not have him guard her? From what she'd seen, he certainly wasn't a man of sentiment. He seemed to be carved from stone.

Shortly, more buildings came into view. From the outside, they seemed to be larger versions of her own. All were raised on platforms and all had slanted roofs. Riley and the man crossed over a short bridge, and the heart of the camp appeared. There was no grass anymore, just the firm feel of hard-packed mud beneath her feet.

It occurred to her then just how good the cool softness of dirt felt under her bare feet. After so many years of stomping through the pounding streets of New York, she'd forgotten the free, renegade feel of bare feet. In Ohio—

Suddenly, she became aware that the man had stopped and was now looking at her intently again. He glanced down at her feet and back up again, and in spite of herself she blushed. Surely he couldn't have known what she was thinking. She

could grant such a sharp-eyed man several things, but she
wouldn't grant him that. It just wasn't possible.

It was then she realized that they had stopped in front of one
of the buildings. And he was—had been—holding the door
open for her all this time. Her face flushed scarlet.

She stepped in and was instantly greeted by the rich, spicy
smells of simmering food. In spite of herself, she sighed and felt
her stomach rumble its agreement. It had been ages since she'd
last eaten.

And the food, brought out by a huge, rotund cook, was just
as good as it smelled. There was warm soup, followed by duck
cooked in oil. Then she had fish paste, cauliflower in oil and
some kind of eggs. She ate it all, savoring each warm bite,
blissfully cleaning off her plate. To end it all there were fresh
mangoes, cool and ripe in her mouth.

For the half hour seemingly allotted to her, she tuned out the
dark-eyed man before her. She tuned out the jungle and the
danger of her own fears. With inborn strength and willpower,
she just concentrated on the rich taste and spicy aroma of a
good meal. It restored her energy and sustained her courage.
When she was done, she was almost ready to take on the man
sitting across from her.

He hadn't eaten; he'd just watched her. As soon as she was
done, she refocused…and found herself alone in the room with
him and already strangled by the silence.

"Are you American?" she asked finally, though she'd already assumed that he was.

Amazingly, he seemed to ponder the question, one ankle
resting on his other knee, staring at the wall just past her
shoulder. Then, with a small, negligent shrug, he nodded.

"Then why are you here?" she managed to prod, though the
words were a little more nervous this time. She didn't really
expect any kind of reply.

And he didn't answer.

"Are you a mercenary?" she persisted bravely, refusing to
back down and let him once again intimidate her with silence.

He looked at her sharply, his eyes seeming to linger on the
soft curve of her neck, the graceful line of her cheekbone. She

became flustered under the stare and could feel the color creeping up her cheeks. *Damn.*

Finally, he nodded.

"And you," he said suddenly in soft, level tones, "are a journalist."

She was taken aback, first by the shock of him actually speaking, and second by the knowledge he already seemed to possess. She struggled to rally her defenses. She'd already figured out her identification was missing. They had obviously gone through all her things. Half-hysterically she supposed that must be proper procedure for guerrillas coming across plane crashes.

But she was still shaken when she nodded in affirmation. Then another thought occurred to her. Maybe she could just go through with her original plan. Maybe she could convince this soldier to tell her his story, and she would tell it to the world. On the condition, of course, that he set her free.

But the moment she opened her mouth to suggest it, he held up his hand and silenced her.

"I don't like journalists" was all he said.

She slumped slightly in her seat and felt the beginnings of tears burn her throat. What was she going to do now?

He watched her sink down, watched her beautiful head bow forward at his words. It hit him harder than he'd expected, like a slam in the gut. No, there was no pleasure in beating down a proud woman. He'd liked it better when she'd looked at him with her head high even as he could see the fear in her eyes, the tremble in her hands. She wasn't what he'd expected. But he fought to hate her all the same.

"You shouldn't have come," he said abruptly, taking his eyes from her dejected figure to focus on the wall. He didn't like what he was about to do and steeled himself against any emotion.

It didn't matter, he reminded himself. Likes and dislikes were not important. Just as long as the job got done.

He rose to his feet, standing before her hard and unyielding. He jerked his head toward the door. "It's time to leave," he told her curtly.

She nodded, slowly coming to her own feet. Then she took a deep breath, and her eyes rose once again to meet his. They were such beautiful eyes. Such a brilliant, proud shade of green.

His jaw tightened, and one hand curled into a tight fist at his side. "Ko Tan wants to see you," he said flatly.

Chapter 2

At first she didn't react. She *couldn't* react. There was nothing in her realm of experience to prepare for something like this. Ko Tan. The world's most dangerous drug lord. A man who, according to legend, had survived over forty assassination attempts. A man known for his harsh, cruel rule.

She'd known he must be in the area. After all, she'd intended interviewing a few guerrillas who fought under him. But his troops numbered well over five thousand, and his hit-and-run-type tactics kept them widely dispersed and peppered throughout the jungle. She hadn't given any real consideration to actually running into the man himself.

Ko Tan.

Oh, God, what had she gotten herself into?

The shattering impact of the news had clearly shown on her face, because all of a sudden she became aware of the fact that Shadow had stopped and was watching her closely. She could only look at him, her green eyes huge with shock. She couldn't find any words to speak.

His eyes were gray, she found herself thinking, the thought way off and distant, as if it were coming through a long tunnel. And the eyes were looking at her with a combination of qualities she hadn't thought to find in a mercenary's face. Pity, perhaps. Understanding, maybe a little. And something more. Something dark and mysterious that she couldn't quite pinpoint beneath the steady current of his control. Regret?

Quickly she shook her head, trying to dismiss such strange thoughts as she struggled to digest and accept this horrible fate all at once. She took a few deep breaths. And swallowed. And breathed in again.

"What does he want?" she managed to ask, her voice studiously even.

No answer.

"Please," she asked again, her voice cracking a little this time. "Please tell me."

He shook his head. But then he hesitated, and as if moved by a force not quite under his control, he relented enough at least to speak. "I don't know," he said flatly.

She nodded, starting to feel a little faint. What was she going to do now?

Escape.

It came to her then, crystal clear. She'd landed herself in a real mess, but there was still hope. If she just kept her wits about her, her mind alert, she could get out of this. She knew she could do it. She had to.

She took another deep breath, and it was steadier this time. She might be young and inexperienced, but she'd never been a quitter. She'd always wanted adventure—well, now she'd found it. She couldn't just decide to quit and let them get the best of her. No, McDouglas, she told herself, it was time to bite the bullet. She'd gotten herself into this, now she'd just have to get herself back out.

Resolutely she began walking, and Shadow fell into step beside her. Her mind racing, she slanted a quick glance at him. What about him? He was an enigma. Silent, controlled, hard. He'd been angry with her at first, harsh even. And now? She almost wondered if he didn't pity her. That made her angry. She had her pride; she wasn't going to just cave in and let herself become a victim. No, she'd show him that she wasn't anyone to pity. She was a fighter!

Then another thought came to her. He was an American, and so was she. And he felt at least some sentiment for her; it had become clear in the last few minutes that he wasn't completely cold and reserved. What if she needed someone to stand up for her? Would he— But as soon as the thought materialized, she dismissed it. He certainly hadn't given any indication that he would help her. He seemed loyal to Ko Tan. Yet maybe... Maybe once he got to know her, maybe if she could prove to him she was a person worth saving... How could she do that? *You're a woman, McDouglas, how do you think?* The thought came out of nowhere, and she almost instantly rejected it. Never in her entire life had she stooped to something so low as using feminine wiles.

Then again, never in her entire life had she been prisoner of a heroin drug lord. Never in her whole life had she been more in danger of *losing* her life. *And,* the insidious little voice spoke up, *he's not an unattractive man.* Of their own volition, her eyes furtively roamed over him. His face was hard, emotionless, his features rugged and masculine, his lips sensuous, his eyes shadowed. A man of mystery. A man of silence. And yes, he was attractive.

Stop it, McDouglas, she ordered herself. It was the riddle he posed, that was all. What woman wouldn't be intrigued by a man who wouldn't even give her his name? But then her eyes wandered down to where his hands swung at his sides. Large, strong, callused hands. Hands meant to wield weapons, to forage, to survive. Elemental, powerful hands. Hands that would be firm as he— The image was so strong, she broke it off, shivering against the night.

He instantly glanced at her, and her eyes avoided his. This time she kept them focused on the sea of grass in front of her bare feet. But already, in her mind, the decision had been made. Her first goal had to be survival. If this man could help her, then she couldn't afford to rule him out. Somehow, she would have to find a way to reach him. Whatever it took.

Unaware of her thoughts, Shadow kept his eyes forward, his mind concentrating on an easy, rhythmic pace through the knee-whipping grass. He didn't allow himself to think beyond the faint slap-slap-slap of the weeds against his fatigues. And he certainly didn't allow himself to feel. After all these years, all these miles, he had no intention of succumbing to that now.

The woman—calling her by her name was too dangerous to his resolve—had made her own choices when she'd rented the plane. The rest wasn't his concern. Could not be his concern. His assignment here had the potential to save thousands of lives if he could just pull it off. There was no way he would risk that for just one woman.

Still, when the large building finally loomed into sight, he felt the smallest temptation to hesitate. Grimly, he squashed it back down, his face cold and harsh as he strode powerfully forward.

With its raised platform and slanted roof, the building at first appeared to be a larger version of the other huts Riley had seen. Then she spotted the four bamboo columns that rose out of the porch to support a small covering. It gave the building a small air of grandeur, but perhaps only enough to point out what it was lacking.

Curious, she gave one pillar a light push as they mounted the porch, only to be impressed by its reasonable stability. That determined, she turned her attention to the raised porch itself.

"The raised platforms," she asked curiously, "why do all the buildings have them?"

His answer was short and clipped. "Snakes."

She looked down at her bare feet, now covered with mud from their journey. Her nerves wrapped themselves a little tighter.

"Should I consider myself lucky?" she asked hesitantly.

He only shrugged, his eyes skimming over her naked feet with indifference.

She sucked in a deep breath under the chill of that dismissive glance, starting to feel the beginnings of hysteria. Grimly, she tightened her hands into fists at her sides and regained some level of control.

Just then the door in front of them swung open, revealing a very large man. His eyes barely registered Shadow's presence, instead skipping straight to Riley with unconcealed interest. Riley felt, more than saw, Shadow tense and straighten next to her. Unconsciously, she drew slightly closer to his lean strength. Was this Ko Tan? God, he was a giant! The hysteria squeezed a little tighter, her face draining of all color.

But with a grunt the large man only turned aside to let them in. Apparently he was only the bouncer. Riley bit back a hysterical giggle.

She turned her attention to her surroundings. Time to notice the details, she told herself. Anything she could learn, anything at all, might eventually be the key to her escaping. She had to remain alert. The initial entrance to the building, she noted, hadn't been anything special; she couldn't recall seeing even a piece of furniture. But as they stepped through an alcove into another small antechamber, she discovered her feet sinking into the rich softness of an oriental rug. In one corner she recognized the deep luster of a cherrywood table, complete with a crystal lamp. A deep couch leaned against one wall, and she ran a hand over its arm to discover soft leather. Further investigation revealed a coffee table complete with copies of *People*, *Sports Illustrated* and *Newsweek*.

"I take it this is the waiting room," she observed wryly.

But her silent chaperon presented her with his infamous shrug and turned the knob on the door to the adjoining room. "Wait here," he ordered, and the sudden terse finality of his words hit her hard and cold as he went into the room, closing the door behind him. This was it. This was really it. She could feel her heart begin to pound.

Before she knew it, he was back, standing tall and shadowed in the doorway. "Ko Tan will see you now," he announced with the same polite indifference. For a minute, she almost couldn't do it. It seemed her legs had no muscles, her knees no tendons. She could only stand there, the clipped formality of the words running over and over in her mind. *Ko Tan will see you now. Ko Tan will see you now. Ko Tan will—*

Stop it, she told herself harshly. Just stop it.

But her face was still ashen when she finally stepped forward. She didn't realize that it accented the brilliant vitality of her eyes and the flaming fire of her hair as she paused one last time, squared her shoulders and held her head up high. But Shadow did.

Once again he was struck by her beauty. It hammered into his gut like a physical blow. She was so young, and obviously scared, but was so determined to go forward. As fragile as she was now, she already possessed the thin strain of steel that marked the truly courageous.

He forced himself to look away. He refused to be taken in by her beauty. He wouldn't succumb to the thoughts of what could very well be her fate, the way her youth and vitality might be crushed—permanently—before this was all over.

It was too late for regrets and hesitation. Ko Tan was waiting.

He held the door open, and without wavering she strode forward into the room.

The carpet here was even thicker, lusher beneath her feet. She was startled to discover that a vaulted ceiling loomed above her with dim track lights rimming its edge. Before her lay a long, beautiful mahogany table, lined with eight leather chairs. In the middle sat an imposing flower arrangement in what she assumed to be a replica of a Ming vase.

And then she spotted him, seated beyond the vase, at the head of the table. He was sitting in one of the plush leather chairs, his back to her as he examined a huge oil painting in front of him. It looked, incredibly, like a Rembrandt, and this time, she wasn't so sure if it was a reproduction.

She stood there, feeling suddenly uncertain. She was standing in a virtual boardroom in the middle of a bamboo hut in the middle of a jungle. Frankly, it should have been ludicrous.

Except that the dark room reeked of money, arrogance and, most of all, power.

Oh, she definitely wasn't in Ohio anymore.

Behind her, Shadow cleared his throat, and on cue the chair swiveled around. The man in it was small, she was surprised to find. She was probably taller. His eyes were jet black in his weathered, stern face, and they were by no means laughing eyes. They were the eyes of absolute, unquestionable authority. The eyes of a man who could stare down death itself. And probably had.

He wore starched military dress, and the tan color was accented by gold stars set against red stripes. He sat rigidly, his hands folded on the table in front of him as, slowly and carefully, he examined her, inch by inch.

She forced herself not to be intimidated by his gaze, forced herself to stand firm and proud under the onslaught of his cold eyes. So this was Ko Tan—a stern, calculating viper.

Abruptly he leaned back, his face breaking into a charming smile that eased the sternness of his face and put crinkled lines around his eyes. She almost sagged with relief, but then looked into his eyes; there with the charm was still the careful calculation. She would have to be very cautious around this man.

"You are a beautiful woman, Riley McDouglas," he said at last, the words fluid though his voice still contained a slight accent. "Even bruised and scraped, you are a beautiful woman. Please, please," he quietly added with a wave of his hand and a benevolent smile. "Have a seat."

She hesitated, suddenly loath to leave the presence of the silent, gray man behind her. He himself had treated her with only indifference, and his face was as harsh and hard as they came. But as she'd observed earlier, there wasn't a trace of cruelty in his eyes. No hidden pettiness in the set of his jaw. With a start, she realized why she didn't want to move away from him. In some strange, tangled way, she trusted him.

And she certainly couldn't say the same of the calculating, black-eyed general before her. But there was no helping it. With one last determined set of her shoulders, she walked away from her guerrilla and faced Ko Tan alone.

As she sat gingerly down on a leather chair, Ko Tan was reaching over casually for a polished wooden box that had been blocked from her sight by the vase. He held it open toward her. "Would you like a betel nut?" he offered, displaying the nuts with an assortment of orange peels, spice seeds, lime and betel leaves.

"No. Thank you," she replied in a carefully even tone. She watched his eyes, trying to catch his reaction. But to all intents and purposes, he was a generous host offering his guest refreshments. Still, she felt uneasy, felt a certain hyperalertness ripple up and down her spine. She decided that she had liked it better when he'd appeared powerful and cruel. She'd expected that. And she'd been preparing herself for how to deal with such a man, if dealing was even possible. But this, the gracious host? She didn't understand this, and for that reason, it actually scared her more.

She worked on keeping the emotions out of her face as she slowly leaned back against her chair. She knew her complexion must be pale, but perhaps he would attribute that to her recent crash. And since her hands were shaking so badly, she was careful to keep them under the table. She actually knew something about this man, she reminded herself. When she'd researched Myanmar, with its part in the "Golden Triangle" of the heroin drug trade, she'd read about Ko Tan. She knew he was a hard, cruel leader. But he had also been educated in the West and was rumored to have a taste for the finer things in life. If this room and his manners were any indication, he seemed to want at least to start with a thin veneer of civility. She would play the game. For now, she would just watch and wait, see the best way to approach him, because she had no doubt that her life depended on it.

Ko Tan seemed unconcerned as he took out one of the betel leaves, spread it with lime, sprinkled it with the orange peels, spice seeds and betel nut, then rolled it up and popped it into his mouth to chew thoughtfully.

"Your English is impeccable," she said at last to break the silence. The words came out shaky, but they came out nonetheless. She took another breath and managed to continue more easily this time. "Did you study in the States?" she asked, though she already knew that he had. She just wanted something to fill the gap. Anything was better than the dreadful silence.

He didn't answer right away, chewing on his nut instead as he examined her closely. Then he reached over for a wooden cup and, turning his head slightly, spit the remains of the nut and leaves into it. Once he'd finished, his eyes returned to her face, dark and measuring. She had to forcibly keep herself from fidgeting under the scrutiny.

"Harvard," he said at last.

"Majored in business, wasn't it?" she asked this time, the words a little stronger. She was a reporter, after all; she'd done an interview a time or two in her life— That was it. She would simply pretend that this was all just an interview. An interview with the most dangerous man in the world. Why, just imagine the story she'd have—if, of course, she lived. She almost broke out into hysterical laughter at the absurdity of the whole thing.

"Yes," Ko Tan said smoothly. "I see you've done your homework."

At that moment, the idea came to her. Born of hysteria, perhaps, it was still the best idea she could come up with under the circumstances. She'd rented the plane to interview some guerrillas and, well, here she was, with the leader of their rebellion. She certainly couldn't beg her way out—he was a man known for his lack of mercy. And as for suggesting they ransom her for money, what sort of money could she offer him when he already controlled a billion-dollar empire? The only thing she had going for her was that she was a reporter, and with the *New York Daily. That* was what she could offer him: coverage, attention, infamy. What could be better for the leader of a rebel movement?

"Tell me, Miss McDouglas," Ko Tan was saying now, his black eyes once more burning. "What is a reporter doing in the middle of the jungle these days, anyway?"

Now was the time, she told herself. Do it.

"Looking for you," she said bravely.

His eyes narrowed at the words, emotion and intellect flickering in the blackness there. Behind her, she sensed her chaperon stiffen at his post. For one long moment, she felt the fear rush through her. She'd made a mistake, a very, very big mistake. Then, abruptly, Ko Tan's face broke into a long, slow smile. In the dim light, she could see his stained teeth and lips as he grinned, and she fought down a feeling of revulsion.

"Intriguing," he said. "Simply intriguing."

The relief rushed through in a wave and she almost sagged in her seat. By God, there might be hope for her yet. Encouraged now, she sat forward a little more, color beginning to flush her cheeks as she searched for the right words to convince him.

"I'm a journalist," she told him, and her cheeks and eyes were flushed with honest pride this time. "I work for the *New York Daily* and I can see to it that your story gets told to the entire world."

He dismissed her words with a wave of his hands, his cold eyes easily cutting her down to size. "If I want a journalist, I can pick up the phone and get the best there is, anytime I feel like it. Why should I settle for some young unknown?"

She faltered then, for a scant moment. She hadn't thought about that, but she did know that hesitation was something she could ill afford. Summoning up a show of bravado, she rushed boldly forward.

"Because I'm the best," she said confidently, her eyes glittering as she leaned over the table in her intensity. On a roll now, she threw down the trump card. "I'm here, aren't I?"

It must have been the right tactic, because once again he laughed. This time, however, she noticed how his eyes lingered on her face, on her neck. The feeling of revulsion crept back up.

"Yes, you are, aren't you?" His voice was suddenly softer, laced with velvet menace. The room seemed too dark to her now, dark and almost intimate. With blinding realization, she saw the true danger she was in. Oh, God, she had to find a way to escape. Soon.

"When can I start interviewing you?" she asked quickly, letting triumph blaze in the green depths of her eyes as she continued playing the role.

Ko Tan frowned at her triumphant smile, his face growing dark and ugly. For a tense moment she was afraid she'd gone too far, but then his face abruptly cleared and he gave her a calculating smile.

"It's not often I have the company of a beautiful woman, but then I am a very busy man." He seemed to debate. "Perhaps I could fit you into my schedule in a day or so. I'm sure that won't be a problem for you. After all, Riley, you will not be going anyplace."

The words sounded deceptively casual, but she caught their meaning. Oh, she'd bought herself some time, all right. He might even actually let her interview him. But never for a minute could she forget that she was still his prisoner. She existed at his whim. And whenever that whim changed, she'd be powerless against him.

She had to get back to civilization . . . and safety. She could use her desire to write a story as a cover to learn more about the camp. Then, at the first opportunity . . .

Escape.

Her mind made up, her next move was easier: retreat. It was obvious from the way his eyes kept lingering over her that to remain would only be to invite trouble. No, she'd pushed her luck enough for one night. Now she would be happy to return safely to her little prison, where at least she was all alone. Taking a deep breath, she rose from the chair.

"If you don't mind," she said softly, "I'd like to get some rest. I think the excitement of the day has caught up with me."

With an according nod, Ko Tan also rose to his feet. They both discovered that she was the taller by a full inch.

It was a small source of power, but it gave her a tiny glint of satisfaction. He was an intimidating man, and to be able to look down on him, well, she couldn't quite stop the faint tugging smile around her lips. Ko Tan's eyes narrowed and darkened in response, the fury building in his eyes like a storm.

Immediately she felt a sharp stab of fear, and she cursed herself inwardly for being so stupid. She waited anxiously, helplessly, for whatever was to happen next. Abruptly, he signaled to the silent soldier standing at attention behind them.

"Shadow," he ordered curtly, and Riley's eyes flickered at finally learning the name of her reticent escort. "You stay here. And you," Ko Tan said, turning once more to Riley, "can wait in the other room."

Riley's fear of just a moment ago disappeared, eclipsed by the curiosity that flared in her at Ko Tan's words. More than anything in the world right now, she wanted to know just what Ko Tan was going to tell Shadow. But caution told her to go out into the waiting room. She'd wanted to retreat, and now was definitely her chance.

She collapsed on the couch the moment the door shut behind her and she was alone. For the first time, she gave in to her nerves, her whole body shaking from the strain. But she'd done it, she thought as both the exhilaration and the fear ran their course. She'd just met with one of the most dangerous men in the world, and not only had she survived, but she might actually get a story.

A story. For one small instant, she allowed her imagination to soar. The look on her boss's face if she came back from Myanmar not just with some boring travel piece, but an exclusive interview with the leading heroin drug lord, Ko Tan himself, raced through her mind.

It was beyond belief. Never in her wildest ambitions had such a thought occurred to her. But then she cautioned herself. She wasn't out of the fire yet, not by a long shot. Fantasies were all well and good. She could be a reporter and try to get a story while she was here, but first and foremost she had to escape. She remembered Ko Tan's eyes, the way they had lingered on her face and neck, the cold, calculating gleam in them. Yes, escape. Definitely escape.

And if she'd known what Ko Tan was saying to Shadow at just that instant, she would have been even more certain.

"You will guard her." The words were short and clipped, as were most of the commands Ko Tan gave his men. Shadow nodded his head briefly in response, keeping his own face passive and expressionless. He didn't have to ask for reasons. One look at the open suspicion and speculation in Ko Tan's face, and he knew.

It was another test, another way to see just how loyal Shadow was, another way to see just how far Ko Tan could push him. By now, Shadow wasn't surprised. After all, it seemed that the last year and a half had been nothing but one long test. So this one was perhaps harder than usual. So this one had the potential to make Shadow choose between his duty to his government and the life of one very beautiful woman. So this one could cause him to lose the last of his self-respect. So what?

None of his rage showed on his face. Not by so much as a flicker in the dark mystery of his eyes did he reveal his feelings. He was a man accustomed to pressure. A man who'd spent so much time with such dark responsibilities, he'd forgotten there could ever be any other way of living. His face remained smooth, even under the sharp scrutiny of the man before him. He simply waited and, eventually, with a small grunt of thoughtfulness, Ko Tan continued.

"I've decided it is time for another interview," Ko Tan told his right-hand man. "After all, it has been years since the movement last appeared in the paper, and much has changed since then. Revolutionary movements are becoming 'in.' All around Europe countries are breaking apart. Perhaps now the time is right to sell the world the legitimacy of our own secessionist plans. And what could be more useful than a young, naive and incredibly malleable journalist?" Ko Tan smiled then, but it wasn't a nice smile.

"You will give her tours," Ko Tan said abruptly. "But guided ones at all times. She is not to go anywhere without you. She will be allowed to see the men training, perhaps even a tape or two of some recent skirmish. Find one that makes our men look good. Allow her to interview a few men. You will, of course, act as an interpreter and edit all comments appropriately. In the end, she is to walk away impressed with our little army and its fight for independence. See to it."

"And the matter of the heroin?" Shadow asked blandly. "Sooner or later, she's going to ask about it."

Ko Tan dismissed the subject with a wave of his hand. "A regrettable tool of circumstance. If only we had outside sponsors, some international legitimacy, then we would not have to turn to such tragic measures." He openly grinned at Shadow now. "I am good at this, no?"

Shadow simply nodded. "Do you really think you'll gain more international support this time?" he asked levelly.

Ko Tan merely shrugged. "It can hardly hurt. There are always a few out there who are willing to part with money, or weapons, to support a 'worthy' cause. Besides, there is nothing wrong with humoring a beautiful woman. She is beautiful, no?"

Once again Ko Tan's eyes were cold; once again they stared at Shadow with calculating suspicion. But Shadow simply nodded again, his face as expressionless as his name.

"You are dismissed," Ko Tan said abruptly. But just as Shadow was reaching the door, his voice once again cut across the distance. "And Shadow," he said, "tell the men—tell everyone—that no one is to touch her. The woman, she is mine."

Shadow froze for a fraction of a second, startled by the raw fury that surged through him at the words. But a year and a half was a long time to play a dangerous game, and it was certainly enough time to learn control. His insides twisted, but his face remained the cold, marble-carved face of a dispassionate man. It was the law of survival. Without a pause, he clipped out an acknowledgment to his superior and walked out.

The anger was still there, however, when he shut the door securely behind him. Anger at Ko Tan for wanting the woman, anger for what he would probably do to her in the end. And there was anger at Riley, too, for having come in the first place, for having thought she could simply throw herself into the big leagues and walk out unscathed. *"Looking for you."* Her words echoed in his head and his fury doubled. Didn't she know she was dealing not with just any corrupt man, but a deadly one? A man who truly didn't care one iota for human life? He'd killed women before; he'd killed children. And none of it kept him up late at night, because he simply didn't care. It meant nothing to him.

What type of fool was she, he thought savagely, to pursue a man like that? And all for the sake of a newspaper story? She was shallow, he told himself, ambitious to the extent she had no respect for her own life. She deserved whatever was coming.

But he still couldn't quite make himself believe that last line, and it only made him angrier. Because after all this time, after all these years, it *did* bother him. He worried about what would happen to her. He remembered the pale dignity of her face as she walked through that door just an hour ago, trembling with fear and determined not to show it. Yes, it bothered him.

He couldn't afford the concern, though. Not now. Definitely not now.

Damn her. Damn Ko Tan. Damn himself.

Then he looked up to find Riley—dammit, when had he started thinking of her as *Riley?*—sitting on the leather sofa reading *Newsweek* as if she hadn't a care in the world, and his rage exploded. One way or another, he swore vehemently as he strode across the room, he was going to get her to understand just what type of mess she'd landed herself in. One way or another, he'd make her see where her ambitions had taken her.

His grip was hard and bruising when it descended upon her arm. He didn't utter a word, but dragged her savagely off the couch and down the hall.

Her eyes widened at the sudden attack, and she let him drag her along for the first few feet. But then, with a spark of the spirit he already knew she possessed, she struggled to pull her arm from his grasp.

"Let go," she protested. "I can walk, Shadow."

But he didn't say a word, nor slow down an inch. Instead, with a grim face and long strides, he continued pulling her out of the house and through the tall grass. The building faded away behind him, and with it the reassuring lights. Soon they were surrounded only by the thin glow of a full moon.

"Where are we going?" Riley tried again. Dammit, but his obvious anger was beginning to scare her. What had she done to deserve this? What was going on? Had Ko Tan just led her along only to kill her now? Oddly enough, this time the thought made her defiant. If she was going to get killed, she at least wanted to die with a little dignity.

"Stop it!" she cried out angrily. Then she added vehemently, "If Ko Tan ordered you to kill me, the least you could do is to shoot me now and get it over with!"

But it was like talking to a brick wall. Not even a single muscle flinched in his face at her words. His fury was so focused, there was no room for anything else. It was frightening. She'd thought earlier that he wasn't a cruel man. Now she wasn't so sure.

What did she really know about this man called Shadow? Nothing. Nothing at all.

At last, when it seemed they must have traveled at least a fourth of a mile, they came to a row of black mounds faintly outlined by moonlight and the smell of freshly turned earth. With a jolt, Shadow came to a stop, snapping his hand back from her arm. "Look," he ordered. The word was deadly soft, underlined with the still-brewing anger within him, laced with purposeful vengeance. She didn't dare disobey.

"I see five piles of dirt," she replied finally, her own hurt anger clipping the words. Then, in a rush, she demanded hotly, "What is it you want from me?"

"What?" he snarled, a muscle in his jaw twitching as he fought to keep his bitter control. "I thought you were this hotshot reporter? Out for the world's biggest story. Well, this is your story, lady. These are Ko Tan's accomplishments."

Suddenly, what she was looking at came to her in a sickening rush that took the bottom right out of her stomach.

"Graves," she whispered in shock. "Five fresh graves."

He pinned her with a penetrating stare. "There's still room for a sixth," he informed her curtly. "So don't tempt him, Little Miss Reporter."

There was a wealth of scorn in the words, but she was too floored to respond. Five fresh graves. Five people who had

lived, and now were dead. She shivered in the night; unconsciously her arms came up to wrap around herself.

It was a particularly vulnerable gesture, and Shadow suddenly felt the anger slipping away. All at once he felt tired and
almost defeated. She was just young and innocent, after all.
Everyone was the same at some time in their lives. Only, in her
case, it would most likely cost her her life. His own words came
back to taunt him. *"There's still room for a sixth."*

God, he needed to leave this place. Leave before it destroyed
him completely. If it hadn't happened already.

"Who were they?" Riley asked softly next to him. "What
did they do?"

For a long moment, he didn't reply. He just stared at the
black mounds where five people now rested.

Then, before her very eyes, she watched all the emotion and
intensity drain from him until, once again, he was just a tall,
shadowed man with a face of granite. Even standing next to
her, he looked all alone in the moonlight. She had the sudden
urge to reach out to him, to lay a hand on his arm, but she was
afraid to see his eyes and all the silent emptiness she was somehow certain was there.

Who was this man? And what was he doing here? After an
entire evening in his company, she was no closer to knowing.

Finally, Shadow spoke, in steady, emotionless words that
gave away nothing, but were nonetheless brutal and chilling on
their own.

"This is the Barber," he said, gesturing lightly to the first
mound. "He gave Ko Tan a bad haircut and Ko Tan shot him
down. Seven times. And here," he said, pointing to the second
mound, "is Mangu, who couldn't stop smoking the opium pipe
after his third warning, and thus was sentenced to death by firing squad. And here is Shan, a fifteen-year-old boy who didn't
hear or respond to a direct order by Ko Tan. So Ko Tan pulled
out his gun and shot him. And this grave—this grave is a
woman's. I don't remember her name. She came as Ko Tan's
mistress, but then she was caught with another man. Her throat
was slit. Her lover is the other mound. You don't want to know
what they did to him."

He looked at her then, looked at her with eyes that seemed
old beyond their years. All the anger and passion were gone,

like a spring that had dried up quickly in the summer heat. Now there was only silence in the gray depths, deadly silence and resignation.

"Do you understand yet?" he asked her quietly. "Do you understand, Riley? Ko Tan is dangerous, and I'm no better. He killed those people, but I stood there and did nothing. That's my job. And I do it well."

There was a wealth of contempt in the words, but who it was aimed at she couldn't be sure. Was it for her, or for what he perceived to be her ambitions? For Ko Tan, and his wanton disregard for human life? Or was it for himself, because he lived in the middle of such a world, and did nothing to change it?

"Why do you work for him?" she asked finally, challenging him. "Why do you work for a man you hate?"

"Hate?" he echoed flatly. "There's no gain in hatred. These people knew the risk of associating with Ko Tan, just like everybody else does. And they accepted that risk, accepted the price it might cost them. Just like I know that on any given day Ko Tan may order my death, if only because he's in a bad mood. That's the price of working for Ko Tan. Now, you tell me," he demanded softly, "how much will it cost you? Because I don't think you get it, Riley. There's a price to ambition."

She hesitated, suddenly understanding what all of this was about. He thought she was here just for the story. In Ko Tan's office, she'd come across as bold and ambitious. In Shadow's eyes, it made her a fool. But she couldn't correct him, she realized. In his own words, he was dangerous, too. No, she knew almost nothing about this man, and at this point, she couldn't afford the risk. In this jungle, both of them stood alone.

So she responded with a bravado she was far from feeling. "I'll be careful," she said quietly.

"Like you were tonight?" he retaliated. "Taunting him with everything from your beauty to your height?"

"Look," she began angrily, becoming genuinely defensive now, "I said I would be careful."

"Tell me, Riley," he whispered, looking straight into her stormy eyes with his own expressionless gaze. "If you weren't willing to die for your story, would you give your body instead?"

The words were softly spoken, but they hammered home with brutal intensity. Without conscious thought, her hand came up and smacked across the plane of his face. It sounded loud in the night, as loud and angry as the red print that now glowed on his cheek.

His eyes narrowed, the anger once again sparking. For a moment he was almost overwhelmed by the desire to hit her back, knock her to the ground so she'd finally understand just how harsh and cold this place was.

With an oath, he clenched his fist tightly at his side. But his anger, having finally penetrated his iron control, welled up inside him like a consuming torrent. He wanted... He needed... His eyes lit upon Riley's face—the vivid eyes, the soft skin, the full, sensuous lips. Without another thought, his arm came out, and before she could so much as protest, he dragged her to his chest. Driven by the raging emotions within him, his lips fell on her own.

At first she was rigid under the attack, caught off guard by the sudden change in her jailor. Then, she began struggling against him.

He was like steel, she thought faintly, his chest an unyielding wall, his arms forming solid bands around her. And the heat... His lips were hot and plundering, seizing her softness, ruthlessly taking. But then they changed, became caressing, almost teasing, nibbling oh so sweetly—

Her body went limp, her mind lost in the confused haze of conflicting sensations. He had seized her in anger, a hard, cold man. She should fight him; she should hate him. And yet...

The heat...

Abruptly it was gone. Cursing, Shadow released her, turning away. What had he done? his mind screamed at him. Had he lost all sense of decency?

Grabbing a woman in anger, kissing her with rage. His jaw tightened with contempt, self-loathing sweeping through him. God, he'd been under too long, he thought dimly. He'd spent one too many years in this cesspool, one too many years of harsh, cruel living to earn the confidence of a hard, cruel man.

He had to stay away from her, he told himself fiercely. Stay away before things got too out of hand. She made him feel, she penetrated his control. And he couldn't afford to lose his control. Not here. Not in this jungle, and not ever. Emotions were too dangerous; he liked his dispassion. He *needed* it.

"I'll take you back now," he said abruptly.

Riley, her mind still dazed, simply nodded. Her hand came up to her lips. He'd kissed her. He'd really kissed her. And she'd *liked* it. Oh, Lord, what was wrong with her?

They walked in silence. Riley did risk one look, only to confirm that Shadow had indeed withdrawn back into his own impenetrable world.

And suddenly she was overwhelmed by the urge to understand him. This man had just seized her, kissed her hard, and then let her go before he did any harm. He'd touched her, and yet she barely knew his name. What had happened in his life to bring him here, to this dark and dangerous land? Who was he, really? Where had he come from? And which parts of him did she believe? The harshness of his words that claimed he was a killer? Or his own actions, the obvious control that had kept him from striking her back?

He was the ultimate puzzle, the ultimate challenge.

Except, she reminded herself, she wasn't here to figure him out. Her only concern was escape, her only interest in this man whether or not he could or would help her. True, he had to have some interest in her to want to prove to her the danger she was in. But he'd given no indication of his willingness to help her out of it. None at all.

If anything, he'd revealed just how dangerous he could be.

Finally they arrived at what Riley had mentally dubbed Prisoners' Row. Her living quarters. Obviously not a man long on goodbyes, Shadow simply opened the door of the prison for her and then shut it firmly behind her.

From the other side of the barred windows, she couldn't resist watching him fade away into the night. Long after he disappeared, she stood there, still watching, while her mind raced.

Hours later, Shadow finally relaxed deep in the darkness of the jungle. He'd matted some leaves down in a tiny alcove and now sat amid them, lightly stroking Nemo's back with one hand. The little monkey had appeared as soon as Shadow had left Riley, and was already curled up in contented sleep. Shadow looked at him with something close to envy.

It would be a long time before he would sleep again.

He knew he was becoming too involved. It seemed the more he told himself that she wasn't any concern of his, the more he worried. But, dammit, he couldn't afford such luxuries as worrying. Not now, and certainly not here.

He'd kissed her. Even now, he could barely believe he'd done such a thing. In his entire year and a half here, he'd never slipped so badly. Worse yet, as he sought to regain his control, he could still feel the sweet softness of her lips. He cursed silently. He should be able to handle this.

After all, the dark side of life was nothing new to him. He'd grown up on the streets, a silent, resourceful boy who'd become a silent, resourceful man. God knows, he would probably still be on the streets if he hadn't met Sabrina Duncan when he was fourteen. She'd believed in him, had cared for him, long before he'd ever been able to understand why. And because of her faith, he'd returned to her shelter for runaway youths time and time again. Until eventually he'd found the courage to stay.

But in the end, even that had only been in passing. There had come a day when he'd realized he couldn't stay forever and that it was time to move on. Sabrina, after all, was happily married now to Thomas Lain. After her own life of darkness as a runaway forced to sell her body to survive, she'd finally found the perfect man and the perfect love. She certainly didn't need Shadow, and at the age of eighteen, he'd known that it was time to see what he could do, who he could be. Maybe, he'd thought, he could find his own happy ending, just as she had. So he'd written her a note and had joined the army.

He'd never looked back, never even written a letter. Perhaps because he knew that, better than anyone, she would understand. Yet sometimes late on nights like this one, or when he happened to be near a television and caught an old Western, he would think back to those days at Sabrina's house. The days when, silently, they would sit side by side on her couch and watch the good guys beat up the bad guys. But he never picked up the phone, never called her.

Because he didn't believe in trying to hold on. Because it seemed the more precious something was, the better the chances of losing it. Like his mother, like Johnny. It was easier to simply accept the loss, lose it before it lost him. He'd been alone throughout most of his past. He would probably be alone through most of his future. That was the way of it.

Once, so long ago the memories were but hazy recollections, there had been someone. His mother, with her dark hair and the soft scent of lilacs. He rarely thought about her these days, for she'd existed in a lifetime that had long since passed and could never be regained. Still, he carried the memory of her comforting scent around with him like a faded photograph of another time in another world.

When he'd joined the army, a buxom blonde had been more than happy to relieve him of his virginity. And over the years, there had been a few others like her. But never relationships. Never anything permanent. He preferred it that way.

So why was it so hard to keep one red-haired woman out of his mind now?

After he'd left her this evening, he'd sat in the shadows between the rows of huts, keeping watch. It had been hours before she'd gone to sleep. Hours when he could clearly hear the rhythmic thumping of her bare feet against the dry floorboards as she prowled the limits of the hut.

She didn't fit into his bamboo world, Shadow thought abruptly. She belonged with the roaring life and hustle and bustle of a big city. He could see her in New York, strolling confidently down the concrete sidewalks, eating hot dogs piled high with relish and sauerkraut. That was where she belonged, in a place larger than life that would never hold her back or shut her in.

He himself had spent most of his life in cities. First in Portland, Oregon, with Sabrina, and then moving eastward to New York. But he'd never felt at home there. In many ways he preferred the slower, natural pace of this misty jungle. But he would be leaving here in a matter of weeks. And there would be no looking back.

But where would he go? Once again, he found himself with that fundamental question. Where?

He had no answer. And as he finally faded off to a badly needed sleep, it wasn't the answer that came to him. Instead he was once more plagued with visions of the laughing green eyes and flaming red hair of a woman he could never have.

Chapter 3

Dawn found her exploring the floor of the hut with her fingertips. She'd already gone over the door again, but with no luck. The inside of the walls was maddeningly smooth, polished with some sort of lacquer that probably served as a sealant against the rain as well. But she wasn't concerned with the rain.

She wanted a way out.

If nothing else, yesterday's events had ingrained in her mind the need for escape. Five mounds under the midnight sky. She shivered as her hands moved over the smooth boards. She'd never heard of such a wanton waste of human life. Ko Tan had killed them because he wanted to. Because it fitted his whim, assuaged his pride. He killed because he liked to.

She *had* to get out of here. She never should have come in the first place, she thought bitterly. She was just a junior reporter from Ohio. What did she know about this kind of game? And how could she begin to survive in this kind of violence?

She was out of her league. *Way out.*

She'd thought about it most of the night—the brutality of Ko Tan. She'd also thought of Shadow, the gray-eyed mystery man who had kissed her with such passion. Sometime in the middle of it all, she'd even given in and cried herself to sleep. But dawn was coming now, the tears were drying on her cheeks, and she knew she couldn't just sob her way home. She was on her own, in a jungle she didn't understand—*couldn't* understand—and she had only herself to rely on, so she would just have to do the best she could. If she could just find a way out. Surely one of these damn boards must be loose. . . .

In frustration she smacked her hand hard against the floor, but as with the door, it didn't do any good. The wood might be old, but it was certainly strong.

With a small cry of despair, she sat back on her heels, running her hand through the tangled mess of her hair.

What was she going to do?

What about Shadow? He seemed determined to keep her at arm's length, determined to convince her that he wouldn't help her. And then there was that kiss. He'd wanted to hurt her; she'd seen it in his eyes. But he hadn't.

In spite of the darkness in his eyes and the threat in his voice, there was something about him that drew her to him. He had to feel *something* for her. After all, he didn't have to show her the graves last night. No, he'd done that on his own as a way of warning her. Certainly you only warned people that you didn't want to see hurt. But then again, even if he *did* feel some pity for her, it didn't mean that he would help her. He'd already told her that he did his job well, even when that job involved death.

Mind spinning from the back-and-forth analysis that was getting her nowhere, she forced herself to face the truth. She was definitely on her own. Her eyes closed briefly under the weight of such a reality, but then she forced them back open to peer out at the lightening sky. Don't give up hope yet, McDouglas, she advised herself. There's no one else to turn to. . . .

Mustering her energy, she directed her attention back to the floor. She'd already lost three fingernails discovering that prying up the boards was much more difficult than it looked. What she really needed was a metal file.

Halfheartedly, she rummaged through the pockets of her camp shirt and khakis. Well, she thought sardonically, now she'd know what type of things to pack in the future. Stumped once more, she resumed sitting back on her heels, a position she was rapidly beginning to hate. Glumly, she wrapped her arms around her legs and rested her tired head on her knees.

This was not going well at all. A drug lord, a heroin drug lord. She was the prisoner of an internationally wanted killer. Why, oh, why hadn't she just settled for the travel piece? She sighed, but tried to bolster her courage. Feeling sorry for herself wouldn't help. The only thing that could save her now was getting out. Her eyes drifted to the cot.

Its frame was made out of some kind of lightweight metal. She could bend it with her bare hands if she tried. But what would that accomplish? Not much. Except ... Yes, not the cot—the screws.

Momentarily energized by this new thought, she proceeded to twist off one of the nuts and withdraw the screw. It looked well made; long and thick. She hoped it was unbreakable, as well.

The sky had completely lightened by now, and she risked one glance out the window before she started. Someone might come by to check on her soon. She'd have to be quick.

Anxious, she wedged the screw between the floorboards, listening with one ear for sounds of approaching footsteps. With a last grunt, she pounded the screw in place, then began to carefully ease it from side to side.

At first it refused to move, but with a lot of pushing and heaving, she was at last able to wiggle it about enough that the floorboard began to move. After a while she stopped. Taking a deep breath, she pushed a long lock of her hair back with a sweaty hand while she decided how to proceed.

Her hands were already a raw red, the blisters hovering just beneath the surface. But she had no other tools to use, so with a diplomatic shrug, she continued.

The goal was to loosen the board enough so that a space would appear between the head of the nail and the board. In which case, she could then use the screw as leverage to pull out the nail. Primitive at best, but as long as it worked ...

Briefly, she remembered Shadow's warnings of snakes. Crawling around in the long grass under a dark hut suddenly didn't seem so appealing. It had been different to walk through the grass in bare feet. Snakes had seemed a dim abstract then.

But crawling, eye level? Now that was a different matter altogether.

What if . . .

Her imagination got the best of her and she was forced to sit back once again, this time to reconsider things for a bit. What kind of snakes did they have in Myanmar, anyway?

A sound penetrated her consciousness, and with her mind still trying to picture Burmese snakes, she jumped back instinctively, a strangled yelp emerging from her lips. Then she realized that the sound wasn't coming from beneath her room, but from outside her door. Frantically, she leapt to her feet and sprang for the cot. She'd barely landed with a painful thunk when the door opened and Shadow walked in.

Once again he didn't say a word, merely looked at her with dark, attentive eyes. It seemed to her that he saw the flushed brightness of her cheeks, the rapid rise and fall of her chest and the smudge of dust she knew must be on her face.

She flushed guiltily and knew that he caught that, as well.

But still he didn't say a word.

"So what's the plan for today?" she asked brightly, babbling as she sought to resurrect her role as the anxious reporter intent only on a story. "More walking, more sight-seeing? When can I interview Ko Tan?"

She was perhaps laying it on a little thick, but Shadow was no longer paying attention to her, anyway. Instead his eyes skimmed the room intently, taking careful inventory of each detail. For a long, breathless second, she waited for him to notice the loose board in the corner and the wobbly uncertainty of the cot, but finally his gaze returned to her, and she breathed a little easier.

Then, for the first time, she noticed the pair of army boots and socks in his hand.

"I've been instructed to give you a tour" was all he said.

Her nerves relaxed a fraction more. That didn't sound so ominous, and she really was interested in seeing the camp—she'd never witnessed a guerrilla movement in action. Also, the more she knew about the camp, the better her chances of escape.

"And what all are you instructed to show me?" she asked brightly as she took the boots and socks and began putting them on. It occurred to her that she might even get a story out of this yet, but then, with an unconscious frown, she pushed the thought away. Story, hell—what she really needed was to save her life.

Shadow, however, didn't answer her question. Apparently he was back to his silent role, his face dark with tight indifference. She looked at him for a long moment, trying to detect a trace of anything behind that control. Last night, for a bare second, he'd lost his iron will to anger. But now he was the man of steel once more.

Abruptly, she felt a small pang of loss.

Determinedly, she pushed the emotion aside, concentrating on her goal instead. This man shouldn't matter to her one way or the other, she reminded herself as she finished lacing the second boot. She didn't need him to make conversation or acknowledge her presence. She just needed him to stop watching her with his eagle eyes long enough to make a good run for it.

Everything else about him was entirely irrelevant.

Unless . . . there was something more than disdain in those dark eyes of his. Unless. . . Once more her mind registered that he wasn't an unattractive man. Once more, she remembered the dark heat of his kiss. What if—

She stopped the thought abruptly. No, she wouldn't resort to such tricks as seduction. She'd always been a woman who used her brain, not her body. Surely her brain could get her out of this.

Shadow was a mercenary, a hired killer. She would be better off keeping her distance. She might like to believe he wasn't cruel, that he wouldn't hurt her, but considering his chosen profession . . . No, given the circumstances, she would be smarter to keep as much distance as possible between them.

She jerked herself back from her thoughts to discover herself the focus of Shadow's sharp gaze. Uncontrollably, her cheeks reddened under the scrutiny as she floundered for something to fill the silence.

"A shower?" she asked weakly. "Is there perhaps someplace I could clean up?"

He seemed to consider this, though his eyes didn't relent in their search of her face. She had to forcibly keep herself from turning away from the scrutiny, determined to meet his gaze head-on. After a small stare-down, he consented with a nearly imperceptible nod. "Follow me," he said curtly.

"All right," she said. "Just tell me one thing," she added casually as she rose to her feet. "What kinds of snakes are out there, anyway?"

It seemed to her that they'd been walking forever. When she'd said "shower," she'd figured at least a nice bucket of water in another hut somewhere in the camp. She hadn't figured on an hour-long trek through an incredibly damp and dense jungle. She was going to end up dirtier when all was said and done.

Already, she'd bitten back the temptation to ask "Are we there yet?" but her control was starting to fade. To make matters worse, the man in front of her seemed intent on not saying a single, solitary word.

About halfway along a little white-faced monkey had come leaping out of the trees to land on her shoulder. Riley had uttered a small scream in shock, but Shadow had simply leveled her with his calm, cool gaze and then, with a few brief hand motions, commanded the monkey over to his shoulder. Even now, Nemo—as Shadow had called him—was perched there, though every once in a while his face would swivel around to peer at her with wide, curious eyes.

"The company you keep," she'd told Shadow dryly, but he'd just dismissed her with his usual shrug. And kept walking.

Just when she felt as if she'd wilted completely, her long hair hanging like rope down her back, they broke into a small clearing with a wide stream. Nemo seemed to be expecting it, jumping onto a low-hanging branch to disappear in the thick foliage.

"There," Shadow said, nodding toward the stream. "It's a bit cold, but the water is clean and shallow. No snakes," he deadpanned, his expressionless face never wavering.

She made a point of ignoring his comment, taking in the wonderful expanse of water instead.

"Perfect," she breathed finally, suddenly overwhelmed by the need for a long, cleansing bath. Without giving it another thought, she unlaced the rigid leather of the new boots, sighing again as she eased out her tired feet and peeled off the thick socks. Automatically her fingers moved to the buttons on her shirt, only to freeze as she realized that Shadow was still watching.

She looked at him pointedly, but he met her gaze head-on. For the first time in hours, she faltered, suddenly unsure of herself. Then, with a determined squaring of her shoulders, she raised her head and looked at him proudly. "If you don't mind," she said with far more bravado then she felt, "I would prefer some privacy to bathe."

"Show me your hands," he suddenly commanded. She looked at him with slanted eyes, but his gaze remained steady and firm. Frowning now, she held up her hands, palms down.

But he walked over to her and turned them over, revealing the raw redness of her palms. With surprising gentleness, he ran a callused thumb over the tender surface. "You know," he said softly, "you really should take better care of your hands."

She flushed again, knowing full well she'd been found out.

"Can you promise me that you won't try to escape?" he asked.

She turned away from him, unable to find the words he asked for while her heart pounded out a panicked beat in her chest. How could he have known? Was the man the devil, or what? Feeling desperate, she tried to hedge. "I h-hurt my hands in the crash," she stammered out.

"I tended you after the crash," he said tersely. "Your hands weren't red then."

The certainty of the words made her blush all the more. He'd "tended"? Her whole body practically shivered under the implications. Somehow she hadn't really thought about who had taken care of her after the crash. Well, now she knew.

And what the hell was she going to do about him? Trust him? Not trust him?

She couldn't. She just couldn't take the risk.

"What would be the point of trying to escape?" she said in what she hoped was a convincing tone. Pulling her hands from his, she attempted a casual shrug under the onslaught of his knowing eyes. "It would be impossible to hide from thousands of trained guerrillas. I'd probably just get myself killed. Surely you don't think I'd be so foolish as to try?"

His gaze clearly gave the answer to her last question. She pulled back her shoulders defensively now. "I'm not trying to escape," she said sharply. "I just want to take a bath. Now could you please turn around?"

He shook his head slowly, his gray eyes still never leaving hers.

Inside, her desperation grew. She was just a girl from Ohio; she wasn't meant for these kinds of things. Subterfuge wasn't her forte. Suddenly she wanted out. She wanted out so badly she could taste it. Even her tiny prison hut seemed preferable to Shadow's silent scrutiny.

But there was no escaping from him.

She licked her dry lips. "What do you want?" she finally asked softly.

"Promise you won't try again," he ordered levelly.

"I can't do that," she said, frustration spilling out in her voice. "You, more than anyone, have emphasized just how dangerous it is for me here, yet now you want me to promise to do nothing? You make no sense."

"Promise," he ordered in the same terse tone.

"No!" she cried now, her fury ignited past caution. Of all the jailers in the world, why did hers have to be the most maddening, stubborn— "I have to escape," she said fiercely. "And you can't expect me to do otherwise!"

"Then," he replied evenly with his dispassionate face, "I can't turn my back on you."

The words burned through her, and she felt her face flushing. Her eyes darkened to a stormy hue. He thought he had so much control, did he? Thought he was above such petty things as emotions. Well, she'd show him. The question was, how?

I know, whispered the little voice in the back of her head. *You're a woman, McDouglas. And he may seem cold, but he's still a man.*

She wanted to push the words away, but her anger had already fastened on to them. Yes, he was a man, a very, very controlled man. But just how controlled was he?

The challenge, on top of all the stress and fear of the past twenty-four hours, was too much. A reckless feeling took over her, and she didn't care if she was latching on to this one small thing to distract herself from the very real threat to her life Ko

Tan represented. Right now only one thing mattered; she would only *let* one thing matter. He'd said he had to watch her—well then, just let him. She'd show him she didn't back down. Let him look at her with uncaring eyes again. She was a woman. Her words didn't get anywhere, her anger accomplished nothing. But this just might.

Her hands weren't completely steady when they found the first button of her shirt, but she kept her head high, her eyes challenging. Her nerves felt wound on edge, tingling from her toes to the roots of her long, long hair, but she ignored them.

He did have such strong, powerful hands, she thought distantly now. And the scar running down the side of his cheek lent him a dangerous air. He looked untamable, completely self-controlled, the ultimate challenge. The first button slid free.

She continued, never looking away as, one by one, she undid the remaining buttons. She took a deep breath then and swallowed hard. This was it, little girl from Ohio. She couldn't back down now. Slowly, with slightly trembling hands, she slid the shirt back, exposing smooth white shoulders and a black lace bra. Next, her hands went to the waistband of her pants, pulling down the zipper with a quiet rasp.

His eyes hadn't flickered away, but she could see a tense rigidity in his jaw now, and his breathing was no longer quite so even. But still he didn't say a word or move a muscle.

She eased the tan slacks down, letting them fall until she could gracefully step clear with one small step. Then, with lingering care, she smoothed the rest of the shirt off her arms, letting it fall away to the soft ground below.

Head held high, she stood proudly before him, clad only in wisps of black lace that tantalized more than covered. Her cheeks were flushed, her eyes overbright with shaky defiance.

And she could see the reluctant hunger blooming in his eyes, the desire. But he made no move, standing motionless a full foot away.

This time her eyes fell shut, and taking a deep shuddering breath, she mustered her courage for that final step. She'd come this far, she could do it.

Her hands came up, and with a small twist, the bra fell free.

Shadow felt like a drowning man, helpless against the on-slaught of desire that surged through his veins and quickened his pulse. Her body was exquisite before him, long and slender, rippling with the ripe curves of womanhood. His hands wanted to stroke the satin of her skin, caress the swell of her breasts and her hips, and then smooth all the way down to the graceful curves of her long calves.

He didn't move, though, his hands staying firm at his side. Only his jaw muscle twitched from the strain of his control. He would not touch her. Yet still he wanted her, still he felt the ache growing from somewhere deep inside and ripping through his body. Unbidden, the memory of her lips rose in his mind—the soft texture, the sweet taste...

This is what she wanted, he thought with a combination of burgeoning rage and overwhelming sensation. She was out to drive him mad. It wasn't enough that she had come here risking both of their lives so she could get some story. No, she had to twist his gut, damn his soul, while she was at it.

He should take her, he thought half savagely, closing his eyes for one precious second. Just throw her down in the jungle and teach her what happened to women who played with fire. She thought he was a mercenary—well, he could be one, all right. Dark, powerful, angry, primitive.

He'd lived here long enough to learn it all.

His hands rose, clenching. Then, with supreme effort, he brought them back down to his sides.

When he looked at her this time, she knew she'd affected him. She could see it in the black flames of passion and rage burning in his gaze. She shivered lightly in fear, but at that moment, she couldn't have looked away from him if she'd tried. His gray eyes fell to her lips, pinned them, plundered, ravaged. Unconsciously, she parted them in acquiescence, her tongue tentatively licking her lips.

His eyes turned molten, and her legs trembled under the impact.

"Go!" he ordered hoarsely. "Take your bath or we leave now."

It broke the spell, and she didn't wait any longer. No, the girl from Ohio had had enough. She turned and fled to the stream.

Slowly, Shadow sank to the ground. It took several large lungfuls of air before he could clear his mind and several lungfuls more until he could ease the tension in his muscles. Then he cursed, long and hard. But even then, the emptiness inside him remained, the remnants of unyielding desire twisting his gut.

To touch her. To simply touch her...

It was at that moment that he realized just how much danger he was in. He'd wanted to remain cold and uncaring, but already she filled him with hollow aches and relentless yearnings. She was a beautiful, stubborn, rash woman. She would get them both killed.

And he wanted her so much he was almost willing to risk it all for one more taste of her lips. Slow this time. Subtle, probing, complete.

He shook his head. No, he hadn't survived this long in a world so brutal just to be undone by a mere woman. She was foolish to tempt him, foolish to think he was still civilized after living in savagery all this time.

But his mission was drawing to a close. With luck it would be over soon—this part of it, anyway. Surely he could control himself for a few more weeks. Couldn't he?

There was no such thing as a sure thing, and he felt the resignation well in his throat, unbidden. He'd been playing the controlled superhuman for too long. Watching all his moves, his expressions, at times even his thoughts. He lived in the darkness, breathed the blackness and fought to remain untouched by it even as he felt himself sink a little every day.

And just when it was about to end, this brutal assignment finally come to a successful conclusion, here came this woman. Reminding him painfully that he was really just a man, flesh and blood, with a man's needs and a man's desires.

He wanted her.

But he wouldn't take her. Duty came first. Duty to his group, and duty to his country. He'd accepted this assignment with the DEA knowing it would be harsh. He wouldn't fail now.

When he trusted himself enough, he slowly rose to his feet and went to a small tangle of roots near the river. There he took out a bar of soap he customarily kept for his own bathing needs and carelessly tossed it out into the stream.

He didn't look to see if she caught the soap. He simply went back to his spot, reseated himself and waited.

Riley had done some pretty serious thinking of her own under the thin protection of the water. She'd been mortified at first, by her own boldness in stripping like that, but also by the pure fact that even when she'd undressed he'd turned her away. What must he think of her? The thought that he had probably lost respect for her bothered her, oddly enough.

She dunked down deep under the cool waters of the stream. She'd thought to seduce him and had only embarrassed herself thoroughly. God, was she out of her league.

Well, she tried to think philosophically, at least she'd established that route was inaccessible. After all, the man had looked at her with blatant physical desire and still had had enough strength to reject her. And to think she'd actually convinced herself that he might possess some small feelings for her. She'd certainly taken care of that!

But once her injured pride finished salving its fragile remains, her mind took up other issues. For example, would a mercenary truly turn away a naked woman? Forget morals, forget respect or scruples. Forget even looks. Maybe she'd read too many novels, seen too many action films, but as far as she'd understood, mercenaries were the type to take whatever they could. And God knows, he could have taken her, so why hadn't he? He could have thrown her down and done whatever he pleased. They were out in the middle of a jungle. No one to see, no one to know.

But he hadn't.

Was she to understand, then, that he was a mercenary with *scruples?* Or was it just that his iron control was so utterly complete? But then again, he'd taken her to see the fresh graves. A savage warning, to be sure, but once again a course of action he didn't have to pursue. Yet he had.

Why?

She was still puzzling over this when she heard the soap land with a thud not far from her. She swam over and claimed it while sneaking a look to the riverbank under lowered eyes. But Shadow was already ignoring her, appearing completely unconcerned once again.

In spite of herself, her fury flared. Resolutely, she tried to push the emotions away while she quickly finished bathing. Now she would have to leave the water.

From the riverbank Shadow appeared to be looking elsewhere, but she wasn't fooled anymore. The man had the attention span of a hawk. The minute she moved from the water, he would notice. So, the best she could do was scrounge together the thin remains of her pride and, holding her head up, walk steadily out of the water.

Her skin was bared inch by inch as she waded up and out of the shimmering stream. She didn't dare look at Shadow, knowing her face would flush and her step falter. Instead she kept her eyes focused on the pile of clothes before her and tried desperately to look unconcerned.

But as soon as her shirt was within grasp, she scooped it up and wrapped it protectively around her, regardless of how uncomfortably it clung to her wet form. The shirt was long enough to reach nearly midthigh, so she took the time to wring out her hair and air-dry a little bit more before struggling into the rest of her clothes. Halfway through the process, however, she realized just how stained and muddied her clothes had become. So, trying to be resourceful, she picked up her pants and underclothing and carried them to the stream for a good scrubbing.

Through it all she didn't afford the silent man as much as one glance, and for all intents and purposes, he was ignoring her, as well. Finally, she dragged on the now soaking-wet garments and sat down on a low stone to drink in the soothing heat of the sun.

Again, Shadow said nothing, the silence stretching on and on. Finally, in spite of her resolution to fight silent treatment with silent treatment, she just couldn't take it anymore.

"Are you really a mercenary?" she asked abruptly. Feeling a little bolder now the words were out, she snuck a glance at him. He appeared to be watching something in the far distance very intently.

He shrugged.

"You don't act like a mercenary," she persisted. "Frankly, you don't act like a bad guy much at all."

Again he refused to look at her. Indeed, he was trying very hard to keep his eyes away from the sight of her lithe figure draped in clinging fabric that clearly outlined every curve of her breasts and hips. "You watch too many movies," he said curtly. He picked up a stick and began to relentlessly pull the bark from it.

She watched his quick, brutal motions for a bit, but then shook her head. "No," she said. "I don't think so. A truly heartless person wouldn't have taken me to a private stream to bathe. A truly heartless person—" she paused for a minute and then took a deep breath "—a truly heartless person wouldn't have watched me undress and done nothing."

He looked up then, and she was taken aback by the blazing fury suddenly raging in his eyes. "What do you want, Riley?" he demanded harshly. "Your story isn't enough for you? I haven't done you any favors, you little fool. I brought you here because back at the camp there are a few thousand men who haven't had a woman for weeks now, and have probably never even *seen* a woman with hair of fire. I brought you here because you're so foolish as to try seducing a man. Had it been anyone else but me, Little Miss Reporter, you would have been raped. And then, both you *and* your attacker would have to be killed. Don't forget where you are, Riley. Don't forget it for a moment."

Her face had paled under the onslaught of his words, but she refused to back down now. "I haven't forgotten," she informed him icily. "Why do you think I want to escape? And what do you mean 'killed'? Ko Tan doesn't allow rape?" She scoffed. "After everything you've said, I doubt it."

Shadow stared at her for a long moment with unwavering gray eyes. When he finally spoke, the words were carefully enunciated and completely devoid of emotion. "Ko Tan has no policy about rape, *except* when the woman has already been selected by himself."

The words suddenly penetrated, and she shivered even under the warming heat of the sun. Her stomach seemed to fall, and her head felt suddenly light. This was like some unrelenting nightmare, she thought dimly. One from which she couldn't quite wake up.

So Ko Tan had already claimed her. She shouldn't be surprised, she tried to tell herself. She'd already noticed how he'd looked at her. But the thought of Ko Tan touching her, the thought of that arrogant, petty man with his stained teeth and reptile eyes . . .

Once more she shivered, her face draining of all color.

"When?" she managed to ask calmly.

He took a deep breath, but forced himself not to back down. She needed to be afraid. It might be the only thing to save her, if such a thing was even possible. He made his voice cold and terse. "Whenever he wants."

In the ensuing silence, she almost pleaded with him, but she knew it wouldn't do any good. He'd already proven his loyalty to Ko Tan. He wouldn't help her.

Oh, God. Absently her hands came up to rub her arms, and her mind struggled to figure out what to do next.

She didn't have any answers. She didn't know what to do. Trying not to panic, she told herself that maybe tonight, when she toured the camp, she could learn a thing or two. Maybe . . .

It was all she could think of, even as she knew it wasn't enough. Her head slumped forward, her shoulders bowing under the weight.

Watching her, Shadow felt something wrench and turn in his gut. Because looking at her now, seeing the white purity of her skin, the sun-drenched fire of her hair, he couldn't stand the thought of Ko Tan touching her. Couldn't stand the thought of that man bruising her skin, twisting her faith and spitting her back out, a used and brittle woman.

Don't care, he reminded himself brutally. You can't prevent it. You can't jeopardize everything for one woman. So . . . just . . . don't . . . care. Funny, after all the years, all the miles and all the losses, he would have thought it would be easy. But it wasn't. It just wasn't.

Abruptly he stood. He had tortured them both enough for one day. It was time to go back. "It's time to go," he said curtly. Then, turning back to the forest, he made a low clicking sound in his throat.

After a short moment, Nemo emerged on a nearby branch, still chewing on a leaf he held tightly in one little fist. Swinging down with the other hand, he landed securely on Shadow's shoulder and greeted them both with a small burst of chatter.

Shadow started walking. Without much choice, she pulled on the rest of her clothes, hurriedly laced up her boots and followed. Trudging behind him with her dreary thoughts and soaked clothes, she was truly miserable. Struggling to recover the last of her sanity, she searched for something to distract herself with. "Where did you get the monkey?" she asked finally. Nemo's head once again swiveled around, and he looked at her with his bright, curious eyes. He really was a cute little thing.

"I bought him," Shadow said shortly.

"When?" she asked, becoming more interested now. Picking up her pace, she was able to get close enough to touch the little monkey with one finger. He rumbled appreciatively, and she smiled for an instant.

Shadow walked a little faster, putting more distance between them. The image of her naked body was still too sharp in his mind. He needed space.

"When did you buy him?" Riley repeated, falling once more back into step.

"A year ago."

"Where?"

"A village," Shadow snapped, starting to sound impatient now. She decided to ignore his tone.

"A village?" she persisted. "What was a monkey doing in a village?"

He shrugged in front of her, refusing to answer. She wouldn't let it go.

"Come on," she prodded. "Surely there's nothing confidential about acquiring a monkey. What? Ko Tan doesn't allow pets?"

She was beginning to really irritate him now, and his voice was razor sharp when he finally replied. "A man had captured him and taught him to do tricks. Satisfied?"

She nodded behind him. "So why did you buy him?" she asked, still curious.

"I didn't think he looked good in a vest," he answered curtly. "Subject closed."

She knew enough not to push him any further. Instead, she digested what she'd learned. So he'd bought Nemo from some village organ-grinder and now let him roam free in the jungle. Interesting actions for a mercenary. Perhaps she'd be doing better if she was a monkey, too.

"Are you assigned as my personal guard?" she asked after a long lapse, her mind once more on her situation. She needed more information. If she could just understand her position better, then she could think of a way out of it.

Shadow, however, seemed to have talked more than enough for the day, and now refused to answer her.

"I haven't seen anyone else," she persisted.

A slight nod was his only acknowledgment.

"But why you?" she asked. "After all, you're a foreigner, too. It seems to me that you would be the most likely candidate to help me escape."

"Citizenship is irrelevant," he told her coldly. "I do my job well, and I won't risk it for some woman, not even an American one."

"Still," she insisted, "why you? Are you the official guard or something?"

He shrugged, not liking this turn in conversation, even as he felt resigned to her questions. It had been a long time since he had met such an insistent woman, a long time since anyone had tried to break through his barriers. Not since he was fourteen, not since Sabrina Duncan . . . His thoughts momentarily wandered and he found himself thinking, once again, about what Sabrina would say if she knew what his life had become.

She would be sad. She'd worked so hard to save his life, and now it had all come down to this. Lying, killing, watching, waiting. Living in a twisted world where truth needed lies and justice called for revenge. It was his job, this deception, and he tried telling himself the end justified the means. To put a man like Ko Tan away would save so many lives. But it didn't make the destruction of the last few years any easier, or the destruction to come—the lies, the tests, the betrayals. All because of Ko Tan. The job had already cost Shadow so much; what was a little more?

But then there was a woman named Riley, a little voice added. A proud woman with glowing hair and flashing eyes. A woman who worked hard to understand him—

He pushed the thoughts away. It was all irrelevant.

"Ko Tan likes to test people," he answered Riley abruptly, his control now firmly back in place. "He tests me—he'll test you."

"What do you mean?" she asked, her brow furrowing at this riddle of an answer.

Shadow stopped then, pinning her with his gray eyes, which were once more devoid of any emotion. "If you escape," he said dispassionately, "Ko Tan will kill me. So either I do everything in my power to watch you, or I leave with you. Those are the only two options—one of obedience and one that most likely leads to death. Now he just waits to see where my loyalties lie."

Riley paled at the words. She hadn't considered this before; that if she escaped, it could cost him his life. Once more, she felt overwhelmed by the situation. What was she supposed to do?

"Do you think he'll kill me?" she asked finally, for ultimately, that was the real issue. Shadow didn't answer right away, and she wished she could see behind the mask to the real man. Now, more than ever, she wished she understood him, wished she could reach him at all. She waited for his answer, but when it seemed he wouldn't respond, she reached out and gripped his arm fiercely. "Tell me the truth," she demanded. "Do you think he'll kill me?"

This time the answer only took a moment to come. Shadow looked at her with his silent, unfathomable eyes.

"Yes," he said. "I do."

He turned away then and resumed walking through the jungle, a tall, lean man with a silver monkey on his shoulder. After a moment, she followed.

Chapter 4

She turned the matter over in her mind for a long time. The desire to escape versus the consequences such action might bring. If she was caught, she would most certainly be killed. Not to mention that Shadow, too, would probably be punished by death. On the other hand, if she stayed, there was always the chance that she might be able to worm her way out of things.

How, though? It was obvious what Ko Tan wanted from her. Not a reporter, not even a hostage. He seemed to have something much more lustful in mind. Could she go along with it? She shuddered at the mere thought. Even with her life at stake, she didn't think she could keep the revulsion from showing, keep from fighting him in the end.

And then? Death.

No, at least escape presented her with a *chance* of making it. To remain here would be to remain like a fly caught in a web, watching the spider encroach ever nearer.

She couldn't do it.

And Shadow? That question was much harder for her. He was a harsh man, coldly dispassionate. But he'd never been cruel to her, and there were times, times when his eyes grew dark with fierce yearnings . . .

Her mouth was suddenly dry and she had trouble swallowing. She definitely shouldn't think along those lines. No, it was better to simply remind herself that he was a competent person, more than capable of taking care of himself. Certainly his odds of survival here were much better than her own. If she escaped, she'd just have to trust that he would find out and act accordingly. He seemed to know the jungle very well. He'd manage.

The decision made, she turned her eyes back to the floorboards in the fading light of dusk. Once night fell completely, there wouldn't be enough light to work by. And she had already been fed for the evening. It seemed that she was on her own. There was no time like the present.

It took hours for her to get the first floorboard up. Twice the screw flew from her hands to disappear across the inky blackness of the moon. With night darkening ominously, and the moonlight only a distant flicker, she had to search with her hands in the dark, hoping by touch she could find what her eyes couldn't.

Her hands were shredded from the deep grooves of the screw, and she'd stopped once to try wrapping the sheet around her raw palms for protection. But it proved to be too cumbersome, so she'd been forced to set aside the sheet, returning to her bare hands.

Judging by the sticky feel, they were currently bleeding profusely.

But whatever doubts she'd once possessed disappeared in the course of the next brutal hours. She was grimly determined, her smudged face a study in concentration.

With a final heave, she felt the first nail finally give. Outlining it with her fingers, she was able to pull it out completely and then set out to attack its companion. With the floorboard already loosened, it went much faster this time. Presently, she'd pulled up two short boards. They revealed a dark hole beneath her, even darker than the night. It wasn't large yet, just six inches by eight. But it was wide enough to attract the attention of a snake or some other creature.

She wondered if they were like sharks, attuned to the smell of blood. Considering the shape her hands were in, she certainly hoped not.

The next floorboard came out more easily, and the hole became an eight-by-eight square. She looked down into its pitch-black depths and swallowed heavily.

She'd picked the corner of the cabin for the express purpose of not having to crawl much under the hut. But somehow she'd counted on being able to see some sort of natural light, like the moon. After all, the edge of the platform couldn't be more than a foot away. But the hole remained pitch-black, and she realized that the grass was so thick it choked out the light.

Oh, this wasn't going to be fun.

She wondered what things lay coiled in that darkness, sleeping in a black pit, just waiting for her to stumble upon them. She would have to go in headfirst, she knew. If something was down there, one wrong move, one quick strike, and it would be over. At least it would be fast.

She debated moving slowly, but doubted it would make a difference. Without any light, probably the first she'd know of its presence would be when she put her hand on it. And no matter how slowly she moved, she doubted a snake would take that kindly.

One last second for contemplation, one last chance to change her mind. Yet it didn't take her that long to renew the old conclusions. There wasn't any choice. No imagined monster down there could be as bad as the one she *knew* lived up here.

Taking a last deep breath, she reviewed her plan in her head, trying to picture a rough map of the camp based on what she'd seen earlier. Shadow had given her a tour of the highly self-sufficient base after they'd returned from the stream. This was the core camp, she'd learned, encompassing well over three thousand men. The rest of the troops were sprawled throughout the jungle to the west, engaged in nameless activities. As the headquarters, the camp included everything from a huge cafeteria to housing duplexes. She'd seen tiny cottages, where the support staff of the camp, including women, lived. She'd seen common latrines, showers and kitchens. Then there had been a small, highly efficient hospital filled with surprisingly new metal beds and some very sophisticated-looking equipment.

Shadow had even shown her a training facility, with everything from a modern weight room to a video room where the guerrillas watched tapes of their latest battle, mock or real. Everything was powered by a generator located on the north side of the camp. It was heavily fortified by thick metal and guarded by at least two men.

It had been shocking to see such modern equipment in the middle of what appeared to be an incredibly rustic camp. Just as the Ming in the bamboo hut had startled her, what she'd seen today made her wonder what other surprises lurked beneath the surface of Ko Tan's camp.

There had been three large buildings, much farther out, that Shadow had been subtle but firm in avoiding. Whatever type of smuggling Ko Tan was into these days, she imagined the inventory was warehoused there. It piqued her interest, and she was half tempted to go explore, but her route was dangerous enough as it was. Besides, she reminded herself in an effort to pacify her reporter's curiosity, from her tour alone she'd picked up enough interesting things for a decent story. Now she needed to focus all her attention on escaping.

Getting her bearings, she'd realized that she was positioned to the west of the camp, with the nearest border—maybe fifty to seventy miles—being on the east. She could try to go around the camp, but with a camp this size that would cost her a few extra hours. Not to mention that the periphery was kept stripped bare for easy sighting of approaching troops. If anyone noticed her escape while she was still going around the edge, she'd be caught out in the open with nowhere to run or hide. No, after a bit of thinking, it became clear to her that the safest course of action, ironically enough, would be to cut *through* the camp. If her absence was discovered then, she could at least attempt to hide in one of the buildings.

With one last deep breath, Riley now looked at the yawning black chasm beneath her. It was late; hopefully most people would be asleep, including Shadow. It wasn't the best plan, but it would have to do. She took a huge gulp of air and, not giving herself any more time to think about it, dived headfirst into the gaping black hole.

She could smell dirt and the musty odor of drying leaves. In her anxious haste, it seemed choking to her, and she fought

desperately to make it through the tangled grass. For one panicked moment, she thought she'd headed the wrong way, then,
with another frantic lunge, she found herself bursting free of
the hut and scrambled to her feet.

Her first thought was that she'd survived. Her second
thought registered why everything had been so dark.

The moon was gone.

It had been blanked from the sky, drowned in a torrent of
teeming black clouds. The air was heavy, sticking her shirt to
her heaving chest, flattening the natural waves in her hair. The
night was completely silent.

She found it difficult to breathe. She moved unsteadily, not
nearly as certain in this heavy, black world. She tried to walk
silently through the grass as Shadow had done, but it seemed
unreasonably loud, slapping against the solid leather of her
army boots in an extraordinarily quiet world.

Up ahead she could dimly make out the faint glow of the
guard lights, posted around the camp at twenty-foot intervals.
But there was no wayward sweep of a guard's flashlight, making the rounds. The entire night seemed to have reached a
standstill, leaving just her, walking through a suffocating night
as thunder crashed in the distance.

She felt the uneasiness buck and roll in her stomach, but
there was no going back now. If anything, she tried to console
herself, a storm might work to her advantage, making it hard
to follow her. At least she hoped so.

She kept her head up as she trudged onward, her eyes peeled
for the slightest change in her surroundings that would give her
warning of someone's approach. Already her hair weighed
heavily on her back, limp and damp with the humidity. Her
clothes stuck to her skin and her hands prickled as mud and
sweat mingled in the dark red grooves of the scratches.

But she gritted her teeth against the discomfort, the pain only
adding to her resolve. She passed over the small stream, then,
with a sudden thought, went back to rinse her hands in its
swollen depths. This water wasn't cool like the river in the jungle, though. Instead, it possessed a grittiness that stung her cut
palms. All she'd probably done was replace mud with silt. It
would have to do.

She'd barely stood up, barely taken another step, when the heavens opened above and water poured down in a thunderous swoosh. She stumbled under the sudden onslaught, thick rain pelting her skin and hair in an overwhelming shower.

She could feel it tearing at the mud and dust on her face, even as it drove into her pores. Within moments she was drenched, the water flowing like tiny rivers down her back and arms. It was a warm but pounding shower, and after the shock wore off, she lifted her arms to the rain, letting it pour through her hair and sweat-stained clothing.

It felt cleansing and rough, beating at the exhaustion in her tense muscles and at the dust smeared in her clothes. She walked more quickly now, invigorated by the thundering force of the night and the rain. The world was still black, but now it had a wet magic that intrigued and captivated her. The mud sloshed under her boots as she began to run lightly through the marshy grass.

The rain, however, obscured her view almost completely until she despaired of ever finding her way around. She stopped for a long moment, trying to figure out her next move. Perhaps she should go back and wait for a better night. But then it occurred to her that this *was* the best night. For just as the rain hid the camp from her, it would also hide *her* from the camp. She was the one on the offensive now. She could move slowly to find what she needed. And then she would be gone, leaving the rest of the camp to scramble through the blackness in vain pursuit. It would work out, she told herself. It had to.

Buildings finally materialized in the darkness, and she slowed to a stop. According to the tour Shadow had given her earlier, these buildings were part of the barracks that bordered the camp on three sides, with the mountain on the fourth. On this side were three rows of houses for the families that accompanied the troops. Inside the small semicircle were also the stables and pens for the animals.

If she remembered correctly, it was the busiest side, filled with the sounds of animals and the bustle of people. A small row of shops outside the stables offered everything from fresh food to handicrafts made by many of the women.

Now she just had to travel unseen through soldiers' barracks and a camp that held well over three thousand people.

Sure, piece of cake.

But the night was still pitch-black, and with the sky raining down its fury, the camp seemed amazingly still, almost like a ghost town. As of yet, she hadn't seen even one patrol guard. Perhaps they figured no one would attack on a night like this, so there was no need? Or perhaps there were only a few men patrolling, and even now one was headed her way....

In which case, she shouldn't stand around and wait. She started forward. Ducking down low, she tried to move as quietly as possible. The rain definitely helped, for the sound of it beating against the hollow bamboo of the buildings drowned out all other noise.

There was one heart-stopping moment when a light flickered to her right and she realized that a guard was indeed coming round, but she was well ahead of him by then, slipping unseen between the tightly spaced barracks.

After that, she passed safely by the row of outbuildings that served as the latrines and showers. Then came the slow, nerve-racking task of weaving quickly in and out of the narrow alleyways between buildings. She stopped at each corner, peering around first before darting forward to the next row, the next alleyway, eyes peeled for the first signs of life that would see her and sound the alarm.

And thus her attention was so fixated on the dark buildings before her, that she was taken completely unaware by the light force that came out of nowhere to clamp onto her shoulder.

She almost screamed out loud, biting harshly on her lower lip as the fright made her jump and spin. But still the force remained, holding on tightly. Only when her heart calmed down did she realize it was a wet and huddled Nemo, trying to find shelter in her hair.

He shivered and chattered against her neck, her own fright having transmitted itself to him. She reached up a soothing hand to calm him as she took refuge in another dark alleyway.

"It's okay, little guy," she whispered reassuringly, wondering why the monkey hadn't taken shelter in one of the thick trees of the jungle. She thought all animals were supposed to know— Then another thought occurred to her.

Shadow. If Nemo was here, then he must be nearby. She felt her heart sink like a stone into her stomach. It was all over then.

But after a long moment, when Shadow still hadn't appeared, she risked a glance around the corner. Nothing moved in the inky night. "All right," she decided with a sigh. "You're in this with me now. So no chattering, you hear?"

Nemo must have, for he contented himself with curling up his wet length against the warmth of her neck, buried beneath the thick mass of her hair. Even more cautious now, she moved on.

She reached another dark building, one she was reasonably sure served as Ko Tan's office. Momentarily she was tempted to go in, but her wet state would certainly leave signs, and she didn't want anyone catching the blame when Ko Tan realized someone had gone through his things. Not to mention the danger to herself if *she* got caught.

She remembered the five dark mounds in the moonlight, and she shivered. Oh, she would be happy to leave this place.

Footing was becoming difficult now as the grass turned into a marshland, swamped by the sudden onslaught of rain. Once she was almost sure she was going to fall, and even Nemo clutched at her hair with a burst of chatter. She regained her balance just in time.

"Sorry," she muttered quietly, and forged on.

She could barely make out the land in front of her through the downpour, having to go slowly in the relentless blackness. A flash of light shone to her right, and she veered to her left to avoid the security guard. But then another light flashed through the downpour, this one so near she froze immediately, standing stock-still while her heart thundered in her chest.

The light flashed by, and with a long sigh, she crept on, shrouded in the black night. But soon she became aware of several more flickering lights bouncing toward her as guards once more approached on their rounds. She tried to anticipate which way they were headed, but in the pouring rain, the lights seemed to bounce merrily from raindrop to raindrop, being in one and three places all at the same time.

To make matters worse, Nemo was shifting restlessly on her shoulder as her own nervousness began to communicate itself. She lifted a reassuring hand, but she could feel him poised beneath it, ready to jump.

"No!" But it was too late. With an easy leap he sprang from her shoulder, sliding in the slick mud as he landed, then bounding through the trampled grass. The lights waved wildly in the night, trying to capture the faint silver blur that leapt frantically on.

In that split second she realized the opportunity she'd been given as both pairs of lights veered madly away, chasing a ghost in the night. Without wasting an instant, she scrambled forward, hoping to make it past their routes before they returned.

Then, abruptly, a heavy hand crashed upon her shoulder. And this time, it definitely wasn't Nemo.

"Just what the hell do you think you're doing?" demanded Shadow's voice in the pouring night. She almost sagged with relief. If it had been anyone else she would, most probably, be dead.

"Oh," she sighed. "It's you."

But he ignored the familiarity in her voice. Dammit, he'd suspected it would come to this. He'd known that a woman like her would never be content to heed his warnings. He should have watched closer, taken her damn cot away. But he had other duties to fulfill, other people such as Ko Tan to watch. Especially now, when everything was coming to a head.

He willed himself to look straight into her green eyes. What he was about to do was for her own good, he told himself. Maybe the fear would be enough to keep her safe.

Without warning, his fingers deliberately dug into the softness of her arm, and he brutally dragged her forward. "You are going back. Now," he uttered coldly. "I will deal with you in the morning."

He had the satisfaction of seeing her look a little more shaken.

"What are you going to do?" she asked faintly. But instead of answering right away, he whirled her around and began marching forward, keeping her in front. She had to jog to keep up with the savage pace.

"Do you know how we punish people here?" he said harshly.

Once again, she felt the fear rear up hard. "No," she whispered, though her own imaginings had told her it wouldn't be pleasant. She hadn't allowed herself to dwell on it, though. A bit of an optimist, she'd always half assumed that she really would make it. Until now. Until this moment, with this hard, unrelenting man herding her through a merciless night.

"Maybe next time you'll find out first," Shadow grated ominously in her ear.

"Why?" Her voice had gone up a little and she fought for control. In the next moment, her own morbid curiosity had her asking, "What do you do?"

"Generally speaking," he said coldly, marching her along, "we whip them."

The color effectively drained from her face. Oh, she definitely hadn't considered this. For a moment she couldn't swallow, couldn't breathe. *Whip.* Whip her. The pure fear she experienced was beyond comprehension. It was sheer unadulterated terror now.

"You would do that to me?" she asked faintly.

This time he came to an abrupt stop, turning her until she was forced to meet his eyes. "I already told you," he uttered slowly, "I do my job well. And if you have any illusion that I'll forsake my job for you, forget it."

The coldness of the words must have penetrated, for she nodded slowly, her eyes still huge as they looked into his. She tried to swallow and found it difficult. She'd thought it would be different. She'd thought that somehow, someway, he would never intentionally hurt her. Why? Because he was so mysterious? Because she was so attracted to him? Because she wanted him to be something that he wasn't?

She wanted him to be someone she could trust.

The pain filtered unconsciously across her eyes, and Shadow felt it slam into his gut. God, he didn't want her to look at him like that. He didn't want her to look at him with green eyes filled with reproach. When he'd first realized that she wasn't in her hut, he'd been seized by the most horrible fear of his entire life. What if one of the other guards had discovered her first? What if they'd already taken her to Ko Tan? What if he'd arrived only to find her shot down in the wet fury of the night?

He shouldn't care. He'd told himself *not* to care. But all he had to do was look into her eyes, filled now with fear, fear of *him,* to know that he already did. And so help him God, but at this precise moment all he wanted to do was drag her against him, enfold her in his arms and kiss that fear away.

With an oath, he turned away. "Let's go," he said flatly. "Quickly, before someone else realizes your stupidity."

Those were the last words he uttered before he once again began cutting through the thick wet grass with his amazingly long strides. She had no choice but to continue, his hand still tight upon her wrist.

She'd done it now, she knew. She'd thought she was invincible, thought she could get away. But she hadn't. Dimly, she tried to imagine what it would feel like to have a whip crash down on her tender skin. It made her feel faint.

So she, too, was silent as she jogged alongside the furious man who'd found her. By the time they made it back to the hut, the rain had ceased, but by all appearances Shadow's anger hadn't. Without a word, he led her back inside, and giving the floorboards a dark look, he began to furiously pound them back down.

"You're lucky you're not dead" was all he said as he put the last one into place. She simply watched from the corner, suddenly too cold, wet and tired to argue. In another fluid motion, he tossed her the rough blanket before throwing the cot out the door. "Be happy you get to keep the blanket," he told her. "Now get some rest and gather your strength. You're going to need it."

She halfway nodded, and for the first time since they had returned to the hut, he actually looked at her. She was standing but four feet away, her face pale and rain washed, her figure huddled beneath the blanket. She was shivering lightly.

He felt himself waver, felt some of the anger drain from his face, but he fought it. He couldn't afford weakness. Yet he was sick of it, he thought suddenly. Sick of playing the role of the cruel, heartless villain. Sick of scaring the proud and beautiful woman in front of him when all he really wanted to do was hold her. He wanted to know if her skin really was that soft, if her hair really did feel like satin. He wanted to taste her lips, to feel her arms around him.

After a year and a half, he wanted to hold someone who was good and warm and wonderful. Someone like Riley.

And just for a moment, her eyes did meet his. Just for a moment the fear left her eyes and he saw a glimpse of something else as her gaze penetrated his. Fear, yes, but beginning to temper it, beginning to burgeon as his own defenses started to crumble, was compassion.

"Don't," he said, but his voice sounded thick even to his own ears. "Don't forget who I am."

"I don't even know who that is," she told him softly. "After two days, I still don't even know."

"Good," he told her shortly. "It's better that way."

She was silent for a moment, and then her face turned away from his to look at the floorboards. "I don't think so," she whispered. "I wonder sometimes . . ."

But she didn't complete the thought, and he used the silence to mend his defenses. Reaching deep down, he found all the emptiness, all the harshness he'd been lacking. "I'm a mean son of a bitch," he told her. "And that's all you need to know."

This time his feet did move, and in three long strides, he was at the door. He didn't turn around, he didn't torture himself with another glimpse of her eyes, her face. Instead he simply left her there, a forlorn bundle in a green army blanket huddled in the corner of the room.

The next thing Riley knew, sunlight was streaming through her window and Shadow was standing next to her. Her head felt thick and was pounding, and every inch of her tender skin burned from the blanket. She had discarded her wet clothes in order to stay warm, but that had left her skin bare and unprotected from the scratchy texture of the material.

She groaned softly and turned painfully away from Shadow. But still he stood there.

Finally, groggily, she mustered up enough energy to ask, "What time is it?"

"Almost three."

"Three?"

"Three."

Even in her current state of half slumber, the lateness of the day hit home. "Why did you wait so long to come?" she asked wearily, and managed to roll over until she could see him, wincing as she did so. "Does this mean it's time for my punishment?"

So she hadn't forgotten, thought Shadow. So the fear had stuck with her through the night to be greeted by the light of day. Maybe that was punishment enough.

"You won't be whipped today," he said shortly.

She peered at him with half-closed eyes. "What? Do I receive that honor tomorrow?"

"No."

"Then when? Or are you going to leave me in suspense?"

He paused for a moment, debating what to say. If the truth were known, he hadn't told Ko Tan that she had gotten out. He should, he knew. It was the first slip he'd made in a year and a half and God knows if anyone else had seen her, if anyone else had mentioned it to Ko Tan, it would all be over. But he just couldn't bring himself to do it. Maybe he hadn't sunk quite that low yet. Maybe there was a bit of compassion in him yet.

He just hoped it didn't get them both killed.

"Don't worry about it," he said abruptly. "The matter's been dropped."

She looked at him sharply now. "You didn't tell them, did you?" she quizzed. But he didn't answer, and for the first time she realized just how worn he looked. He stood with his usual nonchalance, Nemo on his shoulder, and his gray eyes were as calm as ever, but his face looked drawn and there seemed to be new shadows around his eyes.

Even then, she was startled when he pulled a glass bottle of antiseptic and some white strips of cloth out of his pocket. "Give me your hands," he demanded quietly.

She was too tired to protest, surrendering them without a struggle. He looked at them, and then, without saying a word, he quietly sat down on the floor and took the first one in his large, warm hand.

His touch was amazingly gentle, belying the harshness of his words as he slowly and patiently cleaned the scratches bit by bit. The antiseptic stung, but faded to cool the red scratches soothingly. Riley relaxed under his ministrations, trusting the light touch of his hands and the steadiness of his cleaning. He went over the entire palm and her fingers several times, searching out the tightly ingrained mud until each and every scratch had been carefully cleaned.

Within a few minutes, her other hand had been cleaned, as well. But Shadow didn't move away, only looked at her with his dark, steady eyes. "How do you feel?"

"Everything hurts," she informed him honestly, wincing again as she attempted to find a more comfortable position. "I must be getting too old for midnight escapes."

"Muscles?" he inquired, and she grimaced in response. He nodded back, not quite meeting her eyes. "Roll over," he told her.

"That hurts, too," she informed him.

"I know."

She almost argued further just for pride's sake, but couldn't see any point in it. So instead, with a long-suffering sigh, she gingerly turned herself onto her stomach, scratchy blanket and all.

But he had plans for that, too, and in minutes she felt a cool breeze on her naked back as he unwrapped the blanket. She stiffened almost immediately, but he placed a firm hand on her back. "Relax," he said shortly. "I've seen more of you than this, remember?"

He didn't have to remind her, she thought stubbornly, but she forced herself to lie still and unprotesting. His hands positioned themselves, safely enough, on her shoulders, and then starting slowly, he moved them in large massaging circles. She had to bite back a groan at the first penetrating and painful contact, her muscles contracting then melting under the firm, gentle touch. And it felt good, very good. Too good for a man who just last night was threatening to have her whipped. But she didn't want to think about it right now. She just wanted to close her eyes and concentrate on the wonderfully delicious sensation of his hands working away the tension. She wanted to think of nothing but this moment, these hands, this man. If she just shut the rest out and let her mind wander, she could almost imagine...

He shouldn't be doing this, he knew. He shouldn't be touching her, shouldn't be worried about her pain or discomfort. But all night long he'd stayed awake, staring at the sky, remembering how she'd looked so lost, so beaten, wrapped up in the old green army blanket. And no matter what he told himself, no matter what he wanted to believe, he couldn't stand seeing her hurt.

Maybe because the last few years had been so dark. He'd taken on this assignment from his superiors knowing that it would be harsh, knowing that his role couldn't be acted, but had to be *lived*. At the time, it had been worth it. Anything to put away Ko Tan. Anything to avenge the death of his best friend. But now, after a year and a half of living in the darkness, he realized just how insidious it had become. In the beginning he'd thought he would be strong enough. He'd always lived his life on the edge, first as an orphaned street kid, then in the army, and now in this assignment. He'd seen a lot of evil in his lifetime. He wasn't a man with illusions. He knew the types of death and destruction man inflicted upon man.

But he'd never been part of it before. He'd never had to watch people die in front of his eyes, and do nothing. He'd never had to kill. And now he understood that to live the darkness was to invite it inside you. To find out that you had darkness, too. And to feel it grow, day after day, until sometimes you didn't know yourself anymore and were afraid you never would.

He'd seen too much death and destruction in his lifetime. He'd lived with too much darkness, too much loneliness. And now there was Riley, a flash of hope and purity in the jungle. She reminded him of the civilization he'd left behind. And she reminded him of the loneliness that always lurked on the inside, no matter what the job, what the mission.

He wanted to touch her. He wanted to see her eyes sparkle again, see the way she moved when she walked, see the brilliance of her smile. He wanted to bask for a moment in the sharp warmth of her own innocent youth. She was light, where he was dark. She was a flame, and he was only a shadow.

It would never last. They were just two people brought together by circumstance, bonded by danger. But in the end, he was still a man on a mission. And that mission might just destroy them both.

He didn't want to think of it. He didn't want to think of the emptiness, of the deaths that were still to come, for he understood now that Ko Tan would kill her. Ko Tan wanted to bend her to his will, and this was a woman who wouldn't bend. So Ko Tan would break her instead. That was the kind of man he was.

The future was dark, all right, darker than even the present, than even the past. Already Shadow could feel the strain.

He wanted—*needed*—this one moment to actually give in and touch her. One moment to forget the last year, and maybe, just maybe, feel alive again.

So his hands moved gently across her back, then moved all the way down, kneading the firm muscles of her thighs and calves. She felt good, he acknowledged, like firm satin beneath his hands. She felt wholesome, pure. And it had been so long since he had felt any of those things.

His hands continued moving, finding the gentle curve of her bare buttocks. She went rigid at the first touch, but then, as his large hands circled with gentle insistence, a soft sigh escaped from her lips.

Riley felt like she was melting slowly, deliciously. She shouldn't be letting him touch her this way, she thought vaguely. She should be pulling away. But oh, it felt so good....

After a languorous moment, his hands drifted back up, seeking and finding each pressure point along her spine, caressing the silky firmness of her back. Then, seemingly of their own accord, his hands shifted, dipping down, skimming the sides of her torso, brushing her ripe breasts. She stiffened slightly, letting out her breath in small gasps, goose bumps rising on her flesh.

Above her, Shadow had to grit his teeth in an effort for control. Barely able to restrain himself at the tantalizing feel of her softness, he quickly returned his hands to the relative safety of her back.

She relaxed once more, almost purring under the tender ministration. How could a man who spoke so harshly touch her so tenderly? her mind puzzled sleepily. But she didn't think about it just yet. For now she simply wanted to believe the man above her really was that gentle, that caring.

"Tell me something," Shadow asked her at last, his control firmly established. "Why are you risking my life?"

She sighed, knowing the moment was over, reality once again intruding. She had lost the lonely man, the man she sensed she could reach—*wanted* to reach—and was now gaining the mercenary.

Slowly her mind returned to the seriousness of the moment. "I don't have a choice," she told him flatly. "You said yourself that Ko Tan will probably kill me. So I have to try to escape. And I—" the next words were hard to find "—I just have to hope that you can take care of yourself."

He didn't respond right away, his hands lying still on her back. He knew he should stop the conversation right then and there, but before he could, the words just spilled out. "I'm trying to keep you safe," he said tersely.

But she shook her head at him, her own expression disbelieving. "Don't," she told him bluntly, starting to feel angry. "*Don't* keep speaking in riddles. One minute you're calling me a fool, the next you're telling me I'll most likely be killed, then you're threatening to whip me, and now you're saying you just want to keep me safe. You make no sense, Shadow," she declared vehemently. "I've been with you for nearly twenty-four hours a day for the last three days, and I know absolutely nothing about you. And you know what? I think you like it. I think you like keeping your secrets and doling out bits of information like precious gems, because it keeps you in control of the game. Well, I won't play along anymore. You either trust me or you don't. And unless you tell me otherwise, I'm here on my own and I'll take care of myself. So you can stop doing me any favors."

"Take care of yourself?" he interrupted harshly, his own eyes darkening with some unnamed emotion. "How? Like last night? You're just lucky no one else discovered you escaping first."

She shook her head furiously. "It was a risk I had to take," she contradicted. "And so far, I still haven't had to pay for it, now have I?"

The arrogance in the last words inflamed him. His eyes turned black, the muscle at his jaw leaping vividly. He sat back completely, his fists clenching at his sides. "You little fool," he stormed. "You don't understand anything."

"Then tell me," she demanded. "Who are you, Shadow? What is your game?"

"I'm a mercenary," he told her brutally. "I'm a cold-hearted killer for hire."

But she shook her head. "I don't think so," she said. "You may be many things, Shadow, but I'm not convinced that's what you are."

Once more his eyes blazed, but then they narrowed suddenly in speculative intent. "Really?" he taunted in a low voice. "Well, how about this, then?"

And without any other warning, his lips swooped down upon hers.

Chapter 5

He meant it to be punishing, he meant it to be harsh. But even as he absorbed her initial struggling shock against his frame, his lips were reveling in the softness she offered.

She tasted like silk, his mind registered. Silk and heat and honey. And the pressure that should have been brutal suddenly became gentle.

How long had he wanted to taste these lips again? How many times had he fallen asleep only to awaken ablaze with passion, seeing her naked body glistening with the river's caress?

How many times could a man tell himself no?

There was no denial anymore, no refusal of the sweet glory of her body, the blazing warmth of her mouth. He drank of passion like a man dying of thirst, feasting on the softness of her lips. He felt her begin to relax against him, felt the initial stiffness of her lips slowly give way under his. Not waiting, he pushed his advantage, deepening the kiss, finding her tongue, tasting her mouth. She was exquisitely soft, exquisitely tender. Last time, he had demanded in anger. Now, he coaxed her with slow seduction. He could feel her hands raking lightly down his back, then smoothing around to find the buttons of his shirt. But he caught her hands in his grip, pulling them back and out of his way, until he could run his tongue along her jaw to the gentle curve of her neck.

Her hands protested his hold, longing to touch him. But then she succumbed to the wonderful feel of his mouth on her throat. With a groan, she arched against him, giving in completely.

It was the sound that penetrated his consciousness. For a heart-stopping moment, he sagged against her, cursing himself silently.

What the hell was he doing?

The racing sound of her heartbeat gave him answers he didn't want to acknowledge. He wasn't supposed to touch her. He wasn't supposed to get involved. He was the shadow, she was the flame; he had nothing to offer such a woman. He couldn't even give her her life.

"I'm sorry," he whispered against her ear. "Forgive me."

The soft words grated against her until she felt like screaming out her frustration. Her blood was singing in her ears, each nerve ending crying out for release. And there was nowhere for the tension to go, no natural end for all the pent-up passion. Once again, he'd wanted her and rejected her, anyway. And she'd let him, she thought bitterly. She'd given in to his kiss, only to have him pull away. Unable to stop herself, she balled her hand into a fist and slammed it against the solid strength of his shoulder. "Damn you," she whispered brokenly. "Damn you."

He didn't answer; he didn't know any words to say. He could only pull her closer, unable to bear the weight of her eyes. He felt like a drowning man, wanting only to touch her more, and knowing that he couldn't.

He never should have given in. Now he knew the full extent of what he was denying himself, and the self-control would be that much harder to bear. If only they'd met at another time, in another place... One where he was allowed to be Shadow the man, and not this dark creature he'd become.

When Riley thought she could look at him without her eyes growing too bright, she pulled away and with proud dignity wrapped the ugly blanket tightly around her graceful form. "You can leave now," she told him coldly. "I believe you've already proved your point."

The bitterness of her words made him want to wince, but he didn't show the emotion. Instead his eyes drank in her appearance, wrapped in a dark green blanket and a mane of fiery red hair. He wondered if she realized just how beautiful she looked now, clothed in little more than strength and pride.

And he wondered if she realized that a woman with all her passion wasn't meant for a silent man like himself. She belonged to a golden-haired man who would blaze like the sun, not a man who lived his life in the shadows, forever on the outside looking in.

"It won't happen again," he said abruptly, his face once again passive, his eyes dark and steady. "Don't forget who I am, Riley. You certainly don't want to get involved with a man like that."

The very certainty of his words silenced her. They hammered home where she was most vulnerable, ricocheting against all her doubts. She had forgotten who he was: a mercenary, a man who killed for money. A man who worked for Ko Tan.

Oh, what are you doing? she asked herself in near despair. Kissing a hired gun, throwing yourself at a man who kills for profit?

But even as she thought this, a small part of her denied the words. A small part of her wanted to believe in Shadow. A part of her recognized the emptiness in the man before her, the dark shadows that haunted his eyes and left him without peace.

"Maybe I just see who you could be," she ventured softly after a long moment. "Maybe it's—"

But he interrupted her harshly, cutting the words off in her throat.

"Don't," he told her sharply. "Stay away from me, Riley. I mean it."

The words hurt, but only because they were brutally honest. Somehow, somewhere along the line, she'd built up some romantic notion about him. Maybe, in the madness of this place, she simply needed some hope, someone to believe in. Whatever it was, she'd made him out to be a man much kinder than he really was. She'd seen how cold he could be; she'd felt the stinging fury of his words.

And she'd known the tenderness of his kiss.

The thought penetrated, unwanted, but she was still captured by it. On their own, her fingers came up and lightly traced the swollen softness of her lips. How could a man so cruel kiss with such tempered strength? Surely a cold man wouldn't make her feel so unbelievably hot.

The uncertainty made her take a step closer. It forced her to peer deep into his eyes, searching for answers, seeking revelation. But his eyes were too deep, filled with glimmers of eternity. There, in the back recesses, floated the slivers of pain and desire, like a river's hidden current. They were much too distant to grasp and pinpoint, however. Much too distant for definition and understanding.

And she found that, more than anything, she *did* want to understand. Even now, she just wanted to understand. And maybe it showed in her eyes, for his own changed suddenly, emotions peering out from the murky depths—yearning, desire and, most of all, regret.

Softly, gently, his hand came up, and his thumb also lightly traced the tender swell of her lips.

But then, like a pond on a cold winter's day, his face froze over again, the icy dispassion falling in place with startling efficiency. In a space of seconds, he was the distant, uncaring man of before.

It was as if nothing had ever happened at all.

He turned, clicked at Nemo to follow and disappeared out her door.

For a long, long time, she just stood there, watching his tall, lean form and his silver companion vanish in the distance. Then, with trembling hands, she picked up her damp clothing and slowly began to dress.

He didn't come again until almost nightfall, but she didn't notice the time. The simple act of dressing had seemed to rob her of all her strength, and she curled back up in the corner to fall asleep once more. When she awoke again, her lips were cracked and her throat unbearably dry. She was hungry, thirsty and already tense.

Dammit, this wasn't going well at all. With each day the danger increased, and she'd already failed in her only opportunity to escape. What was she going to do now? Where could she turn? There was only one person that she could think of. Shadow.

Even as she thought his name, however, she felt the helplessness grow deep inside of her. Hell, she wasn't getting anywhere with that man. He was so controlled, so...cold. So...lonely. Lonely?

Oh, you *are* a fool, she cursed herself uncharitably. How could a man like that possibly be lonely? From what she'd seen, he didn't even have feelings. For whatever reason, she was seeing him as someone he wasn't. He was just a mercenary, a cold and heartless man.

No, she was on her own and she had to start thinking of another way out. She had to find some other opportunity.

She'd barely made the decision when she looked up and saw Shadow standing in the doorway. He was holding a large pail of water and a sponge in one hand, with a long garment bag slung over his back.

"Ko Tan wants you to meet him for dinner," he said curtly. Apparently his mood was no better than her own, for his face was still completely dispassionate, his eyes remote. He set down the bucket and sponge, and laid the garment bag across the floor. Then he simply leaned himself negligently against the wall and waited.

She frowned down at the bucket, discovering it was filled with warm, soapy water. Apparently it was to help her clean up. She sighed slightly and absently picked up the sponge.

"Dinner?" she quizzed. "Does that mean an interview?" In spite of the danger, she still felt a tingle of anticipation at the prospect. God knew she was half-terrified of the man and what he could do. But the other half of her, the ambitious reporter thrilled by the challenge, still wanted to talk to him. An interview with Ko Tan... What her editor would say in New York!

But Shadow just shrugged, apparently as noncommittal as ever. She decided to ignore him and went over to check out the garment bag instead.

What she found inside immediately killed whatever excitement she'd felt. It was a long black evening dress with a slit up one side and a plunging neckline in the front. She'd seen similar dresses at Saks Fifth Avenue in New York, but on a journalist's salary she certainly didn't buy such items. It must have cost over two thousand dollars. And it certainly wasn't the type of thing worn for an interview. Oh no, there was only one thing such dresses were made for.

"I won't wear it," she said flatly.

"I don't recall your having a choice," Shadow replied stiffly.

"Look at it!" she demanded hotly, whirling around and thrusting the dress under his nose. "Just look at it! Dammit, I came here on business, and frankly, there is only one type of business this dress was meant for."

Looking at it, Shadow felt his own anger grow. He himself hadn't seen the dress. But now he took in the high-slit side and the plunging neckline. Just the thought of her wearing that dress in front of Ko Tan made his blood boil.

Furiously he clamped back down on his emotions, hard. Turning to the side so that only the sharp clenching of his jaw muscle gave him away, he fought for control. He wasn't supposed to care, he reminded himself. He'd screwed up enough for one day, let too much show. But now it was time to get back on track, to get himself under control. This was all part of the test, Ko Tan's damn test to see just how loyal he was. And he would pass it, dammit. He'd worked too hard earning Ko Tan's trust to blow it now. Especially when it would all be over shortly, if he could just hang on. His plan to lure Ko Tan to the States was beginning to come together. Just two more weeks, and it would be over. Ko Tan would be brought to justice at last. Just two more weeks.

When some of the anger still refused to die, he grimly forced himself to remember that night two years ago. The chatter of the guns, the rat-tat-tat-tat ripping through the darkness. And the screams, Johnny's screams, as each and every bullet hit home. Not one. Not two. But over a dozen pieces of lead. Over and over again. Until it was too late, until Johnny didn't scream anymore.

Yes, remember the sound of the bullets, Shadow old buddy, remember the sound of the screams. Remember what that night so long ago cost you—your best friend.

He wouldn't fail now. He couldn't.

"Put the dress on," he said coldly. "Ko Tan doesn't like to be kept waiting."

"What?" Riley retorted angrily. "You honestly think I'll wear this?"

"You'll do what you're told," he said levelly.

It wasn't the response she wanted. She wanted him to snatch the dress away. She wanted him to be upset. She wanted him to care.

Idiot, she cursed herself. She was all alone, vulnerable, afraid. She wanted someone to believe in, someone to give her some hope. She wanted to believe that there was a real, caring man somewhere deep within those layers of control. Savagely she whirled away. No matter what she wanted, she was on her own now. Completely. She couldn't trust this man; she couldn't depend on him.

But at the same time, he was perhaps the only hope she had in the tangled world. Perhaps he *didn't* care. Perhaps he *was* just a cold mercenary. But she was a proud and intelligent woman—maybe she could change his mind....

When she turned back around this time, her face was softer, her eyes more cajoling as she slanted her green gaze at him. She took a whispering step forward until he could smell the scent of soap in her hair, on her skin.

"I think you care," she whispered huskily, her eyes sweeping up to meet his. "I think you don't want me to wear this dress in front of Ko Tan. I think when you kissed me, you cared more than you wanted to."

He willed himself not to look away from this new approach. He willed himself to look straight into her beautiful green eyes and lie away the last small hope he'd held for his future. "Then you're a fool," he said levelly.

He watched her wince at the words, saw their impact in the wounded pain of her eyes. She faltered, searching his eyes for some last sign to cling to. But no matter how long she stared into the gray depths, all she found was the emptiness. With a stifled cry, she turned away, flinging the dress from her.

"I won't wear it," she said abruptly. "If Ko Tan wants to eat dinner with me, then he can take me the way I am."

"Don't," Shadow said, and this time his voice was softer with the warning, but no less chilling. "Don't push him. You'll only lose."

"Don't worry about it," she told him harshly. "After all, you're just a mercenary, and mercenaries don't care."

The very bitterness of her voice almost broke him. Because so help him God, he did care. He went to bed aching to touch her, awoke just wanting to see her. But he couldn't afford to care. He was a man without a future, a man of silence, a man of darkness. And she was everything wonderful, everything bright, everything beautiful in the world.

Perhaps... Perhaps if they had met years ago, when Johnny was still alive, when Shadow had still had hope...

It didn't matter, he told himself. He wasn't the man for her. But just for a minute, he wished he could be. He wished he could bury himself in the warm comfort of her arms, that he could taste her lips, that he could forget all the evil, all the death he'd seen, been a part of. Just for one moment, he wished he could find peace.

She looked at him, waiting to see if he would answer her challenge. And even as she watched, the emotions flickered like ripples across his face. For one instant, his eyes were filled with such pain it almost brought her to her knees. The anger died in her stomach, and in its place she was consumed by the desire to touch him, to simply reach out and offer him one moment of comfort. But she knew by now he would just turn away, leaving her with nothing.

He didn't want her. He'd already made that so clear. But it was okay, she told herself resolutely. She knew she was on her own, and she would find a way to take care of herself. She had to.

She turned away. Picking up the sponge, she started to clean her face and her arms. She worked a little at the tangles in her hair, and then she turned back to him, taking one last deep breath. Ko Tan had called, and there was no denying him.

"We should go," she said.

Shadow could only nod, not trusting his voice. And for the first time in two years, he started to pray. *Just keep her safe*, he asked. *Just keep her safe.*

Because he really wasn't so sure he could.

Ko Tan looked less than happy when Shadow brought Riley in without the dress. For a moment his face turned positively

ugly, and Shadow could feel Riley tense in apprehension next
to him. Neither of them moved, neither of them spoke, and at
last, Ko Tan's face cleared the slightest bit.

"Didn't the dress fit?" he asked tightly.

She was the one to answer. "To tell you the truth," she be-
gan cautiously, trying for a conciliatory note, "I didn't try it on.
Not that I don't appreciate the offer," she hastened to add.
"But I really don't want to impose upon your hospitality."

Ko Tan still looked less than pleased, but after another tense
moment, he nodded stiffly. He motioned to Riley to have a
seat, then turned to Shadow. "You can leave now," Ko Tan
told him.

For a moment, Riley froze. Somehow she hadn't figured on
her and Ko Tan dining alone. But how else had she expected it
to be? Now, faced with the possibility, she felt the apprehension bloom thick and dark in her blood. There was something
reassuring about Shadow's presence, even if he claimed he
didn't care. At least he was still a little bit human, while she
wasn't sure the same could be said for Ko Tan.

Nervous now, she darted looks from one man to the other.

Shadow could feel her eyes coming to rest on him, could feel
the unspoken need pouring out of them. And it took every
ounce of willpower in his body to keep himself from looking
back at her. Because one flicker, one small sign of his weakness for her, would be all Ko Tan would need. He would probably kill them both for the sheer amusement of it.

So he forced himself to stand rigidly still, forced himself to
ignore her even as he knew she needed reassurance. It's not
your problem, he told himself again. But somehow, it was getting harder and harder to believe. Ko Tan was watching, waiting. He just didn't have any choice. He'd made his decision a
year and a half ago when he'd accepted this assignment. Now
he could only play out his bitter role, just as he'd been playing
it for a long time.

He left the room.

The door closed with an abrupt click behind him, and with
a long sigh he headed back out into the night. There was nothing more he could do, he told himself. Now he could only wait.

They were two of the worst hours of his life.

* * *

"Would you like a drink?" Ko Tan asked as the door shut behind Shadow. He was already moving to a black lacquered bar on one side of the room.

"No, thank you. I'm fine," Riley told him, her voice not quite steady.

But obviously the question was rhetorical, for he mixed and handed her a drink, anyway. All the time his face remained pleasantly smiling. Only his eyes gave him away, hard and black and always watching.

"So how have you enjoyed your stay so far?" he asked casually as he pulled out one of the huge leather chairs for her to sit in, and then seated himself in the one directly across from it. He took a sip from his glass, urging her to do the same. She complied, only to have the Scotch and soda burn its way down her throat. Her already flushed cheeks flared at the impact, and the faint pounding of her temples increased fourfold.

She set the glass down gingerly on the dark wood of the table, resting it on the cocktail napkin. A few more sips on her empty stomach and the evening would be pretty much over for her. She had the feeling that Ko Tan wouldn't mind that at all.

"My stay has been fine enough," she managed to reply, and tried to relax her face into a casual, social smile like his own. "Shadow's been an excellent guide," she said. She forced herself to speak with a bit more enthusiasm. She was here, wasn't she? She might as well get more information about the man and his operations while she could. "Would it be possible," she proposed, "to watch the men train sometime? Just to get a better idea of the rigors of being a secessionist soldier?"

Ko Tan nodded slightly. "Perhaps it can be arranged."

"That would be wonderful. I also noticed," she said lightly, "that there are several very modern aspects to your camp. The hospital is especially impressive. Just how do you get equipment like that out here?"

He dismissed this question with a wave of his hand. "Where there is money, beautiful Riley, anything is possible."

She did her best to ignore the compliment, and instead kept her attention on the first part of his reply. "Yes," she agreed, "where there is money. But all these men, all these guns, the equipment. That can hardly be cheap. Just how do you support such an operation?"

He shrugged. "We get a little money here, a little money there. We always manage."

"I see," she said levelly. "And I imagine exporting heroin helps a great deal, as well."

For a long moment he was completely silent, and the room seemed suddenly stifling with tension. Riley blanched. Perhaps she'd gone too far. Perhaps she should have dropped the subject— But then he spoke, his tone polished and smooth from long practice.

"Heroin," he declared grandly, "is but a tragic tool of circumstance. We've tried and tried to attract international donors to our cause, but alas, the support is just not sufficient. Foreigners don't care about a little Southern Asian secessionist movement, you see. But we still believe in our cause, all five thousand of my loyal men, and we still need guns. So, you see, we are forced into selling the heroin and opium. Not by choice, mind you, but by circumstance."

It was a very well-practiced speech, and she wondered how many times he'd rehearsed it. The opium was also news to her; she'd heard only about the heroin.

"That must be very unfortunate," she said, not quite able to keep the dryness out of her tone. "But then, looking at your current life-style, with its Ming vases and Rembrandt prints, it's hard to believe money is that scarce."

His eyes narrowed instantly, and he gave her a long, speculative look. His mouth opened, and for a minute she thought he might actually comment on the accusation, but then he abruptly changed the topic.

"How about eating first?" he said instead. "Dem really has prepared an excellent fare for this evening." He picked up a little silver bell sitting not far from his chair, rang it, and instantly the rotund Dem was bursting his way through a swinging door tucked in the back of the room.

He carried with him huge platters of steaming food, and Riley relaxed a fraction. So far the evening wasn't going as badly as she'd thought, though she still wished Shadow was here. She didn't trust the man in front of her.

The food Dem set out was a large banquet of steaming, aromatic dishes. It all looked wonderful, but the smell was too strong for her sensitized stomach, which lurched queasily. She hadn't eaten in what seemed forever; maybe she'd waited too long.

At the abrupt motion of Ko Tan's hand, the cook disappeared behind the swinging door. Ko Tan turned his smile back to her, holding up a bottle of wine. "For the occasion," he said, and set about uncorking it. Riley wasn't sure what the occasion was, and she didn't feel like asking. All of a sudden her nerves seemed overwound and her head slightly thick.

"Could I just have some water, please?" she asked softly.

He refused her easily. "My beautiful Riley," he said. "while we may have many modern conveniences here, I'm afraid purified water is not one of them. But this wine is good—you will like it."

She wasn't so sure of that herself, but it seemed she had no choice. And she really was thirsty—very, very thirsty. She managed to summon a polite smile as Ko Tan handed her a glass of the chilled white wine.

"A toast, then," he said grandly and held up his glass. "To the promise of the evening."

"Yes," she managed to retort as he went to sip. "To the promise of a good story." He frowned, but it was too late to refrain from drinking. Riley herself took just a small sip, discovering that the wine was indeed excellent, cool and fruity on her tongue. Without thinking, she gave in to her thirst and took a long swallow. It went straight to her empty stomach and rolling head.

She set the glass down gingerly. Where was Shadow? She wanted to go home.

But Ko Tan took no notice, liberally piling a plate high with steaming duck, broiled fish and a few other things she didn't recognize before setting it in front of her. "Dem is an excellent cook," he said smoothly. "I'm sure you won't be disappointed."

In fact, the strong aroma of the food was beginning to make her feel even queasier, but she smiled determinedly and picked up her fork. Perhaps eating would help. And God knew she couldn't continue drinking wine on an empty stomach. She began with a small bite of the duck, finding that it was incredibly tender, almost melting against her tongue. The flavor was also mild, not as greasy as she'd expected.

So, bit by bit, she took small bites from the duck, then tried some of the fish. It, however, was much too spicy, while the eggs in oil were too rich. She returned to the duck, though after a few more bites even it became less than appealing.

Ko Tan wasn't one for conversation while he ate, enjoying his food with gusto while refilling the wineglasses with a liberal hand. But his eyes remained watchful and calculating, making note of what she did and didn't eat, and how much she drank.

She probably drank too much. But the wine was so cool against her throat, and she really was outrageously thirsty. She wasn't a heavy or experienced drinker, knowing that two glasses were clearly her limit. But by the time she reached one and a half glasses, the world was already spinning senselessly and her cheeks were much too warm.

I will not be drunk. I will not be drunk, she told herself firmly, and forced herself to eat more to counteract the heady effects of the wine. Ko Tan was waiting for any sign of weakness, waiting to move in for the kill. *Remember, Riley, he's a snake in a penguin's suit.*

The thought came out of nowhere, and in her current state, it seemed amazingly funny. She almost giggled, catching herself just in time. But Ko Tan noticed the change, as well, and across the table she could see him smile. It had a sobering effect, clearing her mind long enough for her to know that she was in serious trouble.

She needed to stop drinking. But at the same time, she was still so unbelievably thirsty, and there wasn't anything else for her to drink. So she kept taking sip after sip, glass after glass, long after she probably should have.

Ko Tan was finishing up now, pushing back his chair, placing his linen napkin next to his plate. With another wave of the bell, the dishes were magically cleared, and then it was just him and her and, of course, the glasses of wine.

He smiled at her once again, and it seemed a strangely observant smile. But then he rose to his feet and crossed over to what appeared to be a discreetly hidden stereo system. In a matter of minutes, soft classical music was pouring like velvet through equally well-hidden speakers. Another minute adjustment, and the lights in the room dimmed a notch. He turned back to her then, and this time his eyes were smug with expectation.

"How about a little dancing?" he asked, even as he slid back her chair and helped her up with a commanding hand on her elbow.

The sudden rise made her head swim more, and for one instant she swayed against him, watching as triumph flared blackly in his eyes. But the effect of that look was potent, jerking her spine rigidly straight and clearing her mind for a little bit longer. She stood stiffly before him, her arms enforcing a seven-inch space between them even as he tried to force her closer.

He frowned lightly, but allowed her the tiny victory. In the middle of the room, he danced smoothly, his hands lightly but firmly leading her. She was slightly impressed in spite of herself, and relaxed a fraction. He immediately seized the opportunity to drag her closer, forcing her once more to attention.

Whether it was the classical swirl of the music or the heady potency of the wine, she began to sway again, her eyes drooping shut, as she fought for control. But it was no use. The world tilted dangerously, and she felt his hand brush against her hip as she stumbled.

Blindly, wildly, she realized in the last sane corner of her mind that she simply wasn't going to make it. Whatever hope for an interview she'd possessed was long since gone, and Ko Tan clearly had other intentions on his mind. And in her current befuddled state, she'd never be able to fend him off. Calling on some deep instinct of survival, she summoned the last of her energy.

Without another thought, she reacted, lashing out against Ko Tan's shoulder. He stumbled back in surprise, and she seized the opportunity, lurching for the door.

She made it out the first door, hearing his raging stream of curses behind her as she dashed blindly down the hall. Then the front door was there and she pulled it open violently. She felt the cool night air sweep in, welcomed it against her burning cheeks. But then a massive hand appeared on her shoulder, jerking her back with brutal strength even as she cried out in protest.

The bodyguard didn't loosen his grip, and from a distance she could hear the pounding footsteps of Ko Tan as he raged down the hall. In defeat, she sagged against the mountainous mass of muscle.

And heard Shadow's voice.

"Let her go."

"Hold her," corrected Ko Tan as he stormed into the entranceway from the hall. "She tried to run away."

But Shadow was already leaning over, brushing his hand lightly against her burning cheeks. "She's sick," he said flatly. From a long way off, Riley heard him and was grateful.

"It's merely the wine," said Ko Tan, but he leaned forward, too, and placed his hand against her cheek, anyway.

It might just be the wine, Riley thought dimly, but it didn't stop her stomach from rolling queasily. Perhaps her face turned green, because both Shadow and Ko Tan glanced at her again.

"She's sick," Shadow repeated. "Or maybe it *is* the wine. Either way, she needs to rest right now, to sleep it off."

"She can stay here."

There was a pause as that sank in, a pause as Shadow fought for control. He lost. "Why?" he heard himself say. "There's a camp full of healthy women for you—surely you can spare her."

Ko Tan flushed darkly, his face becoming ugly. "You overstep your bounds."

For one moment Shadow felt himself teeter on the brink of insanity. One moment, when after a year and a half of bowing down to the man's pettiness, he really wanted to fight back. But with brutal concentration he fought and won back the reins of his control. "Of course," he said stiffly. "My apologies. The woman isn't my concern."

Ko Tan seemed slightly mollified by the words, though his face was still dark as he looked back down at Riley. "What do you think's wrong with her?" he asked gruffly.

Shadow shrugged, keeping his face impassive. From both his army training in medicine and his own experiences in the jungle, he was fairly good at diagnosis. "She looks feverish and nauseous," he said. "Probably some jungle bug. I imagine she'll be violently ill for a few days, and then it will pass again."

As if hearing him, Riley's stomach lurched one last awful time, and she was sick all over the floor.

Ko Tan gave the mess one disgusted look, then motioned to the bodyguard. "Release her."

The huge man didn't protest, relinquishing his fragile burden gladly. Shadow easily picked up her sagging form, and Riley gratefully encircled his neck with her arms, her head falling against his shoulder.

Moments later they were out in the cool night air, Shadow striding smoothly through the long grass.

Safe now, she gave up her struggle and sank into the swirling, whirling depths of blackness.

Chapter 6

He stayed with her through the night.

He doubted that she was sick and he doubted that it was merely the wine. Instead, he suspected a far more insidious culprit: Ko Tan. Riley was a beautiful woman, but she was also independent, headstrong. And everyone in the camp knew that Ko Tan liked his women willing; he wasn't above using drugs to gain their compliance. Slip a little something in a drink, perhaps in dinner, and even the normally sharpest of women would be caught with her guard down.

The only thing that had probably saved her was her own nauseous reaction. And now, having rid her system of the substance, she seemed to be doing slightly better. Some color had returned to her cheeks, and she'd drifted to an easier sleep, though at times she would moan and toss, wrestling with the invisible demons of her mind. At those times he would stroke her brow until eventually she quieted once more.

If only he could say the same for himself.

He'd known since the day she'd arrived that there would be trouble. He just hadn't figured on so much, so fast. He'd tried to tell himself it wasn't his concern, and he'd tried to convince himself that just maybe it would work out, anyway. Ko Tan seemed to have some interest in a journalist; maybe the matter would end there.

Not anymore.

Shadow could still remember the black menace of Ko Tan's eyes as he'd taken in Riley's fallen form. The man wanted her, and he wouldn't be content until he had her. For under all his trappings of civilization, Ko Tan was really nothing more than a petty dictator, with a dictator's whims and a dictator's rage.

And Riley? She would fight him, as she had tonight. But she couldn't win, not in this land, not in this jungle. Here Ko Tan was the law, and the next time she refused, he would make her pay. Dearly.

Just thinking about it, Shadow felt his jaw tighten to an agonizing rigidity. It was just a matter of time, and not even much at that. Ko Tan wasn't a patient man. Maybe he'd give her one night to recover. And then the next...

Just thirty-six hours, thirty-six hours before this woman, sleeping so softly now, died.

He couldn't just let her die.... He couldn't interfere. He had to think of something.... The matter wasn't his concern. He needed to help her.... The price was simply too high.

He had to let her go.

Desperate now with the conflicting emotions bombarding him, he tried to gather his control, tried to drag up the vision that had haunted him for so many years now. Tried to find his sense of purpose in the dark memory....

Two years ago, it had been a cold fall night in the deep, dark back streets of New York City. The wind had been tinged with frost, and he and the other men from the DEA had drunk cups of coffee as they kept their vigil. Already everyone had been in place for a few hours, but in spite of the cold, anticipation was high. The special group that worked on the heroin drug trade had been on this case for almost a year now and it would close tonight. Shadow's best friend, Johnny, had managed to penetrate one of the main suppliers' operations. All Johnny had to do now was make the trade-off—cash for the heroin—and they would get one of the main men. Not the head drug lord, but a significant player in the operation.

Everything should have gone perfectly.

Except, when the limo had driven up, it hadn't stopped. Instead the window had rolled down, and the gun had come out. *Rat-a-tat-tat-tat. Rat-a-tat-tat-tat. Rat-a-tat-tat—*

Over and over again, each bullet tearing through flesh, each bullet eliciting scream after scream as the DEA men scrambled to deal with this sudden crisis. Until there weren't any screams anymore.

Johnny was already dead.

His best friend . . .

Somehow Johnny's cover had been broken, and the drug lord had instantly ordered his death. That drug lord had been Ko Tan.

Shadow had insisted on going undercover himself, in spite of the objections and concerns of his supervisors. He told them it was the only way. For years they'd been trying to reach Ko Tan through his underlings, albeit his main men, in the States. Now, Shadow told them, it was time for a new strategy, a bigger aim. Go after the man himself.

They already had enough evidence to indict Ko Tan. That wasn't a problem. Getting him to the States was. Ko Tan was a shrewd operator; he knew that as long as he stayed in Myanmar, surrounded by his five thousand guerrillas, he could enjoy the gains of illicit activities in relative security. Other governments, other drug lords, had gone so far as to try to assassinate the man, but he remained untouchable. The ultimate snake in the jungle.

Now, Shadow suggested, it was time to broaden the playing field. All along the DEA had been waiting in New York, seeking second-in-commands. But what about going straight to Myanmar? What about an undercover agent becoming Ko Tan's right-hand man, and then setting the ultimate trap to lure Ko Tan back to New York?

Then they'd have him.

Except that Ko Tan was one very suspicious operator. It would take time to gain his trust. Possibly years. And the stakes would be high. Once in the jungle, the agent would really be on his own, for too many contacts with the DEA would increase the risk of discovery. And the price of discovery . . .

It was a risky bet, an incredible gamble.

At first Group 41, the special task force that was in charge of the Asian drug trade, had been against it. But Shadow had been relentless. Ko Tan controlled nearly sixty percent of the world's heroin supply. He was a known murderer, and the number of agents alone he'd been responsible for killing... No, it was time to take him out, once and for all.

Eventually, still with a few doubts, the higher-ups had given the go-ahead. From there, the rest of the pieces had fallen smoothly into place. Shadow's past was already murky, so the DEA had just added a few new twists. Instead of his actual path of going from the army to the DEA, Shadow's record now showed a dishonorable discharge from the service for illegally trafficking small weapons. Shadow's expertise in high-tech weaponry, training he'd received in both the army and the DEA, was played up, and his record now showed him as under investigation by the FBI. Finally, he was still wanted by the army for his activities in selling weapons.

To complete the cover, Shadow had spent six months building up arms contacts and making small, illegal deals in the States. Once Ko Tan started checking, he wouldn't find just documents, but actual arms dealers who had done business with the man called Shadow. To account for the time he'd spent in the DEA, which had now been deleted from his records, they inserted rumors of his activities with a small insurgency group in El Salvador. Given the underground nature of an insurgency group, it would be a hard story for Ko Tan to prove either way.

Then everything was in place. Shadow took on, once and for all, the role of a suspicious and quietly efficient arms dealer and trainer.

Upon arriving in Myanmar, however, Shadow didn't seek Ko Tan out. He just made sure rumors started spreading about the presence of a former American soldier, now wanted by the law, who had experience in high-tech weaponry. A man for hire.

Then he simply waited for Ko Tan to find him.

That had been a year and a half ago, and the pressure had never relented. A year and a half of endless tests and challenges as Ko Tan sought proof of his loyalty. A year and a half of constantly being watched, even as in the deep recesses of his mind, he plotted the downfall of the watcher. Shadow's background, however, had given him the advantage, for if there was one thing Ko Tan loved, it was computerized smart weapons. The drug lord was a true technophile—the more advanced, the more sophisticated, the better. He wanted—he demanded—the best. It was his weakness, and Shadow had spent a year figuring out how to exploit it.

Now, for the last eight months, he'd been carefully piecing together a multimillion-dollar arms deal for state-of-the-art weaponry. Meeting with various low-level go-betweens in Myanmar, and then one brief sojourn back to the States to negotiate with the main supplier, he almost had the entire deal worked out. Complete with such weapons as computerized defense networks and missile launchers, it was truly the deal of the century.

And it was a deal so large and so crucial, the arms dealer would only make the final deal with Ko Tan. In the United States.

It had taken a bit of careful manipulating on Shadow's part to get Ko Tan to agree, but eventually the man had given in to his own arrogance. He had to have the best, the newest, the most advanced. And this would get it for him.

Now everything was clicking into place. The arms dealer was an actual arms dealer and equally oblivious to Shadow's true identity, which would be an added bonus to the sting: they'd get Ko Tan and a major arms dealer, as well. The DEA had been kept up-to-date through Shadow's periodic reports to another DEA agent—a Burmese native—who was undercover in Myanmar as a local villager.

They were just weeks from the deal now, all the last details finally sliding into place. It was tense, sometimes almost overwhelming. But it would be over soon.

Just two more weeks.

And the life of one red-haired woman.

Shadow's eyes returned to the sleeping form, and for a minute they blazed with dark anger. Why did she have to come now? Now when he was so damn close, and every move was so critical?

He wanted to hate her, he wanted to blame her, curse her.... He wanted to lay it all at her feet.

It was hard to hate a woman with such vibrant eyes and fiery hair. It was hard to blame a woman who showed such courage even when she was deathly afraid.

It was hard to know such a woman and feel nothing.

The end justified the means, he tried telling himself. If Ko Tan got away again, he would continue to murder and to sell drugs, drugs that led to even more deaths. The man had to be stopped at any price, even if that included the life of a beautiful, spirited woman.

But looking at her hit him in the gut with just what was meant by the phrase "easier said than done." Seeing her in the soft embrace of sleep, it was impossible not to want to protect her, to keep her safe.

He wanted to reach out, to lightly stroke her skin. Even now he could remember its silky feel, warm and vibrant beneath his hand. And her lips, so soft and supple beneath his own. The soft sigh of her surrender.

He never should have touched her. Having done so, he just didn't want to stop.

He had no choice, he told himself, turning away from her graceful form. He should just let her go.

He was a man who didn't feel, right? A man who had grown up in harsh city streets. A man who knew just how cold and cruel life could be. A man who, for a year and a half now, had lived and interacted with an evil so dark it had stained his soul.

He'd seen all the wrong parts of life. He knew it was hard; he knew it wasn't any fairy tale. So he should be immune to such things as softness. He should be distant, cold, untouchable.

Uncaring.

But then he remembered how she'd looked at the river's edge, clothed in little more than her pride. He remembered how her hands had shook, but her eyes had remained firm. And later, huddled on the floor of her cabin after having tried to escape, how she'd looked, wet and forlorn. Like a lost waif, needing protection, needing security.

Needing him.

Don't, he told himself. Don't torture yourself with it. But he still couldn't let it go, either.

She was so beautiful. So courageous. So... So everything he'd once thought to find in a woman.

He'd given his life to avenging his friend. But could he give hers, too? Could he really stand aside and do nothing?

From the sinking in his stomach, he already knew the answer was no.

Somehow, someway, that he still couldn't quite pinpoint, she'd managed to penetrate his indifference and disarm the mercenary.

Now what was he going to do?

Thirty-six hours more before Ko Tan would most likely demand her presence again, and everything would come to a head. Thirty-six hours under the watchful eye of a cruel and clever man, surrounded by thousands of well-trained guerillas. All he had to do was figure out how to save a woman's life while keeping his own, and not blow his cover. *Damn.*

His eyes grew weary, and for one moment, his shoulders bowed under the strain. But then, with grim determination, he squared them again and took one last look at the sleeping woman next to him. She looked so peaceful now, so untouched by all the blackness swirling around her. She looked pure and innocent and beautiful, all the things he'd left behind so long ago.

All the things that, after all this time, he'd never get back. His entire life had been in darkness. And the last year and a half had been the finishing touch, sealing in the blackness once and for all.

It was much too late to go back now.

Exhausted, he finally let his eyes drift shut as he sat on the floor of the hut with Nemo curled at his knee. But even then he couldn't find peace from his own mind. Even then, images and sensations swam and swirled into a hazy pool of drowning memory.

A long, long time ago, there was the soft security of being hugged by the woman who smelled of lilacs and always looked at him and smiled with her gentle gray eyes, eyes that he knew cried late at night when she thought he was asleep. There was the dim pain of watching her tall, thin shoulders shake with every hacking cough. And then there was the day he came home and found her sprawled on the threadbare floor. The day he'd cried, *"Mother!"* in that last moment of crashing despair, even as he'd known she could no longer answer.

Then there had been the woman with the golden hair and violet eyes as deep as his own. The woman who had never pushed him too far, but who had understood too well. The woman who had given him help without costing him his pride. The woman named Sabrina.

And there were other faces, too. The rebellious sulk of Mike, the teenage friend who tried to overdose on speed. Then later, lifetimes later, the dazzling smile of Johnny, always trying to charm the ladies. The dazzling laugh...the ear-piercing scream. The bullets hitting home, one by one by one.

And now there was the glowing red hair of a green-eyed woman. Strands that blew and teased in long, tantalizing waves that begged for a man's touch. The feel of her satin skin, the flashes of her quick anger. The stubbornness in the tilt of her chin, her endless pride, standing in only an ugly blanket and the mane of her wild hair.

Her fevered strength sagging against him, the whispered cries of his name.

With a long sigh, he at last let the tension go. Sleep came finally in the long night, and carried him away to a dream-filled land. Somewhere, in the dark of the night, the lilac woman and her gentle eyes lived again, and Johnny, with his charming smile, died.

The sunlight finally penetrated the blackness of her sleep. With a small murmur of protest, she tried to turn away from it, but it seemed to be everywhere. Finally, one eye peeled slowly open.

God, it was bright.

With another moan, Riley closed the eye again. But having now woken up, she couldn't quite return to the gentle hold of sleep. With a deep sigh, she realized she was going to have to face the brightness, after all. Carefully, she rolled over onto her back, eyes still closed, and began to take inventory.

She felt incredibly weak, no stronger than a child. Her muscles were exhausted beyond any hope, but she stretched slowly anyway, gently pulling on each one. It felt nice, but she was still weak. Very weak.

Starting to truly wake up now, she realized she was very thirsty. And her head *really* hurt. With a low groan, she attempted to open her eyes again.

The light was still too bright.

But this time, after a bout of frantic blinking, she actually succeeded in gazing at the world through a serious squint.

A very furry silver-haired monkey was staring back at her.

With a groan, she closed her eyes again. But then she felt something cool and wet against her cheek, so she tentatively peeled her eyes back open. This time she discovered a tall glass filled with juice.

Of course, her foggy mind managed to register. If Nemo was here, that meant Shadow was, as well.

She tilted her eyes way back, and sure enough, a tall, lean man came into focus.

"Boy," she managed to say thickly, "you look like hell."

"Drink your juice," he ordered her.

Too thirsty to argue, she weakly propped herself up on one elbow and greedily gulped down the cold, sweet concoction. It felt wonderful against her throat, quenching the unbearable dryness.

But just as the cool refreshment of the juice swept the last traces of sleep from her mind, it brought the memories of last night flooding painfully back. Holding her head in one hand, she let the glass sink back to the floor.

She didn't want to remember last night. But she did. She remembered the dinner with Ko Tan, his lecherous looks and the cool sips of wine. She remembered the cold calculation of his eyes, the cruel twist of his smile.

Journalist? Hah! He might feed her a crumb or two of information, but his prime objective was unmistakable.

Feeling more lost and uncertain than ever, she squinted her eyes open just far enough to peer at Shadow. His own eyes were gazing out the window, and from her vantage point, he looked as aloof and distant as ever.

For a crazy moment, she thought she might actually cry. Defeated, her head fell forward, and she struggled once more to cope with her situation. But she just couldn't find any more strands of hope. She was being held prisoner in the middle of a jungle by one of the world's cruelest drug lords. And she *was* a prisoner. It was obvious after last night that Ko Tan certainly wasn't going to just let her walk away when he chose. No, he wanted something more from her that she definitely couldn't—*wouldn't*—give.

Fool, she told herself savagely. She should have known better; she should have been better prepared.

But then her mind relented enough to acknowledge that there really was very little she could have done. She'd certainly never planned on becoming Ko Tan's prisoner, and now that she was one, there wasn't much she could do about it.

Escape.

She latched onto the word once again, for at least it offered fragile comfort. She had to escape—the price of failure was simply too high. If only she knew a way. If only...

Her mind drifted to the man in front of her.

There was something between them, she knew that much. Maybe it was just chemical attraction, or maybe it was purely the result of the situation they found themselves in, but a part of her thought it was something more. A part of her was so captivated by him, by the mystery in his eyes, by the tenderness of his touch that—

He had to feel something for her too, she told herself. Maybe not much, but there *had* to be something there.

She swallowed several times, searching for the right words.

"You stood up for me last night. So I wouldn't have to stay there. Why?"

"You were sick," Shadow said simply, his gaze never leaving the window.

"But you've always said that you wouldn't help me. That your duty to Ko Tan came first," she said softly. "Why did you change your mind?"

"I didn't."

"But you stood up to him."

"I questioned his initial decision, that's all."

The words were cold, abrupt, not offering any comfort at all. But grimly she plunged on, anyway, trying a new approach this time. Something had to reach him. Surely he wasn't as remote as he sounded. Surely...

"Shadow," she said quietly, "Shadow...I really am in a lot of trouble, aren't I?"

He only nodded his head, not even bothering to turn around.

"If I refuse Ko Tan, he will kill me, won't he?"

Once again, the short, precise nod.

The despair was back, but she fought it down, taking a deep breath. "Do you think I should give in, then?"

"Do you want to live?" The question sounded strangely cold, impersonal. It did little to reassure her, and the despair grew a little more. *Tell me no,* her heart begged. *Tell me you'll help me. Tell me . . . you care.*

The room was still silent. Even Nemo was quiet as he watched the interplay with his round, round eyes.

"Yes," she said at last. "Yes, I want to live."

"Then you don't have a choice."

The despair mushroomed completely, filling her with its hopeless solitude. She'd wanted to think he'd help her. Wanted to think that maybe she wasn't on her own.

Well, she was. After all the worrying before last night, the assurances to herself to the contrary, she'd still harbored a tiny hope that Shadow might help her. He might have kissed her. He might have touched her with tender hands, but he wasn't her champion. She'd been a fool to ever think otherwise. Funny, but somehow she'd figured there was something between them, something special. . . . Then again, she always did have an overactive imagination.

She was alone now, but strangely, it left her without fear. "I won't," she told him evenly. "I'll take my chances."

For a moment, his own head seemed to sag, but then he was standing as straight and still as ever. It had to have been her imagination. If she could have seen his eyes, however, she would have known the truth. For his eyes were the eyes of a man completely torn between his need for revenge and his desire to protect. He didn't turn around, though, and he didn't offer her any consolation. The safest course for her, he knew, was to keep her thinking he was the cold-blooded mercenary. Then he had to keep Ko Tan equally unaware of what was going on as he sought a way out of this. Because he saw it clearly now. He *would* have to find a way out of it for the both of them. He almost laughed bitterly at the task. Yes, just so long as no one ever knows what you're thinking, what you're feeling. Just so long as you have complete and utter control. . . .

After a long moment, he fought down the bitterness enough to speak. "Don't tell me these things," he said, and the words came out coldly. "I'm your jailer, not your confessor."

It was the very coldness that made her angry, the very biting edge that managed to fill the emptiness within her with rage instead. "What?" she demanded harshly. "Are you going to run to Ko Tan now? Are you that eager to see me die?"

"I told you in the beginning. I do my job well." His own voice was beginning to sound angry now, the frustration finding the only outlet that it could.

"Yes," she agreed bitterly. "You're quite the little gofer aren't you? Ko Tan says jump, you jump. Ko Tan says kill, you kill. Tell me, is the money really that good?"

"Good enough," he said levelly, refusing to rise to the bait even as his fist clenched at his side with the effort of maintaining control. It was better this way, he reminded himself. If for even a moment she suspected who he really was, how he really felt, it would only endanger her life more. And after all, why shouldn't she hate him? After all the things he'd done, after the strain of the last two years, maybe her contempt for him was more accurate.

"Leave," Riley said suddenly. "Get the hell out of here."

He nodded at that, accepting the rejection as his due even as he felt desolation fill his soul. He didn't turn around; he simply headed for the door. There was one moment when he paused, one moment when he went to push the door open and heard her own muffled sound of despair. One moment when he would have sold his soul to be just Shadow the man comforting Riley the woman. But then, clenching his fist tightly, he forced himself to leave, Nemo loping along after him.

Because after all, he wasn't Shadow the man. He'd given that up a year and a half ago in the pursuit of justice. Now he was only Shadow the undercover agent who had sacrificed his future for his friend. And if there was one thing he hadn't lied to Riley about, it was that he did, in fact, do his job well.

The next thing Riley knew, it was late afternoon, and Shadow was shaking her awake from a light doze. She was still weak, consciousness coming to her slowly. She managed to sit up.

Shadow's grim face chased the last of the sleep from her eyes. Belatedly, she noticed he was dressed in dark olive pants and a matching olive shirt already stained with deep circles of sweat. A gun was slung around one shoulder, and a long knife was at his waist.

"Ko Tan said that you were to observe the men's training," he said flatly. "Get up. It's already almost over."

Scrambling now, she managed to get to her feet, swaying slightly. No hand reached out to help, nor did a flicker of emotion pass over Shadow's face. The lack of reaction only served to reinforce her own determination, and she met his eyes squarely as she stood before him. So he was determined to leave her on her own.... She was tough, she told herself. She could take care of herself and she would.

"I'm surprised Ko Tan remembered," she said levelly. "After last night I expected him to drop all pretenses."

Shadow simply shrugged. "Ko Tan is Ko Tan," he said.

"Yes," she agreed, her chin rising up a notch. "So I guess as long as he wants to play his games, I might as well, too. Who knows, I might get a story yet." The words sounded faintly challenging and echoed firm control. Sometime between the hours when he'd gone and the hours when she'd fallen back asleep, she'd reached a final conclusion. She had to stop thinking of any sort of an understanding or attraction between her and Shadow. He obviously didn't care about her fate, and that was just fine, she told herself. She didn't need him. And she wasn't going to care about him, either. As far as she was concerned, they were both on their own.

But that didn't stop her from trying to catch the look in his eye as they left the cabin. That didn't stop her from wondering about all the lines of exhaustion that she found there.

Soon, however, it was her own fatigue that concerned her. After being so violently sick the night before, and perhaps simply due to the aftereffects of the alcohol, she felt weak. After about ten minutes of walking, her steps were already lagging, and the exhaustion returned in force. Stubbornly, she made herself trudge on, determined to last another five minutes at least. She would allow herself a break then.

But soon after, she stumbled, and Shadow automatically reached out a hand to catch her. The minute his hand touched her arm, however, she jerked away as if touched by a searing brand.

"I'll be okay," she said sharply, unconsciously rubbing the spot. "I don't need your help, thanks."

There was a bitterness in the words that wasn't lost on him. Nor did his mind forget how she had recoiled at his touch. But there was nothing he could do, he reminded himself sternly. Nothing at all.

The training field was a long ways away, and her face was openly strained by the time they reached it. Her steps had slowed considerably for the last half mile, though neither had commented on it, and the sweat was rolling in small streams from her brow. But not once did she stop, and not once did he repeat his mistake of offering assistance. Instead they simply walked alone, side by side, without touching, without exchanging a word. The tension was almost palpable. What should have brought them sanity, only served to make each one more aware.

Shadow was visibly relieved to finally arrive at the distraction of the training field.

When Riley had managed to regain her breath, she looked around to find that the field was divided into sections. One part had targets set up for shooting. In another section the trainees fought hand to hand with knives. Another long strip of demarcated land weaved in and out of the jungle as a strenuous obstacle course.

She watched small men coated with dirt and mud squirm under barbed wires, while another group of men grunted through a long set of push-ups. Shadow left her in the middle, where the men moved and milled around her. The men had been briefed that a woman with red hair would be coming. They'd also been informed that she was strictly Ko Tan's property. Not even looking was allowed. And one thing Shadow could say about the men was that they had learned discipline, albeit the hard way. Now, with a beautiful woman standing right in their midst, none of the men so much as gave her a covert glance. These were men who had learned the value of their lives.

Fascinated, Riley watched Shadow head to the hand-to-hand combat zone, where he barked out curt orders in a tongue she didn't understand. Then he whipped out his knife and illustrated a few lightning moves against a stationary student. Instruction complete, he moved to the side, motioning another soldier to take his place, and commanded the two to begin.

The drill was incredible to watch, each student moving fluidly through rapid attacks and counterattacks. Shadow watched, nodding now and then, once frowning, but never interfering until at last one soldier neatly tripped the other and had a knife at his throat before he could recover. The victorious soldier held the pose for a minute, then he, too, stood, adjusting his shoulders a bit smugly, and headed away.

In a flash, the fallen soldier was up and upon the retreating man, felling him in a matter of seconds. With a curt nod, Shadow showed his approval, and the lesson was learned: Never turn your back on your opponent, even when he's down.

After watching that, Riley's gaze wandered to observe soldiers gunning down paper targets and sweating their way through the long obstacle course. Not too far away was a building, and, curious, she headed toward it. No one blocked her way.

The building was larger than she'd expected, and she stepped inside to find that it was a huge room containing a model of bamboo huts and jungle trees. To one side was a small anteroom that contained an impressive array of buttons and other electrical controls. It didn't take much imagination to determine that this was another type of training field, designed to test the reflexes and accuracy of the soldier. Buttons would make different targets appear from the huts or bushes—some civilians, some enemies. The trick was to determine which it was before the enemy killed you or you killed the civilian.

It was a very sophisticated setup—she had seen ones like it for police training in the States. The exercise certainly helped develop amazing reaction times. Importing it to the jungle, however, couldn't have been cheap. Plus it would require sophisticated electrical skill to set up. Now, who provided that skill and who had sold the system?

It was an intriguing question. While most of Ko Tan's troops were straight out of the local villages, Ko Tan himself had been educated in America. So far, the only person she knew who was close to him in rank was Shadow. Had he been in charge of setting this operation up? And if so, why? Probably the money.

It could explain his special position, she thought. After all, an extensive knowledge of engineering and electronics couldn't be that easy to come up with in the jungle. Even more intriguing, however, was *where* the system had come from. Her fingers itched for a pen and pad to take notes, but such luxuries hadn't been made available. All she could do was examine the control panel carefully and attempt to commit such things as model and serial number to memory.

Once she got back to the States, she could check it out. And she *would* make it back, she told herself firmly. She just had to think of a way. She had learned a few things after last time, at least. This time she would try to be better prepared. First off, she should try to get supplies. Drinking water, a little food, a compass, maybe even a map if she was really lucky. After all, it would take at least two days to get to the Thai border by foot, something she hadn't considered carefully enough last time.

Then another thought came to her. The chance of making it all the way to the border undiscovered was slim. But what if she didn't go that far? What if she just tried to make it back to where her plane crashed? She knew the coordinates where she'd gone down, so with a map it shouldn't be too hard to plot a course back to the wreckage. Then all she had to do was hope the CB was still operational. Even if it wasn't perfect, she did have some minor experience fixing airplane transmitters, once again courtesy of her uncle. So there was a chance she could play with it enough to make do.

Then all she had to do was hope someone out there heard her, and arrived before Ko Tan.

Of course, that still left several problems she hadn't figured out yet. Like how to escape Shadow's notice long enough to assemble supplies. Since Shadow had stolen her bed, she could hardly vacate through the floor again to steal items by nightfall. Which left her hoping that he would become busy with something or someone else long enough for her to pay a visit to the kitchen. Somehow, she didn't think the chances of that happening were very great. But she had to hope, because otherwise, she would give in to the fear.

It was definitely something to think about. With a slow nod of her head, she journeyed back out into the sunlight, to see Shadow heading toward her. Taking a deep breath, she composed herself and went back to assuming the role of Riley the reporter.

"Have you seen enough?" Shadow asked her.

She only shrugged. "Oh, I don't know. What else is there?"

Shadow seemed to give the matter serious thought. "Back by the barracks there's a video room where the men watch tapes of their skirmishes."

"Who does the videotaping?"

"There are a few men trained in that area."

"Who trained them?"

"It was before my time."

"And when did you arrive here?"

"Long enough ago."

"Long enough ago for what?"

"Long enough to know what questions not to answer."

She almost smiled at that. For someone who didn't like to talk, he was remarkably quick in verbal debates. What keen intelligence was lodged behind those carefully controlled eyes? And how in the world was she ever going to escape it?

"I'm hungry," she said abruptly. And tired, and thirsty, and in a suddenly bad mood for that matter.

Shadow nodded. "Dem should have something prepared, or you can eat in the mess hall if you'd like to experience more of soldier life."

Somehow, she hadn't counted on being given an option. Well, McDouglas, she told herself. Think fast. Would it be easier to steal things from the mess hall or Dem's kitchen? Considering that avoiding Shadow's attention would be hard enough, let alone hundreds of other watching eyes, she went with Dem's kitchen.

"Could I eat in the mess hall on another day—maybe tomorrow?" she asked smoothly, hoping her voice sounded natural.

But Shadow merely nodded, leading the way to the kitchen.

For one instant, she allowed herself to feel triumphant. For one instant, she allowed herself to believe it really would be all right. But that was before they ate, before Shadow's sharp gaze followed each and every move that she made.

That was before he was leading her back out the door, empty-handed, without hope. Soon, she managed to console herself. Soon she would find a way. If she just held on a little longer, thought a little harder, she would figure out a way. Because there had to be some way.

She had no way of knowing that the silent man next to her was thinking exactly the same thing.

Chapter 7

In the end, opportunity presented itself before she'd even expected it. Not long after sundown, Shadow returned to her cabin, and without so much as a single word, took her to Dem's kitchen for an evening snack, where he promptly deserted her. As she'd spent the last ten minutes bombarding him with questions only to be thwarted by his silence, Riley wasn't in the best of moods when Dem's rotund form came bustling through the doors with a platter full of late-night snacks.

But then, looking at the pile of bread, cheese and fruit in front of her, she grimly suppressed her anger with the realization that this was exactly what she'd been waiting for. Shadow wasn't present with his burning stare, and Dem was still commuting from the room to the kitchen, leaving her alone for short intervals. Quickly, she wrapped up some cheese in a napkin and tucked it into her pocket. The pieces were cut fairly thin, and with a little patting and tucking, would hopefully be unnoticeable.

Then she just needed drinkable water for her journey. That proved to be frightfully easy. She simply mentioned to Dem that it would be nice to have something filled with water in her room because the heat often made her wake up thirsty in the middle of the night. And, voilà, the next thing she knew Dem was handing her a small canteen filled with boiled water. There wasn't much in there, but if she rationed it carefully, she could make it work.

Thus, in the space of an hour, she found herself compiling all the objects she'd decided that she needed. Yet instead of filling her with triumph, it left her feeling strangely empty.

Funny, just a few days ago she was preparing herself for her great adventure of going off and interviewing a real-life guerrilla. And it had certainly turned out to be a far bigger adventure than she'd ever planned. She'd been terrified, intrigued, thwarted and challenged, all in nerve-racking succession. Now she was even on the verge of an escape adventure, *if* she could just finish working out her plan.

At the first sign of an opening, she would be gone.

Back to the States, back to her career, back to a normal life. She'd have her freedom, and no longer be in danger.

And she'd be without one silent, gray-eyed man.

The thought was unwanted, and resolutely she pushed it down. Shadow was no concern of hers. He was a paid mercenary who certainly hadn't shown himself prone to helping her. If anything, he'd tormented her with his cold shrugs and dispassionate stares. Like earlier today, when she'd sought his help, only to be confronted by the cold mercenary once more.

But if she did escape, he would be punished with death.

This thought was a little harder to ignore, but she countered it with cool rationality. She'd seen him train today. She'd seen just how fast his reflexes were, just how adept he could be. He knew the men—he'd trained them. And that would certainly work to his advantage should he need to outwit them. He was the stronger one, the smarter one, the faster one. Her original impression came back to her. Yes, the man was like a panther. She certainly never needed to worry about his survival.

But what about the nights when the shadows shift in his eyes? What about the nights when his guard slipped, and the pain glimmered out? What about when he was no longer the panther, but the wolf standing alone in the darkness?

Foolish drivel, she told herself firmly. Once more she was romanticizing the man, seeing what she wanted to see rather than who he truly was. The man killed people for money.

Straight and simple. He had never denied it, not all the times she'd challenged him—*wanted* him—to do so. And he worked for Ko Tan, a man who killed senselessly and who would kill her if she remained.

No, Shadow wasn't a panther or a wolf. He was one more serpent in the jungle, and she would do well to remember that.

But what about his eyes, the touch of his hands, the scar down his cheek, the feel of his lips—

Quit it, she ordered herself. Only it still didn't quite stop the emptiness burgeoning inside her. Shadow intrigued her. He made her long to reach out, long to understand more. Sometimes he infuriated her, but sometimes he compelled her with the loneliness shifting in his eyes. He was dangerously attractive, yet likely to reject her. But when he'd touched her... When his strong hands had caressed her skin...

The hands of a killer.

No matter what, she thought, it still came down to that.

Shadow was a mercenary. He used his hands and the keen intelligence of his mind, not to build, but to destroy. Once more she remembered the sophisticated training equipment she'd seen earlier—equipment that Shadow must have helped with in some way, equipment that was used to create and hone killers.

"Dem?" she asked suddenly, "Dem, how long have you known Shadow?"

The large man looked slightly shocked to be addressed directly, but after a bit he managed a reply. "More than a year," the cook said in rough English.

"Is he an important man here?" she quizzed.

"Yes, yes," he agreed with a small nod. "Shadow big man here. Important."

"Why?" She prodded softly. And then, after a small pause, she forced herself to add, "Is he that good of a fighter?"

Dem looked shocked, as if she couldn't possibly know what she was asking. "Yes, yes," he told her, bobbing his head much more adamantly this time. "He kills many men. Moves very, very fast. All the other men, they speak of this."

Riley felt herself pale a little at the words, and the next question was even harder to ask. "How many men has he killed?" she whispered softly.

The cook looked uncertain now. "Eight," he ventured. "Maybe ten. I hear stories only. Don't see."

Her hands were shaking violently now under the table, and she had to fight hard for control. She'd tried to tell herself what type of man he was, but it was different to hear it from someone else. He had killed. And unlike the others, it wasn't for some cause he believed in, some faint hope of a different way of life. He killed for money. Cash.

"And the equipment," she found herself whispering hoarsely. "Does he help with the equipment?"

But the cook was merely shaking his head, looking very uncomfortable now. "I don't know," he told her and began to pick up the dishes. "I just cook. I know nothing."

His denial didn't stop her thoughts. Her stomach rolled, and she felt faintly ill.

She'd come to care for a killer.

A *killer*.

Abruptly, she felt her determination solidify, her nerves becoming icy calm. She'd known all along, she reminded herself. This wasn't new knowledge. It was just the first time she'd faced up to it. Well, it was all right. Because she wasn't going to remain here much longer, anyway. No, she had her plan. Tonight, she told herself. She would find a way to go tonight.

When Shadow finally reappeared half an hour later, her eyes were distant, her hands steady, as they hovered over the stash of food in her pockets. Her face was an image of faint politeness. She carried the canteen around her neck.

Shadow looked at her intently, registering not just the canteen, but the change in her demeanor. For a minute, she thought he was going to take her precious water away, but then, with one more penetrating glance, his eyes left her. With a short nod to Dem, he led her out into the night, Nemo astride his shoulder.

They walked in silence at first, neither attempting conversation. Only Nemo burst into chatter once, to have it fade into the tension of the evening. In spite of her best intentions, Riley found herself sneaking glances at Shadow as they went along. She tried to reconcile what she knew with how he looked. This man was a killer, her mind repeated over and over. A killer.

But he didn't look vicious in the night. If anything, he seemed to look tired, the exhaustion rimming his eyes in dark circles. And his jaw, which usually looked firm, appeared positively grim in the deep shadows of the night.

He looked like a man with the weight of the world on his shoulders, she thought suddenly. And then, on the heels of that thought, came the inevitable one. Maybe he cared what happened to her, after all. Maybe he wasn't as cold and vicious as she'd thought.

Fool, she countered immediately. Here she went again, looking for signs, for feelings that simply did not exist. He was a mercenary. A drug runner who was aiding Ko Tan in controlling over half of the world's heroin supply. The only thing he deserved from her was contempt.

And yet she could still remember the passion of his kiss, she could still recall the tenderness of his hands as he gently massaged her back. What was more, all those times they'd been alone together. In fact, they'd been alone together most of the time she'd been Ko Tan's prisoner. He could have used her any way he cared, yet he'd made no effort to harm her, ever.

Fear of Ko Tan, she tried to convince herself. Hadn't he said there were certain pleasures Ko Tan reserved for himself?

The thoughts remained, however, and she cursed herself royally for her weakness. She knew what he'd done, and he himself had made no attempt to delude her about his profession. And yet as much as she wanted to despise him, other emotions tangled and weaved into it.

Sometimes he looked lonely, and she understood loneliness. Sometimes he looked so tired, and she could understand that, too. And sometimes, when he looked at her, there was a blazing hunger in his eyes.

She understood that all too well.

A small, strangled sound of frustration emerged from her throat, and then all at once, she became aware that they had stopped. "Where are we?" she demanded immediately.

But Shadow didn't answer her. Instead, his eyes were roaming the dark depths of the night. At first glance, it would appear that he and Riley were all alone, but his keen eyes slowly penetrated the shadows.

So far two guards had seen them come in this direction. They'd kept a discreet distance, knowing better than to interfere with Ko Tan's right-hand man. Whatever dark errand he might be running, they were better off not knowing.

Still, if questioned later, they could attest to the fact that Shadow and the woman had left the outskirts of the camp together. Shadow was counting on it.

Now his eyes couldn't make out any more shifting shapes in the night, which was how it should be. He glanced down at his watch, registering the time at 11:05. They were actually outside of the camp, beyond the patrols. So all he needed to do was kill a good hour, and then make sure that they were also spotted reentering the camp. It would be best if their clothes were a little messed up, and probably Riley's hair, too. Just enough to give the proper impression of a midnight dalliance.

Then step one of his plan would be complete.

"Wait a minute," Riley's voice interrupted. "Hey, this is a poppy field!"

Slightly surprised that she'd recognized it so quickly, Shadow nodded. This was just one field of the nearly three hundred thousand acres of poppies Ko Tan controlled. Almost two trillion dollars' worth of opium, growing by the rivers, in the jungles, at the bases of the mountains. The villagers harvested it and then dutifully paid Ko Tan his forty-percent tax on the crop. From the harvest, the opium resin was made into opium and heroin, then smuggled out of the country on ships, each rubber-wrapped block marked with his KKK. The first *K* standing for premium quality—eighty- to ninety-percent-pure white No. 4 heroin. The last two *K*s represented the Kokang area of the Shan state. Shadow almost shook his head, looking at all of it spread around him. So much destruction. And it had become his life.

He remained silent, waiting for Riley's reaction. It was not long in coming.

"Who owns this?" she demanded to know.

"A nearby village," he answered simply.

"I see," she stated darkly. "So they grow the poppies and hand them over to Ko Tan. Tell me, does he threaten them with death if they don't comply?"

Shadow merely shook his head. "You don't need force," he said quietly. "Economics is enough."

Riley was forced to acknowledge his point. "Sixty-seven dollars for one pound of opium resin," she recited bitterly, having done her homework before coming to Myanmar, "versus a mere one dollar for a half bushel of corn. And the opium can be harvested several times a year. My God," she breathed, looking at the rows and rows spreading out before her, "we must be standing in tens of thousands of dollars' worth."

Suddenly, it made her very angry. "Doesn't this bother you?" she demanded, turning to face him. "You're standing in a field full of potential opium and heroin. Drugs that people beat and steal and murder for. Drugs that corrupt and kill, slowly but surely. How can you do that? How can you just stand there and feel nothing?"

He didn't answer her. Instead he just stood there, hearing the accusations pound into him, one by one. Feel nothing? How could he afford to feel anything else? He'd learned. He'd closed his dead mother's eyes with eight-year-old hands. For six years, he'd run streets filled with violence, sex and drugs, looking for food and shelter. Then, years later, he'd cradled his dead friend's head on his lap and felt the blood running onto his hands. He'd cared, and he'd paid so dearly for caring, that he had learned never to do it again.

In this land emotions made one vulnerable, and vulnerability led to destruction. So in the last year and a half, he'd become the very cold and dispassionate mercenary he was supposed to be.

Until now, on the eve of his mission's completion, he could look inside himself and know that, for him, it would never end. He'd lost something along the way. Fire, zest, passion. Now he was just a shell of a man, consumed by an emptiness inside he no longer knew how to fill.

His best friend was still dead after all this time. Shadow would have his revenge, though. Ko Tan would pay. And then?

Nothing.

He would go back to another job, another case, another undercover assignment. One not as burningly and personally important, perhaps, but one just as dark as all the others....

Once more his eyes strayed to the woman standing beside him. The woman with such fiery hair and the green eyes filled with angry conviction. A woman of strength and courage and passion. A woman of fire.

Who looked at him with contempt.

For one moment it was too much, and where he'd almost reached out his hand to her, now he turned away abruptly. She despised him, and he couldn't blame her. She thought he was a mercenary, and maybe, after all this time, that was exactly what he was.

"Answer me," Riley was demanding hotly. "Come on now, answer me!"

He didn't have any answers, though. Only the emptiness inside.

He shrugged his shoulders, then glanced at his watch. Enough time had passed. They could head back now. He started to walk.

But he hadn't counted on her reaction.

"Damn you!" Riley exclaimed behind him. "Don't you just turn and walk away from me!" And when that still wasn't enough, she strode forward until she could lay a demanding hand on his arm. Angry and determined, she spun him around.

And was struck by the starkness of his eyes.

The black depths were drowning, filled with slivers of white-hot pain and daggers of dark gray self-loathing. The impact hammered into her heart, silencing the accusations in her throat.

These were not the eyes of a killer. These were not the eyes of a cold, uncaring mercenary. These were the eyes of a man filled with a pain she couldn't begin to imagine, and a man haunted by a darkness she just couldn't understand.

And at that moment, she forgot all the logical and rational reasons to despise him. Whereas just hours before she'd heard that he was a killer, now she could only see the man. She should have felt cold indifference; instead she responded with overwhelming emotion. She didn't hesitate anymore, ignoring the logic and following her instinct. She put her arms around his neck and held him close. He didn't move, didn't step back, didn't reject her. Rather, with a muffled groan, he gave in and buried his head in the sweet curve of her neck.

She was soft, her skin like velvet against his own rough cheek, her hair like silk. And she smelled like fresh soap and rainy days. Good and clean and wholesome.

He shouldn't touch her, he thought. Surely hands stained with as much blood as his would corrupt such purity. But he couldn't let go, either. He was the darkness, the never-ending shadows, and she was the light, the emerging solace.

But it wasn't enough to just hold her, just touch. He wanted—*needed*—more. Affirmation that he was alive after having been cold for so long. Affirmation that maybe she *did* need him, if only for this moment, in this place, in this night.

He could resist many things, like the sight of her naked body magnified by the river, the satiny feel of her skin, the flaming silk of her hair and the green temptation of her eyes. But he was, after all, only a man. A man who'd lived too long without touch or passion. A man with infinite self-control, but not the power to resist the sweet comfort she offered him.

How many nights had he dreamt of touching her? How many days had he longed to feel the softness of her skin? To touch her, to feel the softness? After all these years, all these miles, to finally feel softness. To finally feel at all....

His lips found her neck, and unable to help themselves, they drank of the sweetness there.

She moaned lightly at the first velvety touch, his tongue flickering out to tease her sensitive nerves. Then she felt the gentle nip of his teeth and shuddered.

She'd been attracted to him from the start, and she'd fought the attraction with cool logic and high morals. But now, confronted by his need, she couldn't turn him away. There was a moment of fear, of overwhelming uncertainty. He had turned away before, he might reject her again at any moment, and he was a mercenary, a paid killer....

But then he took her hand, and looked at her with dark eyes filled with burning need. And there was no more room for fear as her hand closed around his.

To return to the hut would be too dangerous, Shadow knew. It was too close to the camp, too close to Ko Tan. Ironically, it was out here in the poppy fields that they had the most privacy, shrouded by darkness and outside the circle of prying eyes. No one ever came here this time of night. And certainly not Ko Tan.

He moved them deeper into the bordering foliage.

They were silent as they moved together, the bond of unspoken need too fragile for words. Instead they communicated purely by touch and look. The feel of his guiding hand, gently cupping her elbow. The burning depths of her eyes, glowing hotly in the night.

With quick hard hacks of his knife, he cut down enough foliage to make a small, padded clearing, safely encircled on all sides by thick leaves.

It was the last moment, the last chance for either to turn back. And for one moment, Riley felt the fear creep back in. Even as she longed to reach out to him, she wondered if the next touch, the next caress, would be the one where he would turn away, leaving her once again alone. She shouldn't risk it— she should end this madness now, while she still could. But perhaps that moment was already gone. For, looking at him now, seeing the dark burning of his eyes, she couldn't turn away. He needed her. For whatever reason, at this moment, he needed her.

She looked at him, waiting, uncertain, and then, with a dazzling smile she opened her arms and beckoned him to her.

There was one moment of hesitation, when the force of his own desire almost overwhelmed him. He suddenly found he didn't just want a moment of passion. He wanted something deeper, something purer in this dark world. He wanted to touch her deeply, to show her a minute of the brilliance she'd so unknowingly shown him. But he had such little experience, and, in truth, he hadn't touched a woman in over two years. The brutality of the military training kept the hunger at bay, and emotionally, there had never been any need. Until now. And now he had no idea where to begin.

But then she reached out, gently capturing his cheek in the warm circle of her palm. It was a small gesture of comfort, and it pushed him over the precipice. He couldn't resist the soft temptation anymore, and with a low groan he succumbed, capturing her lips with his own.

At first it was gentle, tender, as he explored her lips, tasting the lush softness. Experimentally, he touched her lips lightly with his tongue and felt her push closer to him in response. Encouraged, he dipped his tongue inside, exploring the sweet recesses of her mouth. She whimpered low in her throat, but he kissed it away.

He took his time, journeying from the wonders of her mouth to the delicate curve of her ear until she moaned softly against him. Her body trembled as she pushed herself closer. She needed the feel of him, the touch of his callused hands on her sensitized skin, the warm assault of his lips and tongue on her willing body. She wanted him. She needed him.

Dizzy with overwhelming desire, Shadow drew away long enough to wrap her in a tender embrace, his head resting on top of her head as they both fought desperately for control. Less urgent now, Shadow drew back, tracing his finger gently down the curve of her soft cheek. Her eyes were luminous as they found his, banked with the burning embers of trembling passion.

She had never looked so beautiful. Slowly, she took a step back from him, and, her eyes never leaving his, she began to unbutton her shirt. It was as tantalizing as the day at the river, only more so because this time there was no fear in her eyes. Only sweet welcome and slow-burning desire. The blouse came off and her pants slid down to land in a small puddle among the leaves. With infinite care, she stepped over her clothes, standing now in just the thin wisps of her underwear. The next moment, they were gone, as well, and she stood before him, naked silk in the night.

He stared at her for a long time, not touching, not moving, just absorbing the raw wonder of her naked body. It was more than any one man deserved, he thought in wonder. Unable to wait any longer, he spread his jacket over the leaves for comfort; then, in one long stride he was there, scooping her satiny body into his arms, feeling the silk of her hair against his shoulder as he slowly lowered her down to the bed of leaves.

"Let me," she said softly, and her hands came up to find the buttons of his shirt. She felt breathless, half shocked by her own daring and half dazzled by the heady sensations overrunning her body. How long had she wondered about his touch? And now he was here, needing her, touching her, looking at her with the dark burning of his eyes. She wanted to touch him, to run her hands along the rippling waves of his lean, muscular strength. She wanted to share with him the beauty she saw there.

One by one the buttons slipped out. Her nimble fingertips whispered them free until finally, after one last moment of hesitation, he shrugged the shirt free.

His chest was a maze of scars, from a deep circle on his shoulder to crisscrossed lines racing across his ribs. Mesmerized, she lightly traced the raised skin, finding his eyes with her own. So much pain. Long gone, lost in the winds of the past, and yet still there, shifting in the depths of his eyes. Gently, slowly, she raised her lips until she could gently touch his own. Then, lightly, she kissed his chest, a soft apology for the moments long gone and impossible for her to eradicate. The tenderness overwhelmed him, and for one long moment, he clutched her close.

He didn't know what he'd done to deserve such compassion from such a woman. But all his life, he would treasure this moment, he vowed. This one moment when a woman of fire brought a ray of light to the darkness.

He wanted her, he thought fiercely. Wanted her as he'd never wanted anything, anyone, until the very force of his desire threatened to bring him to his knees before her.

He stood, and his hands came to rest on the snap of his pants, while she waited for him in brilliant anticipation. There was one last moment of self-consciousness, for he knew his body, with its lean strength and patchwork of worn scars, didn't match the perfection of hers. But she'd stood proudly before him, so he stood silently before her, letting her gaze sweep over the maze of muscles and scars. And when at last she finished, looking at him with her tender, passionate green eyes, he went to her.

He lay down gently next to her, pulling her close until he could feel the softness of her skin against the entire length of his body. Then, with a groan of surrender, he captured her lips once more and plunged them both into the burning flames.

He was lost in the softness, his hands burying themselves in the magnificent silk of her hair as his lips plundered her own. She sighed against him, one long leg coming up to rub against his as he moved to the hollow of her throat, tasting and teasing with lips and tongue. She gasped as he kissed her throat, reveling in the fiery goose bumps that raced down her body in response.

And then with burning kisses he moved down, trailing his way slowly to the soft curve of her breast. She arched back, giving him greater access as his hands moved from her hair to cup the small, tender swells of her breasts. He felt the tips harden, brushing against them with callused fingertips as she gasped and sighed. And when she arched against him, crying his name in a gasping breath, he captured her breast in the burning warmth of his mouth and lost himself in the softness there.

She moaned low, her hands kneading frantically the corded muscles of his neck as her hips came up, brushing against the burning length of him. She needed more. She needed *him*.

In response he smoothed his hand down to the swell of her hips, capturing the silky curve of her buttocks, pressing her gently against him.

She moaned against his throat, her fingers clutching his shoulders, but he didn't give in yet. He'd waited too long for such softness; he wanted it to last. So he journeyed down, his lips trailing past the soft swell of her stomach, to the top of a silken thigh. With lips and hands he explored her thoroughly, from the long curves of her legs, to the delicate structure of her feet.

He worshiped her body with taste and touch, finding the sensitive spot behind her kneecap until she begged for final release and he thought he would die of need.

But even then he held back, not yet ready for the slow, precious torment to end. Moving back up, his lips found the apex of her legs, and with slow tenderness, he began to pleasure her.

She gasped at the first touch, her hands helplessly entwining themselves in the thick darkness of his hair, pressing him closer. Never in her life had she felt such a sensation. Liquid heat boiled through her blood, and while a part of her said she should pull away, the rest of her knew she would die if he ever stopped. And the heat kept building and building, relentless and sure as she cried out his name.

And then there was that final tenseness, that rippling shudder and her gasping cry of satisfaction. But before the last wave had passed, he had returned to her and penetrated with one smooth thrust, taking her back up the crests of pleasure.

Dimly he heard her cries, felt the splendid pain of her fingernails digging into his back as he plunged into her silken warmth. With gentle fury he took her. With savage glory he skyrocketed them to the top. And with tender ecstasy, he plunged them over the edge, giving himself over to her magic with a last strangled cry of her name.

Riley.

With gentleness he had taken her. With savagery and ecstasy. But most of all, he had taken her with love.

Afterward, she curled up warmly in his arms, falling into a light slumber. But Shadow stayed awake. His mind was prisoner of all the swirling thoughts, all the responsibilities that threatened to send him to the edge of sanity. He had dropped Riley off at Dem's so he could finish his work with his arms contact in the States. So far, everything was going as planned. Except in the next twenty-four hours, he was going to throw a huge monkey wrench into the plans. In the next twenty-four hours he was going to take the biggest risk of his life.

All because of this woman sleeping so softly next to him. All because after nearly two long years of brutality, after an entire life of emptiness, he'd finally allowed himself to care.

He wasn't a fool, he thought, lying against Riley's warm form. He knew that good things merely passed through a life as dark as his own. He could count on three fingers the people who had mattered to him, and they were all long gone, two of them dead. It wouldn't be any different now.

Even if he did manage to succeed in his plan, even if he did manage to rescue Riley, it would hardly matter. Once she learned his true identity, she would hate him for deceiving her. And she would hate him dearly for this night, when he had taken her body, without repaying her with the truth.

No, he shouldn't have let things go this far. But once she'd embraced him . . . He had no defense against such comfort.

So she would hate him, turning away from him and getting back to the normality of her life. That would be the end of it all.

It would hurt, he admitted to himself, but he was a man used to pain, wasn't he? Besides, he'd spent his life in such darkness that things like hope and compassion were too foreign to need in the first place.

He didn't have anything to offer, anyway. Even if everything worked out and Ko Tan was arrested, his life still wouldn't be safe. Ko Tan was a vindictive man, and even behind bars he would have connections and power. Shadow would always have to be on the lookout against the man's revenge. And there was no way he would ever subject a woman like Riley to such a dangerous life.

A small crash came from the tree above, interrupting his thoughts as a small silver ball swung down to land with a plop not far from his shoulder.

"Shh," Shadow cautioned Nemo. "She's sleeping."

Nemo seemed to take this news with quite a bit of interest, eyeing the pair with huge, curious eyes. Not known for his tact, he sauntered over and sat down on Shadow's chest, just inches from Riley's sleeping head. But then, just to make sure his presence was felt, he lifted up the shiny locks of her hair until he could peer down at her gently closed eyes.

"Leave her alone," Shadow warned softly, making a negative motion with his hand.

But Riley shifted softly, murmuring soft noises as she turned to get more comfortable. It was too much for Nemo to resist, and his little hand shot out to find her nose before Shadow could react.

"Go away," Riley said in a clear voice, though her eyes never opened.

Nemo cocked his head in puzzled bewilderment, and Shadow couldn't stop the soft smile from forming on his lips.

"I told you so," he said to Nemo, who was beginning to look decidedly frazzled.

But Riley was starting to wake up, rolling over sleepily to face her attackers. With a deep sigh, she left the last of sleep behind. There was a small moment of awkwardness, when she didn't quite know what to say. But then, with an intense, unreadable look, Shadow reached over and lightly stroked her cheek.

"It's time to go back," he said softly.

She nodded, understanding as well that the moment had to end. She didn't say anything more, unwilling yet to test their newly formed bond. Quietly she began to dress. After looking at her for one last moment, Shadow did the same.

Then came the long trek back to the cabin, two people with rumpled clothes and tousled hair passing discreet guards. His plan had worked better than he'd anticipated, Shadow thought as they walked by. He'd wanted to give the impression of a midnight dalliance to the guards, knowing word would spread back to Ko Tan and thus set the stage for the next phase of his plan. But he hadn't meant for it to actually happen, and now he knew with certainty that he would pay for it later. When Riley knew the whole truth, and his plan, she would hate him for this night. There would be no way she could look at it without feeling set up. No, he would pay for this and pay dearly.

They were two silent people on the way back to her cabin. Two people who'd just communicated in the most intimate way possible, and now no longer knew the words to say.

And there was a sadness in the air as they walked. A feeling of loss so deep it was almost tangible. Even Nemo was quiet, his expression a study in consternation as he looked from face to face. Already the void was growing between them, already a gulf of solitude opening into a yawning chasm.

The moment was gone. The tenderness over. The softness lost.

Now they were preparing to once more stand alone. For though they had just demonstrated how deep their feelings ran, neither trusted the language.

Chapter 8

Dawn found Riley on the floor of the room, giving the door yet another exhaustive going-over. For hours she'd been working on trying to find a way out. For hours she'd gone over each and every possibility in her mind. But now, the sky lightening, her fingertips raw, her body exhausted, she was left with one conclusion: There was simply no way to escape the hut.

She would have put her head in her hands and wept, but she was too weary for even that. Realizing the futility of her initial plan, she gave in to her thirst and drank the entire canteen of water Dem had given her. It wasn't even that much water. If she'd made it out, she most probably would have succumbed to dehydration. Failing that, some soldier's bullet would have taken care of her instead. She took the crushed cheese out of her pants pocket and placed it under the blanket. Perhaps later...

If there ever was such a thing. Time was running out on her, the situation only becoming more complicated. Surely Ko Tan would demand to see her soon, and then...

Then the time would be up.

What was she going to do? She couldn't escape and she couldn't give in.

Only one answer came to her: Shadow.

Maybe, a little voice whispered, maybe he would help her now. Surely, after last night, he felt something. Of course there'd been no grand declarations, but surely a man who touched her that tenderly, a man who looked at her with such overwhelming need . . .

The door in front of her opened, and before she had time to really prepare herself, Shadow himself was there. For a long instant, they slowly stared at each other, the faded sensations of the night hanging between them. And even as Riley searched his eyes, she felt the last of her hope die.

Standing before her, he made no allusions to last night. Not a lover's kiss of greeting, or even a warm touch to spark fresh memories. Instead he stood silently, as alone and unreachable as when she'd first met him.

Hours before, she'd made love to this man, and now he was a stranger.

Without uttering a word, Shadow moved to the side, and a small boy scurried in carrying pails of steaming water. Another boy behind him produced a good-size metal basin to serve as a tub, and then with little bows to Shadow, they both disappeared.

Once again, they were alone. Once again, neither could find the words to speak. Looking at him, seeing the grim set of his jaw, the coolness in his eyes, she wasn't so sure that last night wasn't just some dream her exhausted mind had concocted. Surely no man could make love with that much passion and still look so uncaring in the morning?

Give it up, she told herself tiredly. Just give it up. He doesn't care. He never did. He never will. She'd been a fool to make love to him. She didn't know him, no matter that he'd looked out for her at times. It was just that, in the darkness of the night, she'd thought he needed her. She'd thought there was something there between them that would—

She'd thought wrong.

With a determined set to her chin, she tilted her head proudly and looked him straight in the eye. "I gather all the water is for another bath," she said, managing the words steadily enough.

Shadow nodded, leaning back against the wall. His face was still expressionless, though his skin was starting to pale from the strain.

"What's the occasion?" she wanted to know. "Or is this merely a form of charity?"

He still didn't say anything, and in the silence, the answer came to her.

"Ko Tan," she said softly. "He's asked for me again, hasn't he?"

Slowly, almost imperceptibly, Shadow nodded.

She felt the color drain from her own face as she watched him. The bottom of her stomach fell out, leaving her with a gaping emptiness. The time had come.

Ko Tan had asked for her, and this man standing before her, this man she'd touched, held, kissed, was going to deliver her, anyway. Her throat thickened, and she felt the first sting of tears behind her eyes. Swallowing heavily, she looked away.

She wanted to blame him, she wanted to hate him, but he'd never made her any promises, had he? No, it had been her own wayward heart, her own foolish fantasies that had betrayed her. She'd wanted him to care. She'd wanted him to be anyone other than the man he was. A killer. A mercenary.

Eight men, Dem had said. Eight men.

Yet he'd looked at her with such aching loneliness. A man with such dark, yearning eyes couldn't be so cold. Surely...

Well, now she knew.

Trembling, she rose to her feet. Trying to keep her head up, she managed to whisper thickly, "Can you please turn around now? I'd like to bathe."

He looked at her for a minute longer with his empty gray eyes. Then, quietly, easily, he turned.

One tear trembled out to run down her cheek, but she didn't wipe it away. After all, there was no one to see now. Instead, she concentrated on removing her clothes, and then carefully began to bathe.

There was nothing more she could say, she knew, no accusations to hurl that would change fate. She truly was alone. And somehow, some way, she was going to have to make that work. But deep in her heart, she didn't believe her own reassurances anymore. She was dealing with people colder than she could ever imagine. And in the end, she would be the one to pay the price. In the end, it would be her own death.

Her shoulders slumped forward as she tasted her own defeat. With slow hands, she began to dress. At least there were no fancy dresses this time, she thought, no more charades.

"I'm ready," she finally whispered. "As if I even had a choice."

Shadow said nothing as he turned back around, but for one long instant a smidgen of his control broke. And for just one moment she found herself looking into the eyes of a man caught in the deepest pain of his life. A man who burned with the need to reach out, even as fate held him trapped in a game he simply couldn't win. A man who wanted to help, even as he was forced to hold back.

And Riley felt it all rip at her own heart, until the pain of his gaze forced her to look away. When she turned back, the moment was gone, his eyes once again empty. And for all she knew, it had just been her imagination.

They walked in complete silence to Ko Tan's camp, each lost in a myriad of dark thoughts. There was a part of Riley that kept hoping. A part of her that, with every footstep, every passing hut, thought that now something would happen. Now she would be saved. And all because some part deep inside her refused to believe—*couldn't* believe—that Shadow would fail her so miserably.

Yet with each passing moment, nothing happened—no magical rescue, no sudden change of heart. And then the next thing Riley knew, she was standing at the door of Ko Tan's hut, feeling the squeeze of destiny in the tight ball of fear in her stomach.

There was a moment when she desperately wanted to grab Shadow's hand and beg him not to leave, to beg him to help her. But the iron strength of pride held her tongue. And it was the iron strength of her pride that kept her from weeping as, without another word, Shadow simply turned and walked away.

She found that her hands were balled into fists with the strain, sweat already beading on her brow. The wear of the last few days came crashing down and all at once she felt both ex-

hausted and strangely calm. After all, there was very little she
could do now but try her best. And if it didn't work, well, by
that time, there wouldn't be any more need for regret.

The hulking bodyguard opened the door, leading her down
the hallway with a menacing stare that clearly told her he hadn't
forgotten the events of their last encounter. And then there was
the final knock on Ko Tan's inner room, the opening of the
door, Ko Tan standing, smiling in the doorway.

Riley took one last deep breath to compose her shaking
nerves. Remember, she told herself levelly, you're a reporter
and you're bright and quick. You can do this.

Seven o'clock.

The final confrontation began.

They started with polite chitchat, Riley feeling nervous and
Ko Tan gazing at her with a faintly amused expression. Having learned her lesson last time, Riley crossed to the bar herself. Without asking, she mixed a Scotch and soda for Ko Tan,
then simply filled a glass with tonic water for herself.

She offered him the drink with a small nod of her head, and
after a tense, appraising minute, he accepted. They both sat
down then, and without waiting a moment, Riley dived right in.

"I believe things went badly last time," she began, trying to
make her voice sound light. She had to swallow deeply to continue. "I would like to apologize for my own actions that night,
and thank you for your immense tolerance and understanding."

If Ko Tan detected the faint sarcasm, he didn't let on, nodding his head slightly at her apology. "Indeed," he said
smoothly. "I have hopes that this evening will prove to be a
more...enjoyable affair for everyone."

Riley could only nod, the undercurrent in his words making
her stomach turn. But she was determined not to cower before
him. She'd wanted to get a story, and as long as she was
breathing, she might as well pursue it. If nothing else, perhaps
it would distract him from his obvious intentions and remind
him of other uses for her talents instead.

"I also hope things will go better," she assured him cautiously. "In the last few days I have had the chance to view your
camp, and I must say that I've been very impressed. You're

obviously a man of great organizational and leadership abilities."

The flattery was a bit blatant, she thought, but Ko Tan preened nonetheless. "Was it as you expected?" he asked.

"Actually, no. The amount of high-tech equipment and training facilities I saw was remarkable. Much more advanced than anything I'd anticipated."

"We do what we can."

"Still, the maintenance and training involved must be incredible."

"Indeed, Miss McDouglas. Indeed." He gave her a slight smile to go with the patronizing tone. Then, as if he knew nothing else would sidetrack her questions, he gave a discreet nod and Dem came immediately bustling in, trays heaped with steaming food.

Riley eyed the steamed rice, fish paste and other treats with distrust this time. Her stomach was already rolling from her nerves, and she was still uncertain as to what had made her so sick the last time. But for the sake of appearance, she piled some food on her plate and made a small effort at eating, sticking mostly to her tonic water. Ko Tan proceeded through dinner much as the last time, eating in all-consuming silence.

From time to time, she ventured small glances at him, observing the way he relished his food almost overmuch, taking his fill repeatedly from the steaming platters.

He was a hungry man, she decided after a bit. The sort that had gone without so long that even having it all now couldn't diminish the haunting insecurities of his past. The observation, she found, calmed her nerves. After all, it was the first human element that she'd found in a man so full of power, calculation and arrogance. This was a country full of turbulence and poverty. It wasn't unlikely that at some point in his life, probably his childhood, he'd lived in that poverty. For so long and so hard that even now he feared it.

With a last huge bite and a sweeping wipe of his linen napkin, Ko Tan leaned back in his chair. "Magnificent once more," he declared. "Dem does such excellent work."

Riley merely nodded in agreement, pushing her own plate away, as well. Dinner was over, and her nerves were back in full force. What now?

Ko Tan sat there a minute longer, seeming to debate something with himself. Then, he abruptly pushed back his chair, rose, and crossed the room to the stereo system.

Now or never, she told herself, and took a deep breath.

"No," she said quietly.

He turned, a deep frown marring his face. "What did you say?" he questioned sharply.

"We had music last time after dinner," Riley explained, treading carefully as her fists clenched and unclenched at her side. "I thought perhaps a man as cultured as yourself would provide a few more options in entertainment."

But he didn't rise to her verbal bait. His face merely dismissed her words. "It doesn't matter what you thought," he told her coldly. "I do things as *I* intend."

She felt her stomach take a deep plunge, the despair building within. So this was how it was going to be; without even a thin veneer of civilization to hide behind. She swallowed, closing her eyes momentarily as she felt all the last vestiges of hope desert her. *Oh, please,* a small voice in her mind prayed to whatever powers were listening. *Please don't let this happen.*

"We shall dance now," Ko Tan informed her.

"I'm sorry," she tried again, summoning the words with effort. "But I'm still feeling a bit weak from having been so sick. Could we possibly wait a moment longer?"

"You can wait as long as you'd like," he said with a shrug. "You'd only be delaying the inevitable for an hour or two. You can even persist in your silly attempts at questioning if you'd like. It doesn't change anything. You will not be returning to your hut this evening, Riley," he said silkily, using her first name with apparent relish. "I do hope you understand that by now."

So there it was out in the open—blatant, naked, revolting. She turned away.

"I don't think I feel so good," she whispered weakly.

He almost smiled at that. "Perhaps a glass of wine, then," he suggested smoothly.

"No. Thank you," she replied quickly. Resolutely, she rose to her feet. He watched her from across the room, but he didn't move. Trying to appear casual, she walked around to the other side of the table, examining the paintings on the wall there.

"This really is a beautiful Rembrandt," she said as she edged a little closer to the swinging door leading to the kitchen. "It must be difficult to protect it from the humidity."

It was an inane comment, but Ko Tan seemed to be willing to go along with it. He was watching her carefully from the other side of the table, though he still hadn't moved.

She toyed with a strand of her hair and pretended to examine the painting with enraptured interest. The swinging door was so close, just a few feet. Should she run, just make a break for it?

Out of the corner of her eye, she saw Ko Tan move, and she stiffened instantly. Now, Riley, she shouted at herself. *Go now!*

But the opportunity was already lost. Ko Tan, having anticipated her, had smoothly moved to stand directly in front of the door.

"I have other paintings," he told her easily. "They are down the hall in my room. Since you have such an interest in art these days, perhaps you'd like to go up and see them?"

His eyes were mocking her even as she shook her head. Once again she felt helplessness assail her. He was playing with her, like some cat with a trapped mouse. He knew he had the ultimate control. He knew he'd already won.

She stepped away from him, walking back around the table. It was feeble protection, but she preferred to keep it between them for as long as she could. At a loss for anything else to do, this time *she* turned on the stereo, selecting a more modern CD.

Ko Tan smiled and began moving toward her. Unable to help herself, she automatically stepped back, only to see his eyes turn black with anger. His patience was clearly wearing thin.

"Let us dance, sweet Riley," he said darkly, and not giving her time to take another step, he caught her by the arm. His grip was tight, sinking into her forearm. She stiffened immediately, but there was no place to run anymore.

"I like to dance," he told her under his breath. "And I like the feel of your body pressed against mine. *Now move, Riley.* Dance with me."

Mutely, her eyes large and trapped, she shook her head. The feel of his body pressed to hers was making her sick. His face darkened even more. Then suddenly, without waiting any longer, his mouth came down, landing on hers with brutal intention. There was no place to turn; her shoulders were trapped in his clawing grip. Vainly she tried to fight, only to have him grab her head and hold it in place as his mouth ground against hers.

She could smell the sharp stench of fish and alcohol on his breath, taste the rusty tinge of her own blood as her lip cracked. Suddenly all feelings of revulsion vanished, replaced by white-hot fury. If she was going to die, this was *not* going to be the prelude. In outrage, she forgot all caution and her knee shot up, catching him just to the side of his groin.

With a muttered curse he raised his head and retaliated with a vicious blow to her cheek, never loosening his grip on her with the other hand. Bright lights danced before her eyes, and she felt as if her entire cheekbone had exploded under the impact.

Rage enveloped her, even as she dealt with the pain of his blow. Rage that he had struck her, rage that Ko Tan thought he had the right to take whatever he wanted. And, most of all, rage at the thought of death. She was too young to be crushed by a disgusting rat like Ko Tan. Too young to go down without a fight.

Without another thought, she struck back, her leg kicking out once more. He reacted fast enough to intercept her boot with his thigh but the movement threw him off balance.

She didn't wait for another opportunity, pushing him down completely as she dashed blindly to the other side of the table toward the swinging doors. But she didn't have the chance to run through them, because the main door crashed open at that very moment to reveal the bodyguard's hulking form.

"Fire in the barracks, sir," the bodyguard barked, and Ko Tan's face turned a mottled shade of red as he finished picking himself off the floor.

Practically exploding in fury, he pointed one sharp finger at the mountainous man. "You, stay with her," he ordered. "Do *not* let her out of your sight until I return. Do you understand?"

The bodyguard nodded, and Ko Tan turned back to her, his dark eyes flashing a black fire that sent chills up her spine.

"This is not finished," he enunciated slowly and surely. "You are a naive, stupid woman, Riley McDouglas. In a matter of hours, you will realize just how much."

Then, with another meaningful glare at the bodyguard, he left the room.

The bodyguard assumed his hulking stance in front of the doors, his beady eyes never leaving Riley's shaking form across the table. Her nerves were overwrought, her stomach heaving and the adrenaline surge was still buzzing in her brain. But through it all, including the surprising interruption with the bodyguard, her mind had been working with dazzling clarity. Now was the perfect time, now, before Ko Tan returned. The man before her might be huge, but she would bet that he was slow. He had a gun, but she doubted he'd shoot to kill, as it seemed that Ko Tan had dibs on that right himself. She'd just have to move fast and hope for the best.

But just as she was about to spring forward, the kitchen doors suddenly swung open on their own. In bounded Nemo, scrambling up her shocked form with ear-piercing screams. Even the bodyguard jumped to attention. Nemo leapt from her shoulder onto the stunned man, tweaking his nose with another round of screams.

Covering her ears with her hands, Riley didn't question it. She simply took the hint and ran. Behind her she could hear the angry roars of the man as he fought to disentangle his hair from the quick monkey's persistent grasp.

Then Shadow was next to her, guiding her out a back door and leading her along the house in a crouched run. Riley could scarcely believe it. He had come. Shadow was going to help her. A weight seemed to lift from her shoulders and her spirits rose. Maybe, just maybe, she had a chance of getting out of this mess, after all.

There was no time for questions right now, however, no time to thank Shadow, or even ask him how they were going to escape Ko Tan's wrath. There came a huge crash inside the house, causing them both to turn in concern.

"Nemo," Riley breathed.

Shadow didn't reply, but he pushed her forward, forcing her to run. Keeping low and moving fast, they skirted the outer ring of the camp. Shadow didn't look back, but he wasn't so sure about Nemo's safety. Inwardly he grimaced. That damn bodyguard was so large. . . .

There was no time to think of such things. No time for worrying or counting losses without risking more. He had Riley out—the first part of the plan was moving along. The men and Ko Tan were now occupied on the other side of the camp, putting out a simple blaze that wouldn't keep them busy for long. He had to get them into hiding before then.

He kept Riley running until at last the cabin loomed before them.

"Where are we going?" she gasped as he pulled her close to the back of her hut.

"Nowhere," he said curtly, his eyes darting through the night for signs of pursuers.

"What?"

But he didn't explain. Instead he picked up a bamboo pole he had dropped in the grass earlier, and passed it beneath the building. He encountered nothing, no angry hisses or retaliating strikes against the pole.

"Crawl under," he ordered tersely.

"What?" she asked again, beginning to get her breath back. Was he crazy?

"Now," he commanded, barely sparing her a glance.

Riley took one look at his hard face, heard the shouts in the distance, and went. God knew she didn't want to escape from one serpent only to be struck down by another, but Shadow was looking at her now with dark gray eyes that brooked no argument. So, with a deep breath and a final prayer, she got to her knees and then lay down, wiggling into the black depths. The smells assaulted her at once, the musty, rotten odor of decaying grass and plants. But she forced herself to keep going until she was all the way toward the middle, blackness surrounding her on all sides.

She could hear Shadow behind her, fluffing the grass to hide their tracks, and then the sound of him wiggling across the moist ground on his stomach. He came up next to her, placing the pole between them.

"I don't understand," she began, but he silenced her immediately with a harsh motion of his hand.

She wanted to ask more questions. A million questions riddled her mind. She'd thought he wouldn't interfere with Ko Tan, yet he had. Why? And why, if he had done this for her, was he still as uncommunicative and distant as before? Unless... Had she merely traded one prison for another? Was this all part of some dark game of Ko Tan's?

There were no answers in the darkness, nor would Shadow provide them. Instead he turned away from her, keeping his eyes riveted on the bordering darkness. She was alone with her doubts. But at least she was still alive.

She might have dozed for a bit. Looking back on it, Riley couldn't have explained how she could possibly have slept. But she felt safe with Shadow, and since it was obvious they would have to stay put for a while, well, somehow the stress of the past few hours just caught up with her. Eventually the sound of footsteps roused her, and she realized that there were soldiers around the hut. There was a click from above, and then more footsteps, this time above her.

She realized then that they were examining the hut, and with a crushing sense of dread, she wondered if they would notice the floorboards had been taken out and then replaced. Tense now, she waited for one of them to spot it. Waited for the trained eye to note the discrepancy, pull up the boards and find her and Shadow lying facedown, completely defenseless, below.

More footsteps, the unmistakable sound of foreign curses. A sudden shout, and she tensed. She heard the pounding of running feet and braced herself for the worst....

Silence.

The sounds faded away, pursuing some other mystery. Once again they were alone in the darkness. She didn't find any comfort in it, though. The shadows dragged on, leaving her increasingly filled with fears and doubts that twisted among one another until she dozed off into strange, unnatural nightmares. She bolted back awake in wide-eyed terror. *Where was she?*

For a moment she just lay there, heart racing, feeling the hard earth and grass beneath her tired muscles and bones. She remembered where she was. A moan of despair escaped her. And then came the noise.

Subtle little scratchings from the blackened distance. The sound of rustling grass as it parted to make way for another's entrance. And then the odd sound of movement upon mud. Drawing closer and closer.

Something touched her hand, and she jerked back in panic, banging her head on the solid foundation of the hut.

"Quiet," ordered Shadow, his whisper sharp and immediate. And then came the murmured chatters of a sufficiently frightened Nemo, who had crawled under the building, a long ways from his natural habitat of treetops, just to find them.

"I'm sorry," Riley whispered back, and Shadow could hear the beginnings of hysteria edging her voice.

"Everything's all right," he told her, but his voice was cold, offering little in the way of reassurance.

"I'm cold," Riley burst out, and, as if to prove her point, her body broke into a long wave of shivers.

Shadow bit back a curse. He wanted to remain distant from her, wanted to remain the cold mercenary as long as possible, just in case they were discovered. The less she knew of his true identity and motives, the less danger she would be in and the smaller the chances of a year and a half's worth of work being destroyed completely.

But he could sense her fear and feel the cold shudders of her body. His arm came out of its own accord, and even as he reminded himself to keep his distance, he was pulling her closer.

He absorbed each tremor into the solid warmth of his own frame, until eventually, bit by bit, they subsided, and he felt the full impact of her slender body relaxing against him. He had to grit his teeth to keep from running his hand down her gently curved hip, and he physically restrained himself from burying his head into the silky comfort of her hair.

He'd given into the weakness once. He would not give in to it again.

Soon, Riley drifted back to sleep, leaving Shadow alone with his grim thoughts. Nemo ventured closer at last, his eyes glowing huge and bright in the black depths. He cocked his head a bit, murmuring low in his throat at all the new and strange things unfolding. Shadow raised one hand and stroked the furry back. "It would have been better if you hadn't found us," Shadow whispered knowingly to the little monkey. "But I'm glad to know that you're all right."

There was more silence after that, and Shadow dozed off himself, sleeping fitfully as he kept a watch of sorts for any sounds that would indicate they'd been discovered. Eventually, after another five hours had elapsed, he knew it was time. Grasping the bamboo stick, he moved it across the dirt surface until he had checked the entire area. When he once again encountered nothing, he gently untangled his arm from the still-sleeping Riley, and crept to the edge of darkness.

He poked his head out from under the hut, clearing the grass, to find that it was now late afternoon of the second day. In another hour or so, it would begin to darken, and then, only then, would they be on the move once more.

Tonight would be a long night. He would have to push Riley as hard as she could go to cover the vast distance of the mountains. After they reached a certain village, he knew they could arrange for transportation. At the Thai border, they would be safe to fly back to New York.

But Ko Tan had over five thousand men at his disposal who would be only too happy to join the hunt for a traitor. His eyes keenly surveying the deserted area, Shadow surmised that the majority of the search had probably gone on last night, with Ko Tan's men scouring the vast expanse of the hills.

By now Ko Tan was left with two options. He could assume that they had simply vanished and thus give up the hunt, or he could assume that they had made it farther than he anticipated and keep the men scouting deep into the mountains.

Either way, Ko Tan wouldn't be looking for two people starting out from their very own camp one day later. And perhaps with the supplies he'd hidden, Shadow could even fool them into believing that he and Riley were merely another scouting party, that is, if there was ever a chance encounter. He hoped it wouldn't come to that.

He'd planned this out just the day before, and in theory it seemed sound. For motivation, he had deliberately set up the midnight journey to the poppy fields with Riley. The guards now had the impression that Shadow and Riley had left the camp, only to return hours later in a distinctly rumpled state. That they'd actually made love hadn't been planned, but had reinforced the impression considerably. No, when Ko Tan started asking questions, he'd be left with the impression of his right-hand man becoming very involved with his prisoner. Hopefully then, Ko Tan would blame his defection on personal grounds, and not question his cover.

It was risky, but essential. Shadow had to make sure Ko Tan wasn't spooked into abandoning the arms deal. This might even give him greater incentive to come to New York, for Ko Tan didn't suffer humiliation lightly. No, he would want to make sure Shadow paid for what he'd done.

Which meant that rescuing Riley shouldn't endanger his mission. Just their lives, he thought ironically in the fading light. Just their lives.

Crawling back under the house, he woke Riley with a light touch while Nemo looked on in apprehension. The sleep had calmed her nerves and she woke quietly, not saying a word. With gestures, he motioned her back out from under the house, though when they finally emerged in the waning light, she had to pause for several minutes to adjust her eyes and senses.

Riley felt completely cramped and disoriented, unsure of time or place. It seemed to her an eternity had gone by in that pitch-black hell, but now it looked as if it had only been a day. She was unsure of what was to happen next. She wanted to ask questions, but Shadow still looked at her with stern and unapproachable eyes. She'd followed him this far; it seemed that was all she could continue to do.

As long as she got away safely.

When he motioned her to fall in behind him, she obeyed. Exiting the immediate area of the camp was hard and slow. Shadow kept them low, moving along in a painful crouch. Once they passed within feet of a returning soldier, and they both dropped to the ground immediately, faces pushed into the grass to avoid detection.

Already she felt tired, unaccustomed to the tension and the intense rigor of running flat out, and having to stop and crouch every so often, keeping still for countless moments until all was clear. Her clothes and face were caked with a deep layer of mud that itched and pulled at her tender skin. Her cheek throbbed where Ko Tan had hit her, and she knew without being able to see that she was probably developing a nicely colored bruise. But she didn't say a word, mumble even a hint of protest. If she understood anything at all, it was that their lives depended on the silence.

Eventually they cleared the area, disappearing into the deep jungle. Rather than cut a new path which would be easily followed, Shadow found the freshly cut trail of the soldiers. Any new footprints there, especially as they all wore the same leather boots, would be taken as additional scouts setting out.

It was a good piece of strategy, Riley thought. They were following their pursuers. But there was no time to dwell on it; the situation was still much too tense. Even Nemo was quiet, sitting wide-eyed and silent on Shadow's shoulder.

They had slowed to a walk now, which continued, it seemed, for hours, on and on. Finally Shadow stopped and looked around, straining his ears for sound. Then, with a halting motion of his hand, he disappeared under a seemingly solid bush, only to reappear a few minutes later, motioning her to come. Unsure, Riley followed.

On the other side she found a dim clearing covered by a thick green carpet of leaves, but with room enough for two people to sit down. Shadow disappeared again, moving silently through the jungle. When he reappeared, he had a rather large bundle in a military knapsack which he quickly unwrapped.

Soon Riley found herself completely dressed in military fatigues, her hair securely tucked under her hat while Shadow obscured her face with thick black paint. His thumb slowed once, gently tracing the outline of the developing bruise while his lips thinned into a grim line. His eyes met hers, dark and unreadable. After a long moment, he continued again.

"You're still too tall," he told her brusquely. "Remember to slouch if we meet anyone. And if they figure it out right off the bat, I want you to duck and roll the hell out of the way. Understand?"

She could only nod, these sudden turns of events way beyond anything in her realm of experience. She'd taken a city survival course once. Basically it had covered how to carry Mace, and how to defend oneself with car keys. But she was a long way from the simple dangers of muggers, and right now, her face muddy and painted, she almost missed them.

Shadow painted his own face, then pulled out some *kaukhyin*, rice fried in bamboo. Having tried it before, Riley welcomed the food gratefully, her stomach rumbling. She wanted to question him then, the need to finally understand what was happening burning in her gut. But he kept his back to her, ignoring her completely with unrelenting dismissal.

After that he pushed them on in silence, again following the main trail, though he abruptly pulled them off behind a tree when they heard footsteps up ahead. Sure enough, small groups of the men were beginning to return.

Shadow seemed to expect it, and after a moment, took out his curved blade and boldly began slashing down a new trail through the tamarind trees, making it seem as if a few groups had decided to branch out and search a new area on their own. Hopefully it would work, though there was always the chance of new soldiers deciding to joining them.

Progress was slower now, but no less draining for Riley. They walked all night, until she felt as if each muscle would collapse in screaming pain, and her feet began to drag hopelessly. "I should have done more aerobics," she told Shadow with a wan smile as she wavered before him. "I'm out of shape."

In response, he offered her his arm for support, but continued to push her beyond all endurance. They had to keep moving. Then, when he thought there was an inkling of a chance of them being remotely safe, he let her rest.

But the minute the running stopped, the questions started. Inwardly he stiffened. He had known this would happen. Riley was a reporter, after all. There was, however, nothing he could tell her right now—nothing that wouldn't endanger her life, that is. So he did the only thing he could, what he'd been doing all along—he remained silent.

"Why?" Riley asked bluntly. She was determined to get some answers. "Why did you do all this? And what is all this, anyway? Where are we going? What are you going to do with me?"

He looked at her for a moment then, gray eyes unreadable, all traces of the man she'd once touched completely gone. If she'd thought he would suddenly transform, his face suddenly revealing all the emotions he'd been hiding, she was wrong.

Shadow swung his gaze out to the horizon. The moment he told her the truth, he knew that she would hate him. She was proud and courageous, and he'd lied to her. He'd even half seduced her and still hadn't told her the truth. That they'd both been overwhelmed by the moment, had reached out to each other in need, wanting to black out the situation they were in, didn't matter. He'd deceived her.

It was for her own good that she be kept in the dark. He supposed he could try telling her that, but he had a feeling her injured pride would still block out the words.

No, it was best if he didn't tell her anything yet.

They still had a good two days of traveling ahead of them, and they certainly weren't out of danger.

If they were caught, she still only knew him as a mercenary. The less she knew, the less she would be at risk. Besides, maintaining his cover was critical to keep from jeopardizing the mission, and that was a priority.

Or so he told himself.

Because he certainly didn't want to dwell on the fact that once she knew, she honestly would hate him. And then whatever brief light she'd brought into his life would be gone forever.

"We're heading for a village near the border," he said finally, keeping his voice clipped. "There, we can get some transportation to an airport. With any luck we'll be heading back to the States within the next twenty-four hours."

"And then?" she demanded. "What then?"

He shrugged. "We'll deal with that when the time comes. Now get some sleep, Riley. We've got a lot of miles to cover tomorrow."

"But—"

He cut her off with a sharp motion of his hand.

"Sleep," he ordered. *"Now."*

Against her will she finally lay down. But even as exhausted as she was, the questions buzzing in her mind kept her peering out into the darkness long after she should have been asleep. She'd touched her jailer. She'd hoped to despise him, but had made love to him instead.

And she still didn't know him at all.

Chapter 9

They rose with the sun for another long and grueling day. Shadow pushed them on through the thick and heavy foliage of the jungle to the slightly cooler terrain of the mountains. But even then the sun beat down hot and relentless upon their heads.

Riley still wasn't completely recovered from her short illness, forcing them to rest for short intervals. At each stop, though necessary, Shadow chafed with impatience. The area wasn't safe, and he wanted to put as much distance between them and Ko Tan as possible. Finally, when Riley couldn't go on any longer and fell, he picked her up and carried her for as long as he could. He drove them both mercilessly, until they were lean and tired from their exertions.

Twice they saw soldiers in the distance. Twice he pulled her down sharply onto beds of leaves, covering her startled cries with his hand until the men had passed. Twice her heart leapt against her chest until she thought it would surely explode from the fear.

Finally they were headed back down from the mountains, into another long tangle of mosquito-plagued jungle. There, they stopped long enough to eat cold duck and rice with the feathery-leaved fruit from the tamarind trees. When it got too dark to continue, Shadow allowed Riley to collapse once and for all in exhausted sleep. He remained awake, though, his keen eyes keeping guard through the night as Nemo sat upon his shoulder.

At the first sign of light, he had them up and moving again, his own face pale with the strain, but grimly determined. Halfway through the third day, they cleared the mountain range altogether, passing beyond the natural barriers that marked Ko Tan's territory. There was always the possibility that he might send men beyond the mountains looking for them, but it was slight. Ko Tan possessed a cunning mind that understood very well the dangers of stretching his troops too thin. In the valley of the mountains, his guerrillas reigned supreme. But if he allowed them to drift beyond that, he ran the risk of losing his advantage.

Shadow didn't think Ko Tan would break policy just to pursue one love-struck mercenary. So at long last, they could finally ease their brutal pace. And it was also time to take care of Nemo. Now, when the little monkey was in no danger of being spotted by the soldiers and used to follow their trail. Now, before they hit the first outpost of civilization, and Nemo lost his freedom.

Nemo had been a prisoner of society when Shadow had first found him. He couldn't allow that to happen again. But even with the best of intentions, he didn't know of any good way of enforcing his friend's freedom. There was a small sensation of loss deep in his chest, for though Nemo was just a monkey, he had been the only friend Shadow had allowed himself in the past year and a half. With a heavy heart, but grim resolution, Shadow planned what he had to do.

"Wait here," he told Riley on the third afternoon.

The minute he turned away, Riley felt the weariness and uncertainty rush in. Where was he going? Why couldn't she follow? There was so much she still didn't understand about Shadow. For instance, what exactly were his intentions? What were his plans? Unreasoning panic overwhelmed her as the jungle seemed to close in on her. What if he abandoned her here? What if he was setting her up for some far worse fate?

The uncertainty was too much. Forcing herself to move, she swallowed nervously and followed him.

Nemo was sitting on Shadow's shoulder, quieter now, but his eyes were still bright, his hands fast. Shadow waited until they had reached a small clearing. Turning his head, he spoke quickly, sharply. "Go," he told Nemo.

But the monkey didn't move, not understanding, merely cocking his silver-framed face at this new command. Shadow followed up with a sharp hand motion, clearly designating the order. The monkey still didn't move.

Shadow frowned. This wasn't going to be easy. But he had to make Nemo leave. There was no other way. "Go," he said again. Then more sternly, *"Go!"*

Watching from her hiding place behind a tree, Riley flinched at the steel in Shadow's voice. What was going on? She glanced at Nemo, who remained motionless, unwilling to leave his post on Shadow's shoulder. Finally, in frustration it seemed, Shadow swept him off with the broad side of his hand. "Go," he repeated again. "Now, Nemo. Go!"

The monkey landed on the ground and looked at Shadow in open confusion, retreating a few steps, and then sitting down restlessly to consider this new turn of events. After a moment, his eyes cleared, and even Riley could see the glint of mischief that crept into them. He thought it was a new game. With light chatter he leapt forward, already reaching out with long fingers to clamber back up to his usual post.

But Shadow blocked the monkey's flight with another side-swipe, sending the creature reeling back with a shocked screech.

Riley almost cried out herself. Now she knew what Shadow was trying to do. He was trying to free Nemo, because there was no way he could come with them into civilization. Her eyes teared as the rest of the scene unfolded before her.

"Please," Shadow said, his head falling down, the hoarseness of his voice creeping through. "Go away, Nemo," he said, but there was less force now and more pleading. "Just go away."

Once more Nemo was confused, but he was hurt, as well. With low murmurs he advanced again, and at the sight Shadow's head came back up. Riley sucked in her breath at the naked pain in his eyes as, never hesitating, his hand swept forward, making full contact with Nemo. A solid thunk sounded in the silence.

Riley watched helplessly as the monkey fell back with another screech of distress. If Shadow heard Riley, he gave no indication.

Nemo sat back now, openly distraught, looking at Shadow with huge eyes that innocently sought the friend he once had.

"Go away!" said Shadow, and this time his voice was stronger. He seemed to call upon something within him, rising up to his full height. "I said go," he ordered sharply. "Go away!"

And when Nemo continued to sit, continued to look with his wide black eyes, Shadow stomped suddenly forward, growling in his throat. "Go, damn you, go!"

Riley saw a shudder go through Shadow with the force of the words. But then, with a last chatter, a last wide-eyed look, Nemo turned, bounding off for the safety of his trees, disappearing in a crash of branches as he leapt farther and farther away from the friend he no longer knew.

He'd no sooner disappeared in the trees than Shadow's head fell forward.

"Go," he whispered hoarsely, his back to Riley. So he *had* known she was there. "I asked you to stay away. Now just leave me alone."

But Riley couldn't move, her own eyes overflowing with the tears that streamed silently down her face. And he must have sensed her pain, even through his own.

"Don't," he said harshly. "How much do you think I can take in one day? Leave me alone, Riley."

And in that instant, Riley suddenly understood. There were many mysteries about Shadow, many things she could never hope to explain. But now she understood part of the torment in his eyes. This was a man, who, with all his remoteness, was capable of a deep and humbling love. A love so powerful, so giving, that it brought him the strength to do what he thought was best for a friend, regardless of what it cost himself. A love capable of undying loyalty and sacrifice. A silent, lonely love that asked for no acknowledgment, that accepted that all good things must come and go, leaving him behind—alone—in the isolated world he'd created for himself.

For one blinding moment, Riley wondered what it would be like to have that kind of love focused on herself. Empty dreams, she thought, because when all was said and done, Shadow was still the man who had turned away from her. Throughout this entire ordeal, he had shut her out and kept her at a cool distance. Even after they'd made love, he'd guarded his emotions from her.

So she didn't go to him, alone in the steaming foliage. She turned instead and walked away, knowing that there weren't any words she could give him. Nothing she said would assuage his grief, and even if it would, it was clear he wouldn't let her near him.

This afternoon, this last afternoon of her stay in Myanmar, she saw the silent man who had risked his life for her cry, and in her heart, she wept with him.

"What I'm about to tell you," Shadow was saying intensely, "is to be kept in the strictest confidence."

They were standing in a small airport, having rented a truck from a village the day before and driven to the Thai border. In just a matter of hours, they'd be on a plane back to the States. And now, standing in the sweltering midday heat, Shadow couldn't avoid her questions any longer.

"Too many lives depend on it," he continued. "I need you to swear to me, Riley. Swear to me that you won't use this information until the proper time has come."

"The proper time?" she quizzed skeptically. If she'd thought she was going to get straight answers for a change, obviously she'd been mistaken. So far she didn't understand all this melodrama, and after the strain of the last few days, she was feeling less than patient with it.

Shadow nodded his head. "Promise," he ordered.

She gave in with a small nod of her own head. If it would make him start talking, she would do it. But she certainly wasn't prepared for what he said next.

"I work for the Drug Enforcement Administration of the United States," the man before her uttered, clear and low. "I've been undercover for nearly two years in an operation to capture the heroin drug lord Ko Tan. As part of this operation, I came across an American civilian whose life was in jeopardy.

In keeping with the oath to defend and protect, I acted accordingly."

The words were flat, and they drained all the color from her face. She could only stare at him. This wasn't happening. It was too much. *"What?"*

"You heard me," he repeated evenly. "I work for the DEA."

She shook her head, but the words remained lodged in her brain. All of a sudden, the pressure of the last few days caught up with her, and she almost laughed out loud in hysteria. Oh, God, she thought. All along she'd been wondering if he was Dr. Jekyll or Mr. Hyde when he was really James Bond. And she wasn't even sure which of them she'd slept with. She felt an overwhelming urge to giggle and was afraid that if she so much as moved, she'd lose control completely.

What had happened to reality?

"An undercover agent," she finally whispered. "An undercover agent."

Shadow nodded, his eyes remote and unreachable.

"Then," she breathed out, "that, of course, must make me the civilian in need of rescue."

Her voice cracked a little with the words and she felt the sudden sting of tears. She'd thought that he cared. That maybe the mercenary had feelings, after all. But it had never been feelings for *her,* because he'd never really *been* a mercenary. Duty. All along, it had only been his duty.

He was nodding again, his face still giving nothing away as he confirmed her words.

Unable to help herself, Riley began to pace around, struggling for some measure of bearing with this new information. "I don't understand," she said finally. "What were you doing undercover?"

"Luring Ko Tan back to the States," he said simply. "There, he'll be apprehended and charged."

"And now?" she challenged, wanting to get some reaction from him. "Haven't you blown your cover?"

He didn't answer right away, and that should have been her first warning. His eyes avoided hers as his jaw muscle clenched and his shoulders suddenly squared themselves. "No," he said finally, "I haven't blown my cover."

She could only look at him. "You rescued me," she argued, confusion in her voice. "Surely that's got to make him suspicious."

He didn't want to say this, didn't want to explain all, Shadow thought fiercely. But she deserved the truth, regardless of what it cost him. After everything they'd been through, she deserved at least that much.

"I set it up," he said softly, "so Ko Tan would believe I had other . . . motives."

Her eyes narrowed, and she stopped pacing long enough to pierce him with a long, suspicious look. "And how exactly did you do that?" she asked.

"That night," he said, "when we went into the poppy fields. I made sure someone saw us leave, and I made sure someone saw us return. Given our appearance upon returning, they could infer the rest."

Her face paled, and she could only look at him with wide green eyes as the full extent of his betrayal hit her.

"You what?" she asked faintly.

He had to swallow heavily to continue, but he didn't back down. He'd known this moment would come. He'd known she would hate him. There was no way around it. Still, he found himself struggling for the words. "I didn't mean— It was never my intention," he began finally, "that we would actually make love. I just wanted to plant that impression in everyone's mind, so Ko Tan would assume later that my helping you escape was motivated purely by . . . personal, uh, interests. What actually happened that night, I hadn't planned, Riley. I know it may be hard to believe, but that's the truth."

"Why, thank you very much," she said bitterly, her voice cracking as she retaliated in hurt anger. "It's so much more comforting to know it was an accident instead." After all this time, he was talking, finally talking to her. Only she wasn't so sure she liked what he was saying.

Made love, her mind whispered. He'd said *made love.* But she wasn't ready to examine that just yet. Wasn't ready for anything but the overwhelming pain and anger that rushed through her.

"Riley—?" he began, but she turned away from him.

"No. I don't want to hear anymore." She cut him off sharply. "For all I know, it's all just more lies, anyway." Her voice broke, and she stared hard at the dusty ground, blinking the tears back.

She felt violated, betrayed. She'd trusted this man, dared to believe that maybe she'd reached him somehow. That maybe there existed a bond of understanding and feeling between them. But she hadn't known him at all. All along, he'd been someone else. All along, he'd kept her in the dark. Even after making love.

She'd been such a fool. She'd trusted her heart, and it had betrayed her. *Damn him.* He could have told her. All those times she'd felt so alone, so afraid. He could have at least told her he was one of the good guys. He could have allayed her fears. Especially after... Well, especially afterward.

They stood apart for long minutes, neither moving. Watching her, Shadow wanted to reach out. He couldn't stand how she looked, so lost and alone and hurt. He'd done that to her. He hadn't had any choice, but still, he'd done that to her.

Cursing silently, he faced the bitter truth. He'd been in the darkness too long. He didn't know how to keep from hurting people anymore. It was better to let her go. In time, she would forget him, forget this whole affair. She was better off that way.

But, unbidden, the "if onlys" ran through his mind, taunting him. If only they'd met two years ago. If only he'd found her before all the madness had begun. If only—

"What happens now?" Riley asked finally as she gained some measure of control. "Do you really think your plan will still work?"

Shadow shrugged, "We'll know in a few days."

"A few days? What happens then?"

He shook his head. "Classified information," he said curtly. "I can't tell you."

On top of everything else, it was the last straw. A part of her understood it was his job, but the rest of her just felt the rejection. Even now, he still kept her in the dark. Even now, *he didn't trust her.*

She gritted her teeth, grimly squaring her shoulders. If he could play so damn cool, so could she, she told herself. She'd show him. "Well, then," she said briskly, keeping her eyes on the dusty airfield before them, "I guess it'll be over with soon."

"Yes," he said softly. "Finally, it will be over."

There was a wealth of exhaustion in those words, enough to penetrate her own stiff resolution. For the first time, she found herself wondering what it must have been like for him, having to act as someone else for almost two years. And the five people he'd told her about, killed before his eyes, there had been nothing he could do. For a fraction of an instant, her own hurt abated, and she felt the first glimmering of real understanding of Shadow. He'd had a dirty job to do. And it hadn't been his fault she'd landed in the middle of it. It had to have made his job all the more difficult for him. Not to mention that, in the end, he had had to risk all, including his life, to save her.

But he'd lied to her. Used her.

And she'd never even known.

She sighed then, and at that moment she wished more than anything in the world that she could just lie down and sleep. Maybe it would all make more sense in the morning. Things were supposed to be better in the morning, weren't they?

But then another, darker thought struck her. If there was anything that she had learned in the last few days, it was how Ko Tan operated. He was arrogant, dangerous and incredibly powerful. Once he learned of Shadow's betrayal, he wouldn't let it go unanswered. He'd use every means, every connection at his disposal to get revenge. And even if the DEA managed to arrest him, he was a man with enough contacts to reach beyond the jail cell.

"Shadow," she said softly, turning to face him, forgetting her anger for the moment, "do you really think if you arrest Ko Tan, that'll end it all?"

He looked up, and once again she was struck by the gray starkness of his eyes. His shoulders were straight, though, and his voice was level as he spoke. "No," he said. "No, I don't."

There was no time for questions after that, and truly, Riley wasn't sure she could handle any more answers. The plane arrived, Shadow made a brief phone call, and the next thing she knew, they were both on their way to the United States.

There was a sense of unreality to it all. For one thing, after seeing so much bamboo and wood, the plane seemed more metallic than she'd remembered. And the softness of the plush seats seemed strange, as well as the stifling whiffs of air puffed out by the plane's air-conditioning.

But most of all, the man beside her had become a complete stranger. He was no longer Shadow, a mercenary who played clever games, manipulating her and seducing her with his silence.

Instead, he seemed even more alien than before. His silence was still deep, but instead of the cold chill of before it held a quiet sort of resignation. Despite the strength and virility he still exuded, it also seemed to Riley that lines had appeared around his gray eyes, that the scar streaking down his cheek was somehow less menacing now and more vulnerable. And he was unbearably unapproachable, not even acknowledging her with a look or a touch. He'd done his duty, and now it was as if she had ceased to exist for him at all. She wasn't even sure if she knew his right name. So she continued to think of him as Shadow, for it fit him better than any other name she could imagine.

She spent the long hours trying to sort through her thoughts, trying to understand all that had happened, or perhaps most important, *not* happened, in the last few days.

Upon review, she'd accomplished, even overaccomplished, her major goal. She now had a story on Ko Tan. And maybe she could even do a piece on his downfall, once Shadow's secret operation ended. Regardless, just to be able to write up a first-hand account about the man and his camp would be a major coup. When her editor heard about this . . . Her career would soon be taking off; there'd certainly be no more travel pieces for her. And after all, wasn't that what she'd been after all along?

Just imagine . . .

But in all her wonderings, Riley kept her mind assiduously clear of the main issue. Shadow. She didn't allow herself to dwell on the tenderness of his touch, the gentleness of his kiss, or the magic of his lovemaking. She didn't want to think of jungle beds, of his hands on her body, her name driven from his lips.

She couldn't look at the man next to her, so remote and distant now, and bear to think of those things. Duty. He'd done his duty.

Duty.

She closed her eyes and, unable to take any more, willed her tired mind to sleep.

The next thing she knew, they were in New York.

No sooner had they disembarked from the plane than the awkwardness began. Suddenly it was New York that seemed alien and foreign. They were both dressed in camouflage and leather boots among satin blouses and business suits. They had no luggage in a sea of people swamped by bags. And they had no words to say, lost in the buzz of sound around them.

So the time had come. Time to simply smile as if she hadn't a care in the world, as if everything was just fine, and then simply walk away. He'd been a good agent, she'd been a good reporter, and now it was all over with. Fine and dandy.

Her hands were already trembling with the strain.

"Do you have a place to stay?" she asked to fill the gap as the people swarmed around them like a surging sea.

He shrugged. "I'll contact the DEA now that we're in New York. I didn't want to do so from Myanmar in case Ko Tan ever made the connection. I'm still operating under cover, so they'll find me something appropriate. It'll all work out."

"Well, if there are any problems, you can always come to my place," she said brightly. Inwardly she winced, but he *had* saved her life, she reasoned. She might hate him for his methods, but at least he'd accomplished what she herself had been incapable of doing—getting her out of Ko Tan's clutches. And maybe, just maybe, even after the intensity of the last few days, the thought of not seeing him at all ever again was just too much for her. She was still angry with him, still hurt. But she didn't want to part so abruptly. She needed time, she told herself. A little time to ease the transition. "You can look up the address in the phone book," she found herself saying.

"You should change that," Shadow said quietly.

"Pardon?"

"Go to an unlisted number. Maybe even leave town for a few days. When Ko Tan comes to the States, there's always the chance he may try to find you. Remember, he's a man known for his vengeance.''

"All right," she agreed at last, her hands shaking a bit, not from fear but from the strain of saying goodbye. God, when had she begun to care for him so much? "I will."

"Good."

"So, I guess maybe I'll see you around," she chimed lightly, though her smile was much too brilliant to believe.

"No," he told her quietly. "No, you won't."

And there it was, out in the open with a brutal bluntness that threatened to bring her to her knees. *Remember, you're a professional, McDouglas,* she told herself. *You're back in New York now, and it's time to remember your priorities.* She was the ace reporter, on her way to the top. And he was just an agent, his task completed. All done.

But those words were getting harder and harder to believe, let alone speak. A sudden sense of loss overwhelmed her and tightened her throat. She didn't want to let him go, she realized suddenly. Despite his lying to her, despite the fact that she wasn't supposed to care about someone like him. Somehow, in the course of the last few days he'd managed to fill the emptiness inside her. He challenged her; he intrigued her. And once, once she'd even believed that he might need her. No one had ever needed her before, and no one had ever made her feel like he made her feel. Now she was so afraid that once he walked away from her, she would never feel that way again.

But what could she do?

"Good luck," she managed to say at last, the words tremulous, her eyes misty. "I really hope you get him."

"Don't worry," he told her. "I'll see to it that someone in the department gives you first dibs on the story if we do."

He'd meant it as a thank-you after everything she'd done for him, as a kind of repayment for all those bright moments she'd brought to him. But in the end, he couldn't have hurt her more than if he'd slapped her.

She recoiled from the words, the pain flaring sharp and hot in her eyes. Too late he realized how cold he must have sounded, how he'd unknowingly implied that the story was her only concern.

Time stood still, and for a moment he thought he'd lose it. He wanted to break down, to throw all this damned control to the side and hold her, comfort her. Hold and comfort her until they both forgot the pain of the past, until they both were lost in the wonders of the present.

But he didn't. Because he had nothing to offer her. Because she deserved so much better than him. In a matter of days, she would likely forget all about him and get on with her life. And what a life it would be; she was young and talented and beautiful and wonderful. She really did deserve the best.

And what about him? He smiled bitterly. He was just a dark and shadowy man who had earned his nickname too well. He didn't belong in this concrete world of New York. He didn't belong in any world. All his life he'd drifted. All his life he'd passed in and out of other people's lives, and none of them had really cared. Those who did, those who might have made him stay, had eventually been lost to him, anyway. Like his mother, who had smelled of lilacs. Like Johnny. Even Sabrina, in her own way, had belonged to others—the runaways she helped, her husband, Thomas.

He was a man without a home, a man without a future. He accepted that. He really was just a shadow, flitting through, paying his dues, and knowing it was all going to end soon, anyway. He'd risked his own life in this mission, knowing full well that Ko Tan might be able to kill him even from a jail cell. But he'd been willing to give his life to avenge his friend. It was all he had to give.

Only too late had he found a person who might have made it worth keeping.

"Goodbye, Riley," he whispered softly to her, even as her eyes misted up. "Goodbye."

And then he was gone, swallowed up in the mass of people who went about their normal lives as if nothing was wrong. One minute he was there, and the next he was gone.

Riley stood there for a long time afterward, in the middle of busy La Guardia airport, not moving, feeling the tears spill out and stream down her cheeks. Then, slowly, she began to walk. She was back in New York, she told herself. She even had her story.

She'd managed to get out with her life, after all. She should be happy, ecstatic. And she would be, if only she hadn't lost her heart instead.

It was ironic, really, she thought as she walked. She'd gone and fallen in love with a man whom she didn't even know.

Looking back only a few days later, it seemed, at times, that Myanmar had never been at all. Her apartment was still the same, her friends still the same, even her desk at work hadn't changed in her absence.

And her editor, Chuck Flannigan, was still somewhat grumpy, his belly still slouching over his belt, his tie still stained, his eyes still sharp as a hawk's. He chastised her for pursuing dangerous guerrillas all alone, keen blue eyes punctuating each movement, each gesture. But when the interrogation had finally ended, when he had finally turned off his gaze with a thoughtful nod, he had agreed that her story on Ko Tan and his movement was good. And so it had appeared, on the third page of Tuesday's edition of the *New York Daily*, without any reference to Shadow or undercover operations.

There was a feeling of pride to be had in reading the byline, an intense feeling of satisfaction and accomplishment. She even called home to share the news, only to rediscover once again that her parents would never truly comprehend the ambitious desires of their daughter.

In the end, though, coming back to the same old apartment, eating the same old food, typing away at the same old computer, she knew it just wasn't quite right.

She wanted someone to notice.

She wanted someone to look at her and honestly say, "So, Riley, how *was* Myanmar?" Someone who would ask that simple question so she could pour it all out, all the pent-up emotions caused by one week of turmoil in her life. So she could tell that person about a mysterious man with calm gray eyes who had captured her heart and simply walked away.

And she knew nothing about him.

Did he have a family? Where had he gotten his nickname, and what was his real name? Why the DEA? Had he ever been in the service? Had everything they'd shared really been only a matter of duty?

Shadow's words kept spinning in her mind. *Made love.* He'd said, *made love.*

Where was he now?

Deep in the dark hours of the night, restlessness twisted her sleep, the emptiness in her soul eating her up alive. Over and over again, she woke up, wondering where he was now, if he was safe, and why he couldn't have cared enough to contact her.

And then one morning her period began, and she realized for the first time that there had been the possibility of her being pregnant. Something neither had thought of. Tears overflowed. There was nothing left to remind her of him at all.

He'd left her, but for the life of her, she couldn't get him out of her mind.

Trite but true, Shadow was thinking to himself, twenty blocks away. He'd left Myanmar, but it refused to leave him. The dreams were bad, worse now than ever, so twisted he didn't know what to expect anymore. Some nights he dreamed of death, of the dying screams of Johnny as he fell down, down, down. Except when Johnny hit the pavement, his face became Shadow's. And other nights, when he thought he couldn't take it anymore, *she* was back. With her flowing red hair and long white arms. Laughing with beckoning eyes and smiling lips.

And he would bolt awake in his hole of an apartment, covered in sweat, his heart bursting in his chest until he wanted to die. Wanted anything to get her out of his mind.

He needed peace. After all these years, he simply wanted peace.

But all he could do was wait. He'd reported back in to the special task force he worked with, and all the details had been arranged. His cover was still in place, so accordingly he'd moved into some little trap of an apartment on the less respectable side of town. Sources had revealed that the arms deal was indeed proceeding on schedule, and Ko Tan would be arriving shortly for the final transaction. So now the DEA men were getting into place. It was all a matter of time. Just a day or two now, just a day...

When the phone finally rang, Shadow wasn't overwhelmingly surprised at who the caller was.

"Hello, Shadow," said Ko Tan. "You didn't really think I'd let you live now, did you?"

And then there was a click, the dial tone returning to hum in his ear. Slowly, he set the receiver back down, releasing his pent-up tension in one long breath. It had finally come.

Ko Tan was here, and once again the waiting was over.

He didn't hesitate after that, didn't pick up the phone and make the call he knew he should make to his boss, Bob Hartwood. Hartwood had agreed to put him on the case, but when Shadow had checked in a few days ago to tell him of everything that had just transpired in Myanmar, Hartwood had informed him that he was much too involved. That might be the case, Shadow thought grudgingly, but there was nothing he could do about it now. After all, it was his life. No, Shadow didn't want to hear any lectures, and he didn't want to be told to sit tight. Besides, not everything was in place yet for the bust. He would just have to take care of matters on his own.

After all these years, he was tired of sitting back and waiting. So he went through the small bundle of his few possessions and grabbed the shiny chrome gun. He slipped it into the waistband of his jeans, donned his woolen jacket to hide the bulge, and then he was gone.

He stayed on the streets for nearly twenty-four hours, but never left the general area of his apartment. He figured by now his best bet was to let Ko Tan find him. Sooner or later, a scout, or perhaps the man himself, would come to the apartment to find Shadow and exact revenge.

So Shadow kept to the streets, and in his lean, laid-back way, was soon completely absorbed into New York City life. He ate hot dogs covered in relish, read the *New York Daily*—not a bad story there on page three—and basically ignored everyone, and everyone ignored him.

At night he walked to keep warm against the cold, a beer bottle wrapped in a brown paper sack for a prop. He wasn't uncomfortable. The street scene wasn't new to him. The nights had been his life for years, and the streets had been his home for six of those years. So he walked, letting the emotions well up until his eyes grew dark and impenetrable.

The second day, a man came. Shadow didn't recognize him right off the bat—he wasn't anyone Shadow had seen before. But that was to be expected in an organization like Ko Tan's. And he *was* one of Ko Tan's goons. This particular man spent too much time staring at buildings for just an ordinary observer, and, sure enough, when Shadow walked right past him, he could see the slight bulge in the man's jacket.

So now the games began.

He let the man keep watch all day, understanding that restraint was the key. Finally, when it started to grow dark, the cold creeping down, he saw the man grow impatient, stomping his feet restlessly.

Still, the man was persistent, Shadow had to hand it to him. He didn't leave, just kept waiting for Shadow to arrive. But eventually the cold and the dark grew to be just too much, and with a shrug, the man started to walk away.

Shadow obliged him by following.

After the first eight blocks, though, he was no longer so sure it had been such a good idea. They seemed to be headed into the seamier side of town, and while that didn't bother Shadow much at all, it was very out of character for a man like Ko Tan.

Ko Tan, after having been poor once, insisted on never living like the poor again. Traveling with him meant first-class tickets and the finest hotels. Maître d's in every major city knew him by his first name, though it was always a fake one, of course.

So after avoiding the United States for seven years, Shadow didn't exactly think Ko Tan would return just to stay in the slums. If anything, he was doubtless passing himself off as a wealthy Asian entrepreneur. Deeper and deeper into the slums they went, however, Shadow dropping farther and farther behind until there were two blocks between him and his quarry. The population around them kept thinning out; all that was left were a few rolling bums. Unless the man he was keeping in his sight was half-cracked, he would know he was being followed.

And just when Shadow was about to give up, his sixth sense kicked in, sweeping suddenly upon him with such force he threw himself to the ground before conscious realization struck, only to hear the sound of a gun explode up ahead.

No bullets whizzed by, no plaster exploded behind him.

But the feeling of dread wouldn't leave him, and he knew suddenly that he had guessed wrong. Somewhere along the line, something had changed, and he still didn't know what.

Cursing softly now, he ran stealthily forward, his tennis shoes making no sound on the pavement. And then the warehouse loomed to his right, door still swinging open, the acrid smell of gunpowder in the air.

His feet seemed to go forward on their own, while his mind scrambled to escape from what he sensed would be worse than any nightmare he'd had so far.

It was. Through the open doors, through the smoking darkness, through the choking decay, he cautiously stepped, keeping himself ready should someone try to jump him. Until there he was, alone in the center of the old building.

Alone with a dead man at his feet.

He didn't have to roll him over; he didn't have to see the face. He already knew who it was.

Ko Tan.

The knocking bolted Riley awake, making her sit straight up in her bed. A quick glance at the alarm clock told her it was three in the morning, and she'd only been asleep for an hour as it was. But the knocking wouldn't go away, so in spite of her better intentions, she swung herself out of her warm bed.

A good New Yorker, she grabbed a rolling pin from the kitchen on her way to the door. The peephole revealed a tall, incredibly distorted man who could have been almost anyone. Her first reaction was to identify him as someone who couldn't possibly be standing at her door at three in the morning.

Just to be sure, she drew back the first bolt lock. The knocking instantly stopped, and the silence made her pause. She listened for a moment for anything, a sound of shuffling feet, a wayward hiss of breath. But no sound came, none at all, and it confirmed her initial thought.

There was only one man who could be that silent.

In her sleepy frame of mind, she was half-sure that this was just another dream after the many other nights of dreams. Shadow really wouldn't come back now, would he? He didn't want to see her, did he? All of a sudden, she grew anxious. Quick, her mind thought. Let him in before you wake up. She drew back the rest of the locks in a rush, throwing the door open wide.

He simply stood there, his face looking thin and tired, the lines harsh around his eyes, the scar vivid against his cheek. A wave of dark hair had fallen forward, lying lazily above his gray eyes. He looked tired and worn and incredibly wonderful.

She opened her mouth three times before any words came out. "Why?" she finally managed to ask.

But he didn't say anything right away. The only movement was that of his eyes as they roamed down the length of her figure. She was wearing a short satin nightgown that brushed the top of her thighs to reveal long, long legs. Her shining red hair was in complete disarray, tumbling exotically across her arm and down the front of a deep emerald gown that matched her eyes. And a rolling pin was in her hand.

"Ko Tan's dead," he said finally.

The words hung in the air for a moment, heavy with impact and importance. She felt her face drain of color, and all sorts of thoughts rushed to her at once. Where? When? How? Why?

"I don't understand," she said at last. "You'll have to explain." A small pause, then she reached her decision. "Come in," she said quietly, "before someone calls the cops about a strange man lingering in the halls."

He nodded, coming forward, and in that split second of time, she noticed the subtle change. His smooth steps were off, his shoulders too tense, his eyes too busy. He looked strangely out of sync.

"Do you always answer your door at three in the morning?" he asked gruffly.

"Only when it's a strange man I met in Myanmar," she whispered back.

"You should have asked for my name first, Riley."

"I knew it was you."

"You should have left the chain on until you were sure."

"I have my rolling pin."

He looked up sharply at that. "Yes," he said. "So I see."

"Talk to me," she urged softly, the words coming out stronger than she'd intended as she shut and locked the door behind them. She really did want him to talk to her. She wanted him to trust her, to stop shutting her out. Maybe then she'd learn about the man that affected her so much. She motioned him over to the couch, arranging her short nightshirt around herself carefully. No way would she risk his disappearing on her while she ran to get a robe.

"I don't know what there is to tell yet," Shadow said flatly, sinking into the old couch. His head was still reeling from the shock of his earlier discovery. Of all the things to happen, he had never anticipated this. Never. And all of a sudden he was swimming in negatives. There were things going on here that he didn't understand, but he was going to have to find out. He already knew that his life depended upon it. He also realized, for the first time, that he couldn't do it alone. With his renegade cover still in place, he would be a prime suspect. He needed outside assistance, but after what had just happened, he didn't know who to trust anymore.

Except . . . Riley.

He could always trust her.

"Start at the beginning," she was saying calmly. "How do you know Ko Tan's dead?"

He took a deep breath. He was going to have to tell her everything now; it was the only way she could help him. Hell, maybe after everything, he owed her that much, anyway. But then another thought came to him. Nothing had changed. The more she knew, the more danger she would be in.

He wanted to swear out loud. Dammit, when would all this end? When could he just get on with his life? He didn't want to jeopardize this woman, this beautiful, wonderful woman. He wanted to hold her. He wanted to keep her safe. Maybe he even wanted to believe that someday, someway, they could build a life together.

But he was a man of shadows. His life was so twisted, all he could do was plunge ahead. He needed answers, he needed access to a computer for information. She could help him with these things, and then maybe, just maybe, he could solve this riddle once and for all.

He started talking.

"I told you I was a DEA agent. What I didn't tell you was what my cover was, or what I was doing." He paused for a moment, but continued in a low, serious tone. "I'm currently undercover as a wanted man for arms dealing. Since returning from Myanmar, I've maintained my identity, waiting for the final sting. See, I've spent the last nine months setting up a huge arms deal to lure Ko Tan to the States. It involves lots of high-tech weaponry, state-of-the-art, million-dollar hardware. After we escaped, I'd worried things might fall apart, but since my cover *wasn't* blown, Ko Tan considered the deal as still being on, especially since all the arrangements had been finalized before our little escapade. Well, he came to New York, all right, and he called me, basically letting me know he wanted revenge. Rather than wait for him to take action, I decided to find him first. I followed a man I thought he sent to shoot me, and wound up finding Ko Tan's body."

She nodded, though the story was hard to absorb all at once. High-tech weaponry. Arms deals. Not to mention that Ko Tan was such a vital, powerful man, it was hard to believe he was actually dead. She tried to force her mind into action. Obviously this was not a dream. Even she couldn't have dreamed all this up.

"I don't see a problem," she said. "So he's dead instead of being in jail. At least he's gone now, and your mission is completed. Can't you just call your boss and be done with it?"

"I don't think so," Shadow said slowly. "No, I think that's what they want me to do."

"*They?*" she asked, and then gave a furious shake of her head. "You've lost me again."

"I went to call my boss," Shadow began, "but then I started to wonder how I'd managed to witness his murder like that. It was a bit too easy, too much like a setup. So I went back to my apartment first. Someone had gone through it. Thoroughly. They didn't do a very professional job of it, either, so they definitely weren't from the DEA. There was a gun planted under the bed. I imagine it's the murder weapon."

It took a moment, a horror-filled moment, but then it all sank in. "Someone's trying to frame you," she whispered softly. "Shadow, they want you to be blamed for Ko Tan's death."

He didn't say anything, only nodded, his gray eyes dark and unreadable.

"But who?" she asked abruptly. "Who could possibly benefit from such a thing?"

He shrugged. "Men like Ko Tan have lots of enemies," he said. But then he hesitated and let out a long sigh. "Honestly, Riley, I can think of only a few suspects. Other drug lords might want to see Ko Tan dead as a way of eliminating competition, but they wouldn't have any reason to want to frame me—if they even knew who I was, that is. In fact, managing to assassinate a man like Ko Tan could make for a lot of prestige. They'd probably take credit for it. On the other hand, the main arms dealer knows us both. But it makes no sense for him to kill a man about to pay him millions of dollars. The only logical reason I can figure out right now is if someone paid him more to double-cross us. That's a possibility. And there's always the few guys from the DEA who knew about Ko Tan and me, too. I can't think of a motive there, though, unless someone's dirty. Unless someone there was also paid to double-cross..."

His voice faded off, leaving Riley with only the impact of his words. Shadow might have been double-crossed by his own cohorts? She shook her head. It was unthinkable.

"What did you do with the gun?" she asked finally.

"I left it," he told her evenly. "It's been wiped clean, and it's only circumstantial evidence, anyway. I figure it's less risky there than if it was actually found in my possession."

She nodded her head. "What are you going to do now?" she asked quietly.

He looked at her long and hard. "I need time," he told her directly. "I need more information so I can figure out what the hell's going on. I need someone with a computer, someone with a few contacts. I need you, Riley. I need you."

They were the words she'd been needing, longing to hear. *I need you, Riley.* She closed her eyes, thinking furiously. Shadow was a secretive man. A man who touched her with his eyes, only to pull back again. He'd lied to her, he'd saved her life. He'd hurt her, he'd held her. And everything faded to the background the minute he said those words. He needed her, as he'd needed her that night. And once again, she couldn't refuse him. No one had ever needed her as he did, and no one had ever made her feel as he made her feel.

"Honest this time?" she whispered. "No more games, no more deceptions?"

The irony of the words was almost too much. Shadow smiled bitterly to himself. There had never been any games with her. From the beginning, the way he felt about her had been painfully real. The rest of his life was probably just some dark game, but what he felt for her, what he'd fought against . . . It was the only real thing he had.

"No more games," he said quietly.

"I'll work it out, then," she said. "Everything will be fine, you'll see. You'll need a place to stay for the night."

"Yes."

"I have a sofa," she whispered tentatively, and all of a sudden, she couldn't quite seem to meet his eyes.

"A sofa, Riley?" The soft words had come out on their own; he didn't know where they'd come from. But all of a sudden, the need, the desire for her, overwhelmed him. He didn't want to sleep alone tonight. Tonight, more than any night in his entire life, he wanted to be with her. He wanted to hold her, he wanted to touch her. He wanted to make love to her so long and so hard that the darkness would finally fade, the dreams would finally cease, and at last, lying in her arms in the aftermath, he would find peace.

His thoughts showed in the darkening depths of his eyes, showed in the tightening of his jaw. She took one look and felt herself drown in the passion there. Those dark eyes had beguiled her before, and once again she couldn't refuse them. She didn't utter a word; she simply took his hand and led him to the bedroom.

There were no words spoken. Instead, he showed her his need with gentle touches and tender caresses. In the light feel of his hands running through the thick mane of her hair. In the softness of his lips pressed against her own.

He showed her his need with trembling hands and burning desire. With raging kisses that swept across her neck and shoulders and blazed trails to the tender mounds of her breasts. There were questions both needed answered, doubts both possessed, uncertainties both maintained. But they let the confusion slide in the night, finding solace instead in the touches both had longed for. In the heat of his kiss, she forgot about her doubts and learned again just how wonderful he could make her feel. In the tenderness of her touch, he let go of his fears and rediscovered the haven of her arms.

But simple touches and caresses weren't enough. Both had denied themselves too long, hungered too much. Now, gentleness gave way to urgency, and when she sighed, pressing against him in feverish need, he pulled her short gown over her head while her hands fought with the buttons of his shirt.

But the buttons took too long, frustrating them both until, with a low growl of need, Shadow ripped the shirt open with his own two fists. And then her hands were there—soft, wonderful hands that spread across his chest and ran trails of lightning across his stomach as he sucked in his breath in agonizing desire.

Her hands found the snap of his jeans, ripping the waistband open, moving down lower and lower. He couldn't think or breathe anymore. His world had become Riley. Riley with her satiny skin, soft lips and silky hair. With another groan, he grabbed her close, burying his face in her neck, nipping its sensitive curves as she arched against him.

Now, while the need was burning hot. Now, when his body cried out for hers. Now, when he needed her more than he ever had. Now, when the world was falling apart and she was his only refuge.

They didn't make it to the bed. Instead he dragged her down to the floor, then stood to finish the job of taking off his pants that her fingers had begun. And then he was above her, naked and scarred and vulnerable.

Her love.

With urgent hands she guided him in, with urgent need she pulled him closer, until they were as close as man and woman could ever be.

And it was wonderful, a sinking, piercing kind of wonderful that caught her breath in her throat until only his name came out in ragged gasps. But he absorbed each one in his mouth as he drove in, setting a rapid, roaring tempo that her hips quickly captured.

Now, when he was hers at last. Now, with his strong shoulders in her embrace. Now, when she could take him with all the love that lay in her heart. Now, when he needed her.

Now.

The world exploded in her mind, falling about in thousands of tiny, glittering pieces. But Shadow was there, falling and gasping with her until they both sank back down to the warm glory of the aftermath of their loving.

They lay there for a long time, simply lying in each other's arms on the floor of her bedroom. She ran a long finger down his chest; he caressed the soft curve of her cheek as it lay on his shoulder.

They didn't speak, and in this moment of contact, they told each other more than mere words ever could.

Need. Desire. And most of all, love.

Chapter 10

She didn't sleep much that night.

Instead, she lay in the darkness, listening to the rhythmic sound of Shadow's breathing, feeling the weight of his arm across her chest, touching the rippling outline of his muscled back. These were rare sensations, so she rested quietly and savored the moment.

She liked him in her bed, Riley decided. She liked the feel of his body next to hers and the warm comfort of his sleepy embrace. She liked knowing he could stretch out against her in trusting sleep, relaxing fully.

Trust. In Myanmar, he had kept her in the dark. Now he was starting to talk to her, starting to let her in. But then, what choice did he have? It would appear that even his own colleagues were suspects, leaving him alone, with no one to turn to. Lying against him, she shivered lightly. What would it be like to be so alone?

When she'd first met him, she thought she'd never seen a man so alone. Now she was beginning to understand. He operated in a world of darkness, where every friend was also a potential enemy. She shook her head slightly, amazed. Such an existence was beyond this girl from Ohio. She needed people. She needed friends to trust, people to share with.

But this man had no one.

No one at all.

She hugged him closer, smoothing a hand down his shadowed chest. What if it was someone he knew? What if someone in the DEA's office was dirty? His life was in such jeopardy, and the framing was only a small part of it. Shadow was a good agent, from what she'd seen. He wouldn't rest until he knew the truth. Surely the people from the DEA knew that, as well. They might kill him.

The irony was almost overwhelming. She'd thought she'd seen the last of danger and doubts when they'd left the jungle. Instead she'd stumbled upon another nest of serpents, only this time in New York. And she wasn't convinced she could fight them any better here. She was still just a junior reporter. She'd never worked on any major stories, developed any major contacts that could be of use to Shadow.

She was smart, though, she told herself. She was resourceful; she thought well on her feet. Surely she could come up with something—*anything*—to help Shadow.

The faint light from the window bathed his naked body, accentuating each glowing plane. Even in sleep his face didn't soften, but the lines had eased around his eyes and his mouth was slightly parted. Dark stubble shadowed his cheeks, and she could still feel the light burns on her face and neck from its impact. But it was a sexy feel, she thought, tingling and alive.

He stirred, the burden of his dreams causing him to murmur and frown even in his sleep. With a gentle touch she sought to calm him again, running a soothing hand down his cheek. He turned, snuggling her closer, and drifted to quieter sleep. In this new embrace she discovered that she could run her hand across the smooth expanse of his chest, sharply defined by lean, corded muscles. When she drew her hands down farther, to the rippling washboard of his stomach, the muscles reflexively contracted and he moved closer.

Sighing softly in the night, she rested her head once more in the curve of his arm. It was so warm here, warm and cozy and wonderful. She could watch the soft shadows as they played across the room, enveloping her and her lover.

The shifting darkness gave the night a mysterious hue, fitting for the man next to her. Watching the dancing light play across the features of his face, she could almost imagine that the shadows had followed him here.

And why not? He was a man of darkness, with gray eyes that seemed to be ageless, eyes she would never quite be able to describe. Eyes she was sure would haunt her even after the man himself had left.

Now, under the glow of the moonlight, he seemed a greater mystery than ever before. The pale light reflected off the long thin scar curving down his cheek in brilliant relief through the dark shadow of his whiskers. Her fingers found the rest, carefully defining what she'd seen only briefly when he'd stood before her, naked and passionate. But now she took the time to explore. Now, in the comforting embrace of the darkness, her fingertips traced the myriad of scars that riddled his body.

There was the remnant of a jagged cut in his left side and a similar scar glowed glossy and puckered on his thigh. She found an uneasy indent not far from his spine, but she had neither the light nor the angle to actually see it. His hands—large, callused and capable—seemed to be interwoven with thin, spidery lines racing along the back to reach his fingers.

But the largest of them all was on his right shoulder. She'd glimpsed it before, and the sight had impressed her with what must have been deep violence and pain. But now she was close to the round scar and she could examine it, note with sadness the way the skin was raised and puckered along the rim.

She couldn't help it—with a small murmur for the past pain, she moved the final inch forward and planted her lips on the shiny patch. "I'm sorry," she whispered softly, though there were only the shadows to hear.

She rested her forehead against it for a long time, absorbing the impact. Frowning dreams, shadowed eyes, gunshot wounds. And once again, she realized just how little she knew about this man she slept with. He was a man who'd suffered, who bore secret burdens, even now, that he wouldn't share. Before she'd feared she'd fallen for a mercenary. Now she had the thin comfort that he was really one of the good guys. But despite this, how many unspeakable things had he been forced to do while under cover? How many atrocities had he been forced to see?

And would he ever trust her with any of it?

She wanted to know, if only because she wanted to understand this man. When he looked at her with the dark need in him unleashed, she found she couldn't turn away from him, even if her very life depended upon it. But afterward he would still shut her out. In the cold light of day, he kept a distance between them, and became, once more, a stranger.

She thought that it was quite possible she loved him, but what did *he* feel? And even if he cared a little, how could there be love without trust? How could there be caring without openness?

Once again, she was forced to wonder if what she was doing was right. He'd said he would be honest this time, but that didn't mean openness. He was a man who clung to his secrets, who truly operated best in the shadows.

Perhaps she should just turn him away now, before she was drawn in deeper, before her feelings ran even stronger. After all, what kind of a future could they ever have? He was a virtual island, sharing with no one, trusting no one. And he would most likely go his solitary way even at the expense of her heart.

She couldn't hold him. And even if she could make him fall in love with her, in the end it might be too late. The world seemed to have gone topsy-turvy, with the bad guys dead and the good guys suspect. Shadow had been framed, and in the morning the police might take him away. Worse, he might be killed.

Killed.

Once more she shivered in the night. She wanted to help him; she wanted to save him. But nothing in her life had prepared her for this kind of darkness. The reporter in her had dreamed of someday uncovering a government scandal. The woman in her cringed at the price such corruption might exact from the man beside her. In the jungle he'd seemed almost invincible. But he'd known the enemy then. Now, now there were only the shifting shadows.

Who would kill a man like Ko Tan? Who would frame Shadow for such a crime? What would it cost him to find out?

In the silent night the fear wrapped cold around her heart. She wanted it all to end. She wanted safety, sanity, back. She wanted, for once, just to be with this man. His body told enough stories of pain and misery. Maybe, in time, with her own persistence she could reach beyond the lessons of such a past and gain his trust.

But now? Now there was no such thing as time. Now there was only the fear.

It was irrelevant, she told herself brutally. Even if the situation changed, Shadow had no interest in her. His need of her was merely temporary.

Once he cleared everything up, he would journey on, perhaps to another mission, another jungle. And what about her? She would move on, too, she supposed. After this latest story, she could possibly get a promotion. Onward to Europe or South America or Africa. It was all the same to her. Travel, travel, travel. Search, search, search. And maybe this time, in this country, on this assignment . . . Maybe this success would fill the void, ease the restlessness. Maybe.

What did it even matter? She would simply search as she'd always searched. And some small part would whisper that maybe this was what it was all about, these quiet moments in the arms of a scarred, gray-eyed man. Maybe she'd already found what she needed and let him go, anyway.

Yet how could she ask him to stay? She didn't even know his true name.

Parents? A past? All she knew were the fragments she'd seen: the scars on his body, the haunting depths of his gray eyes, the frowning turmoil of his dreams. And the moments they'd shared, like the first time she'd seen him, the lone panther deep in the shadows of the huts. Then there had been the night they'd gone into the poppy fields, Shadow watching her undress with helpless hunger and desire in his gaze. The last night, head bowed in the jungle, brutally rejecting Nemo's trusting innocence, since the monkey would never be happy away from his natural habitat.

She'd seen him in anguish, she'd seen him in passion, she'd seen him in complete control, and she'd seen him deluged by doubts. She had seen enough of him to etch the memories like fire in her heart.

Maybe Shadow *was* what she'd always been searching for.
But that wouldn't help her now.

Not now when the darkness ruled again, and deep in the
heart of the city, the serpents waited.

He awoke when the sun was just beginning to fight its way
into the New York sky. He'd watched it before in the mountains of Myanmar, and he watched it now with the red-haired
nymph in his arms.

He could capture only glimpses through the thin cracks of the
blinds, but it was enough to make out the soaring gray of the
skyscrapers and the hazy yellow of the morning sun. How long
had it been? How many years since a New York sunrise?

Too many, perhaps. Too many years in the jungle, too many
years of constantly watching and guarding and waiting. Too
many years too far from this world. It seemed alien to him now.
The smell of the smog, the darting yellow of the taxis, the glitzy
sparkle of the lights. He'd forgotten the impact of such sights.

A stranger in a strange land. . . .

But it wasn't too bad as long as he stayed here, buried in the
comforter, holding the soft warmth of Riley's sleeping form.
Here was comfort. Here, for the first time since hazy days of
other lifetimes, was home.

But he didn't allow himself the time for savoring. Too much
time had already elapsed, too many hours he should have been
at work. The cops would be looking for him by now, and it
wouldn't take long to trace the recent connection between him
and Riley. All they had to do was trace the purchase of two
plane tickets from the border of Thailand to New York.

No, they would find him soon enough. Perhaps two days at
the most. Two days to figure out who had killed Ko Tan. Two
days.

So little time. He looked once more at the simmering world
beyond the blind. He looked at the rising sun, the soaring
buildings.

And he wondered how long it would be before he could see
such things again.

Riley woke to the aroma of sizzling bacon and brewing coffee this time. For a befuddled moment she simply lay in her

bed, thinking dreamily of home. But then it came to her that she was in her own bed in her own apartment.

And Shadow was no longer beside her.

With a last sleepy stretch, she threw back the covers and wrapped herself tightly in the jade silk of an Oriental robe. She gave no thought to her hair, knowing by now that it was well beyond all hope.

Instead she followed her nose and the rumble of her stomach, padding softly into the small kitchen. There, she was greeted by the oh-so-pleasant sight of a man cooking. She hesitated for a moment, feeling uncertain once more in the light of day. But then, with a determined breath, she plunged forward.

"I've died and gone to heaven, haven't I?" she teased.

Shadow turned, his gray eyes muted. He looked tense, but after a small pause, his shoulders relaxed slightly, and his face creased into the faintest hint of a smile. "You haven't tasted it yet," he warned her.

"Don't have to," Riley informed him. "As long as someone else cooks, it tastes great to me."

"Don't you cook?" he asked, folding over the omelet with an efficient twist.

"Of course I do. Leftover Chinese, canned soup. And, on a good day, maybe microwavable waffles."

He shook his head, cutting the omelet in half and sliding it onto two plates. He added two pieces of toast to each, then handed her her plate. Without another word, he moved to the table. At a loss for what to say, she followed. Summoning up a bright smile, she took a bite of the omelet, chewing without really paying much attention.

"It's very good," Riley said after a minute, realizing that the omelet really was good.

But Shadow only shrugged, and the conversation dwindled again. Left to her own devices, she watched him under shuttered eyelids. He ate with quick, efficient movements and polished off his omelet in no time at all. Evidently he was in a hurry. Feeling even more uncertain now, she finished her own breakfast in halfhearted bites.

"What's the plan?" she asked finally.

"I need to go back to my apartment," he said quietly, rising and taking the plates over to the sink.

She gave his back an incredulous look. "You know that's the first place they'll look for you," she admonished.

He shook his head. "Check the paper," he said.

She picked it up, flipping through the news section. "It's not in here," she said finally. "There's no mention of the murder at all."

"Actually," he corrected, "I believe it's in the local section of the paper, small print, nearly last page."

She found that section and flipped through it, as well. "'Businessman shot in back alley,'" she read. "They don't know yet," she whispered. "Of course, he's carrying fake ID and they just assumed it to be real. But they'll check it out. And once they clue in to his real identity, they'll also discover your connection to him. Which will lead them straight to your apartment."

"Then I'll have to get going right away."

"But, Shadow," she insisted, "you've already been to your apartment once. What in the world can be so important to you to risk going back?"

He shrugged, running water on the dishes with infuriating calmness. "There are just a few things I didn't have time to grab before. There was somebody coming up the stairs so I had to exit through the fire escape as it was. That's all."

"What is it?" Riley demanded to know. "Dammit, Shadow. That same person could be waiting for you even now. It's too risky."

But once again he simply shrugged her off.

Suddenly the whole situation filled her with rage. It was just as she'd feared, dark with need the night before, cold and unreachable the next morning. One moment he was telling her he needed her; the next minute he was shutting her out. She just couldn't stand it anymore.

"Do you really have a death wish?" she exclaimed hotly, rising to her feet. "Couldn't manage to die in Myanmar, so you thought you might as well take care of it here? Or is it simply that you don't trust me? That's it, isn't it?" She shouldn't be saying these things, one part of her realized. But they'd been on her mind for so long, and now she just couldn't hold back. He didn't trust her. He didn't care. As so help her God, she wanted him to so badly. The intensity of the desire just made her angrier. "Well, let me tell you something, Mr. Mighty and Silent," she snapped, "it's about time you started, because I don't sleep with just anyone and I certainly won't sleep with somebody who doesn't trust me!"

"Riley?" Shadow said softly.

"What?"

"I trust you."

"No," she shot back. "No, you don't, not really. Not enough to open up completely. Not enough to really let me in." Her last words trailed off, the earnestness creeping through the anger. "Shadow, you've got to let me in."

There was a long silence while the man before her said nothing. He simply stared at the sink, hands clenched into fists on the counter. "It's too dangerous for you to come," he conceded finally, though it really wasn't anything she didn't know already. "Whoever framed me could be waiting. I won't take that risk."

"But then, you shouldn't go, either," she added softly.

"It's my job. I've been trained for it."

"Shadow, there's got to be another way. Look, you said you wanted to use my computer. It's free. We can access records on who owns the warehouse. Don't you know any federal access codes as an agent? We could probably check on the activities of both the arms dealers and other DEA agents from here. And while you do that, I can go around the area, asking questions, finding out if anyone saw anything. As a reporter I can even call up the police station and check on the status of the case. See, there are plenty of things we can do from right here. So *don't take the risk.*"

"What you're suggesting," he began slowly, "makes a great deal of sense. In fact, those were the actions I was considering this morning. Since the killer must know both Ko Tan and me, that narrows it down to either the arms dealer or someone from the DEA. But that's assuming that someone was paid to double-cross Ko Tan. And that could be anyone within either group. Ray Thornwall, the arms dealer, has several layers of people under him. In a deal that large, any one of them could have been the weak link. And I didn't memorize everyone's name, just the people I was in immediate contact with. I do have them recorded, though, on disk. Unfortunately, that disk is still at my apartment.''

"And thus," Riley concluded for him, "you have to go to your apartment."

"Exactly."

She sighed, still not wanting him to go. But there really didn't seem to be any other way. "All right," she said at last. "We'll both go."

He immediately looked as if he was going to protest, but she cut him off.

"They'll only be looking for you," she observed. "One lone wolf. They won't be looking for a couple."

He still wanted to argue. She'd been through enough—he didn't want to expose her to any more. He didn't want to further taint her with the darkness that had become his life. She was so bright, so unbelievably precious. He didn't even think she realized the impression she'd made on him, the lightness she'd brought to his life.

He couldn't risk her, he told himself. He wanted to believe that the perpetrator had been one of Thornwall's men, but what if it wasn't? What if it was someone from Group 41? It wouldn't be the first time someone had given in to the lure of incredible riches. And if so...

If so, the danger was too great. And once more he didn't know where to turn, who to trust. Except Riley. He cursed silently. He wanted to protect her, but it seemed he was going to jeopardize her a little longer instead. She was right. They would be looking for him. But a couple... a couple just might work.

Finally, he gave in with a nod. She knew better than to expect anything more, so she excused herself from the table to dig through the closet. It was there that inspiration hit her. After all, Shadow might be determined to be cold, and Shadow might be determined to be distant, but nobody had ever said *she* had to play by his rules.

Her green eyes were gleaming when she finally selected the outfit. She had only a few days left to make an impression on Shadow, and she'd never been a quitter. The man would never know what hit him.

* * *

A little before ten, a nicely dressed man in a tan overcoat and low-pulled hat turned onto Maryland Street with a tall, laughing redhead draped on his arm. In a slim, short skirt that revealed the most incredible pair of legs, she walked with careless strides, leaning forward until she could pull the man's head down for a breathtaking kiss without ever breaking step.

The man tried to chastise her, but she only kissed him again, the sound of her laughter floating down the tired street like rich music. And just when all heads were turned, she stopped, threw her arms around the man and pulled him down for yet another kiss. This one a deep, passionate kiss that earned more than a few calls of encouragement from the passersby.

The man took the hint and, without waiting another moment, scooped the woman into his arms, kissed her again and carried her grandly into an apartment building while the onlookers cheered and whistled behind him.

But once the door was firmly shut to the outside world, the man magically turned into Shadow, and the woman into Riley. And Shadow was less than happy.

"Could you have attracted a little more attention?" he said sharply as he looked her up and down once more, eyeing her maddeningly short red skirt. His pulse was still pounding and he was trying to convince himself it was from adrenaline, but looking at the long curve of her legs, he wasn't so sure. He never should have brought her here, he thought abruptly. Hell, he never should've showed up on her doorstep in the middle of the night. He should have forgotten all about her, forgotten he'd ever seen eyes so green, hair so red. And legs so long . . .

His scowl deepened.

"What?" Riley prodded. Her own cheeks were flushed from the excitement and heady thrill of acting as Shadow's date. Her blood was singing, her nerves tingling, and her whole body seemed ablaze in the rush of mischievous adrenaline. She couldn't stop herself from teasing him further. She leaned over and pinned him with a slanted look. "Do you think they were really looking at you?" she purred.

His eyebrows drew together in an even deeper scowl, proving her point. But refusing to rise to her bait, he abruptly turned away, turning his mind to more urgent matters. Doing his best to ignore her completely, he peered out of the crack between the drawn blinds and the window, observing the people in the street. At one corner was a hot-dog stand; he recognized the man who worked there as the usual vendor. By the post for the bus stop, a group of five men stood, three in suits, two younger and in jeans. He spotted a jogger moving up the block on the other side of the street at a slow and steady pace, as well as four more pedestrians at various points.

He observed that one of the men at the bus stop glanced at the window several times, and the jogger seemed to slow just a tad upon reaching the apartment building. But he recognized none of the men, and from a distance he couldn't tell if either was carrying a gun.

"All right," he said at last to Riley, who was still standing behind him. "The apartment is up the stairs, first door on the right. Stay away from the windows, and don't touch anything."

She bristled at his tone, but held her tongue only because she realized that in such matters, his knowledge was definitely superior.

With a nod, she headed up the stairs, and he followed closely behind, sparing discreet glances at her legs as they ascended. Damn, she looked good in the short red skirt with high red heels. With another scowl, his jaw tightened further.

By the time they reached the top of the narrow staircase, he had his thoughts firmly in order again, forcing his mind to the business at hand. Motioning her to stand back on the landing, he began to meticulously examine the doorframe.

Riley watched him as he went carefully around, inch by inch. Finally, about two inches from the doorknob, he slowly pulled out a three-inch piece of dark brown thread.

"A marker," Riley breathed out. "So they'd know if someone opened the door."

Shadow nodded. "Very good," he said softly as he unlocked the door with an imperceptible click.

"Hey. I've seen the movies."

He motioned her to silence, putting his ear to the door for a long moment. Finally, when he detected not the slightest intrusion, no hiss of breath as someone poised behind the door, no click of a gun barrel, he was ready to proceed.

He moved Riley behind him, guarding her with the shield of his body, as he slowly turned the knob and then thrust the door open.

He leapt in, keeping the door in front of him as he sprang low, dropping instantly to the ground.

He was greeted with silence. He maintained his defensive stance for another instant, scoping out the small quarters of his one-room apartment with attached kitchen. The bathroom door was wide open, revealing emptiness, but he checked behind the door, anyway.

When he was satisfied that all was well, he motioned for the wide-eyed Riley to enter, shutting the door firmly behind her.

Riley gazed around the old, run-down apartment with interest, taking in the narrow bed with its bare coverings. There was a small shelf unit overflowing with books, a brilliantly colored ethnic tapestry on one wall, and a poster of a city at night with the word *Portland* beneath it.

Most of the things were his own, even though he was still operating under cover. He personally found it very ironic that his real life had already been so dark, it had required very little revision to become his cover.

"Oregon?" Riley questioned, pointing toward the poster on the wall. "Were you stationed there?"

Shadow looked up from the small kitchen where he was rummaging through the cupboards. He looked at the poster for a quiet moment, then turned back to the cupboard. "No," he said offhandedly. "I lived there."

"Lived there?" This was news. Her curiosity was immediately aroused. "When?" she prompted.

"A long time ago," he evaded.

"How long?" she persisted. "When you were a child?"

There was a small pause, then the rummaging resumed. "Yes."

"And how old were you when you left?"

This time the pause was longer. "Eighteen," Shadow said at last.

"There now," Riley said, unable to keep the sarcasm from her voice. "That wasn't so hard, was it?"

He might have grimaced, but it was hard to tell from where she stood. Smiling secretly, she decided she was definitely intrigued at this rare glimpse of his life, and she wandered over to the bookcase. There she discovered an incredible collection of poetry. Ranging from Byron to Sandburg, there were books of German poetry and Hispanic poetry, all told spanning over twenty volumes.

She pulled out a thin paperback book entitled *Rimas* by Gustavo Adolfo Bécquer. "Do you speak Spanish?" she called over her shoulder.

"A bit," came the reply, and she heard another clang from the kitchen.

She opened the book to a poem that had a small, carefully penciled-in translation next to it. " 'The sighs are wind and go to the air,' " she read. " 'The tears are water and go to the sea. Tell me, woman. When love is forgotten, do you know to where it goes?' "

She read it one more time, then closed the book softly. "That's nice," she said aloud to herself. "Beautiful and sad." She turned back to the kitchen, from which Shadow was now emerging holding the disk triumphantly. "Are you a romantic, Shadow?"

The question seemed to startle him, and he didn't answer. Finally, he simply shrugged. "I like poetry," he said quietly.

She nodded slowly, putting the book carefully back. "It's a very nice collection. Could I borrow a few books to read later?"

"I guess."

"So where is the disk?" she asked abruptly.

"Someplace safe."

"Did you enter the military when you were eighteen? Is that why you left Oregon?" she questioned in another brisk change of pace. It was a reporter's trick to keep the person off balance and unprepared. And before her eyes, she could see Shadow react. She watched him simply fold up within himself, his face smoothing out, his eyes turning a quiet, impenetrable gray. Like a hermit crab returning to his shell, leaving her once again on the outside.

"I had reasons," he said at last.

In frustration, she turned away. For he wasn't just some subject for a story, a challenge for her to break. He was the man she cared about, the man she'd given herself to, and he wasn't giving her much in return.

"Should you grab a few things to wear?" she asked quickly, proud of the steadiness of her voice, but keeping her back to him. "Or would they notice?"

"They'd notice."

She didn't know what else to say, and she could feel the quiet intensity of his gaze upon her back. Restless now, she took a few steps forward, her glance falling on a small picture lying next to the bed. She picked it up.

It was a sun-drenched photo with an incredible blue sky and the faint spot of golden beaches in the background. In the foreground was a younger Shadow, standing—more relaxed and easy than she'd ever seen him—next to someone else. The other man had one arm draped around Shadow's shoulders and was openly laughing at the camera with warm brown eyes. Both sported the short-cropped hair of military men. She turned the photo over, but there were no names or markings on the back, nothing to give away the identity of the man.

"Who is he?" she asked curiously, and when she didn't hear an answer immediately, she turned around to see Shadow staring at the picture with startling intensity. "He's someone close," she guessed. "Your brother?"

"No," Shadow replied quietly, and she could see the furious clenching of his jaw muscle. She recognized the look now, the intensely restrained signs of his deep grief.

"He's dead now, isn't he?" she said gently.

"Yes."

"But you still miss him. Did you love him that much?"

"Yes."

She understood that, understood the wealth of meaning in the one simple word. And in that instant, she missed the man in the picture, as well. With his open, laughing grin he looked so full of life and zest. A man of energy and magnetism. Exactly the kind of friend Shadow needed, one who could draw him out, teach him to relax. Judging by Shadow's easy manner in the picture, the man had succeeded.

She looked at Shadow now, so tense, so tight in his pain, shutting her out more forcefully the deeper she touched him. So, once he'd relaxed a bit, allowed a person to get close. And bore the pain of the loss still. "Tell me about him," she said softly. "Please, Shadow. I want to know."

He stood there silently, muscles clenching, eyes looking so far away, seemingly drowning in memories she couldn't understand. "I can't," he said at last. "I don't know how. It's just . . . not my way."

"I'll help you," she urged gently, walking forward until she could place her hands on his chest and search the depths of his eyes with her own. "Just start at the beginning. What was his name?"

"Johnny," Shadow whispered, perhaps more to himself than her. "Johnny Dolerman." As if to distract himself, he shook his head and firmly removed her hands from his chest. He returned to the kitchen, bending down to carefully return all the pots and pans to their exact previous positions.

"Where did you meet him?" Riley prodded quietly, following him into the kitchen.

His hands paused, and she could see the muscle in his jaw twitch. "In the army," Shadow said abruptly, his hands moving once more. "Then we worked together for the DEA, as well."

An inkling of something began in the back of her mind, working its way slowly forward. A friend in the DEA . . . and a friend who was killed. When the thought finally burst into full-fledged understanding, she was staggered under the weight of its impact.

"Tell me, Shadow," she said urgently. "Tell me how he died."

"Ko Tan's man shot him down," he said quietly, replacing the last pan and closing the cupboard door. "Shot him fourteen times with an AK-47 before I could reach him. Fourteen times." And in his mind, the rat-tat-tat-tat ripped through his control, ripped through his tight hold on his emotions. Once again his jaw flexed, and this time his eyes closed under the onslaught.

"What happened?" Riley whispered, aching for the strain evident in his rigid stance. "What went wrong?"

"Someone broke Johnny's cover." The words were ragged, having rarely been spoken out loud. They made him clench his hands into fists on the kitchen's countertop so tightly, his knuckles turned white with the strain. "Johnny went to make the deal. Five of us watched as backup. Someone shot him down. Just . . . shot him down."

"You did it for him, didn't you?" Riley said. "All the years under cover to get Ko Tan, even when you knew it might cost your life. It wasn't just your job—you did it for him."

"He was my friend," Shadow said. He straightened, turning until his eyes met hers, a dark, tormented gray. And then, before he could stop them, the words simply poured out in a soft torrent. "I still hear the screams. Deep in the night, there are always the screams."

The starkness of the words sliced through her, hammering home his own pain.

"I'm sorry," she said at last, feeling a wealth of inadequacy. Not knowing what else to do, she stepped forward urgently and put her arms around him, holding him tight.

For one brief moment, he let his control break. He let himself return the embrace, clutching her tightly in his arms as if the scent of her hair, the softness of her touch, could blot out the memories and the pain.

Then the moment was gone, and he was pushing her away, closing himself from the softness even as he closed himself from the pain. He was a man who had lost too much in his life to make any distinction between the two. He was a man who'd lost too many things that were precious to him to try to hang on to anything—or anyone—ever again.

And looking at the woman before him, the woman with her brilliant eyes and fiery hair, he already knew the truth. He would lose her, too. It was the way things went in his life. Simply the way things worked. He would bear that loss, too, of course, huddle it deep inside. He didn't know of any other way.

"Come on," he said abruptly. "It's time to go."

She nodded, searching his eyes one last time, only to confirm that once again, he'd shut her out. He'd allowed her a small glimpse this time, but he'd pulled away completely in the end. For a moment, she experienced a brief flare of pain, a brief flare of frustration. Would he ever trust her? But with a small sigh, she accepted the defeat. If he'd cared more, if he'd wanted her more, he might let her in. But he didn't. So he wouldn't. And that was something she would just have to live with—for now, anyway. For now, she would take what she could get.

She put the picture carefully back down next to the bed. She spared one last look at Johnny, who seemed to laugh right out of the picture until he could have been standing with her now, smelling of the sea, dusted with sand.

Shadow's friend. Dead now and lost forever.

Another victim of Ko Tan.

Chapter 11

They left the building cautiously, Shadow carefully replacing the brown thread in its assigned place and pulling his hat low over his features. But Riley led him out the front door with a swagger, her long legs striding boldly into the street as she flashed a brilliant smile at the goggling men who were still outside. Then, really getting into her act, she threw her arms around Shadow's shoulders and laughed sexily, slanting him a hot look beneath lowered lashes.

With her easy manner she quickly tangled him up in the small charade. Surprised and enchanted despite the danger he knew surrounded them, Shadow found it easy to smile, easy to saunter casually down the street with Riley's arm linked through his, her eyes sparkling merrily. And even as he told himself it was just pretend and nothing more, he found himself being drawn in farther. For the first time in his life, he was part of a couple, strolling openly down the street on a sunny afternoon. He could hear her laughter in his ear, watch the flashing of her wonderful legs as they ate up the blocks, and it made him wonder....

And then something else stirred deep and low in his stomach. Something that he'd told himself he wouldn't feel anymore, told himself wasn't really there. But it was. He watched her until his blood boiled hot, until he wanted to swing her around in his arms, kiss her passionately on the lips and take her right then and there, in the middle of the block, in the middle of the street with the hard strength of the concrete beneath them. And the picture was so vivid, the vision so strong, he had to clench his fists to keep from giving in.

So his attention was elsewhere when they finally entered her apartment building. All his thoughts were captivated by how her hair had felt—would feel—against his chest, how her lips would taste under his own, how she would sound, whimpering beneath him. The desire ran hot, and his eyes couldn't get enough of her.

Riley turned around with some small comment, took one look at Shadow's eyes and felt all coherent thought flee. She couldn't even speak; all her being was focused on the intense gray eyes burning into her own.

The smile disappeared from her lips and they parted in tingling anticipation, tongue whispering out to moisten them slightly. She pressed the button for the elevator with one long perfect fingernail, and, watching it, Shadow could still feel it raking across his back from the night before. He shuddered visibly, eyes darkening to a black obsidian.

With a ding, the elevator arrived, doors whizzing open to welcome them into the dimly lit interior. Without a word, he followed her in, watching the light sway of her hips, imagining their feel against the palms of his hands.

The elevator seemed too slow. He watched her like a hawk. She stood just an inch away, so close in her tantalizing short skirt with her high red heels. Each small click as they passed the floors reverberated in the silence with the heated gasp of their waiting breaths. Each long floor passed by, one by one by one, until his hands couldn't take it and reached out, desperate to touch.

With another ding, the elevator stopped and the door flew open.

His hands came down. Together they walked forward unsteadily, their breathing still decidedly erratic. One more corner to turn, one more hallway to journey, and then, Shadow vowed, she would be his.

He swallowed deeply, and once again he could almost feel the soft luxury of her lips under his own. Her hair, running like silk between his fingers, cascading like fire down his chest. And her skin, raw satin...

They turned the final corner, and her legs brushed ever so lightly against his own. Though he felt like grabbing her then and there, he tamped down his desire. In seconds they would be in her apartment. In seconds he would rip that red skirt off and set them both on fire. Impatient, he looked ahead toward the apart—

There was a dark-suited man standing in front of the door.

With a snap, Shadow whipped back around the corner, pulling her quickly behind him, catching her startled cry in the bruising pressure of his lips. She relaxed instantly beneath him, her back against the wall, her arms pulling him closer. And for a fraction of an instant, he let the flood of adrenaline and passion loose, kissing her brutally as she responded in kind. There was a moment when the passion threatened to send them over, beyond the realm of troubled reality to a place where only their desires existed.

But with a harsh curse, he brought them both back, pulling his lips swiftly away. "DEA," he whispered savagely.

She could only nod, her senses still reeling. Absently her fingertips came to her swollen mouth, registering the loss. With an effort, she pulled her thoughts together. "Are you sure?" she asked softly.

He nodded. "I don't recognize that particular agent, but the look is the same, the style of suit. You can recognize these things after a bit, believe me. Besides, sooner or later they'd send an agent to track me down. Now the only question is, are they here to help or to hurt?"

He spoke the last words quietly, but the uncertainty underlying them was plain. He didn't know who to trust anymore. Even his friends could be his enemies. Except for Riley. She would help him, she vowed, straightening up against the wall.

"What do I do?" she asked softly.

"Go meet him," Shadow instructed. "Answer his questions as honestly as you can. Feel him out, see if you can establish why he's here. But Riley, whatever you do, *don't* tell him you've seen me. Not yet. And don't worry, I'll be here if anything goes wrong. Now, go!''

She nodded, squared her shoulders and pushed away from the wall. Taking a deep breath, she rounded the corner, smoothing her hair with one hand as she straightened her skirt with the other.

The stranger was still standing there, decked out in a conservative dark blue suit. He stood at rigid attention before the door, his head turning as he heard her approach. Her presence didn't seem to surprise him.

"May I help you?" she began, a note of casual inquiry in her tone.

"Riley McDouglas?" he asked, his voice deep and authoritative.

"Yes."

He gave her a shrewd looking-over with cold blue eyes that seemed to linger on the fresh wrinkles in her blouse, the tumbled disarray of her hair, the swollen puffiness of her lips. She had to fight the temptation not to fidget, not to once again smooth her skirt or hair and thus confirm all his calculating thoughts.

"May I help you?" she asked again, and this time her voice was sharper.

"Yes," he said, "I believe you can." He reached inside his jacket to pull out a small wallet. He flipped it open to reveal ID, but snapped it shut again before she had the chance to really see it. "Scott Weinard, DEA," he informed her in a curt tone. "I have a few questions, Ms. McDouglas. Perhaps you'd like to go inside where it would be more comfortable."

She gave the idea brief consideration; after all, it would give Shadow an opportunity to hide. But then instinct reared up hard. She didn't like this man with his sharp, all-knowing eyes. One quick glance at her kitchen, with dishes for two in the sink, then the rumpled sheets on the bed, and he would know. Maybe not have proof, for she could always claim a different lover, but he would know. And that, she already understood about this beady-eyed man, would be dangerous.

"No," she said firmly. "Out here will be fine."

"And your neighbors?" he asked quietly.

"I believe most of them are at work right about now."

He cocked his head at that bit of news. "What about yourself?"

"I'm working on some independent research, as my editor will be more than happy to confirm for you."

"That won't be necessary."

She nodded her head in acknowledgment, even as a trickle of uneasiness began at the base of her spine.

The hall seemed darker to her now, and much quieter than she remembered. Not more than twenty feet away, she knew, Shadow stood separated from them by a mere corner. But twenty feet away seemed suddenly far.

The man was talking. "Tell me, Ms. McDouglas," he was saying. "Have you ever met a man that goes by the name of Shadow?"

"Of course," she said loudly, too loudly in the silence. "I met him in Myanmar."

"Yes," he replied smoothly, "I know." He moved forward a step, and instantly she retreated a step. But then she realized what she'd done, not only giving in to the man's intimidation, but leading him closer to Shadow, as well. Swallowing bravely, she raised her chin and stood her ground.

"What is this about?" she asked coolly, letting a bit of confused indignation rise into her voice. "And if you already know the answers to your questions, why are you wasting taxpayers' money in asking them?"

He merely raised an eyebrow, his cold eyes once more raking her. When his eyes came back up, they met hers with an intensity that was startling. *Come on, Riley,* they seemed to say. *We both know you're lying.*

She shifted a bit uneasily, fighting to maintain her composure. He just wanted to rattle her, that was all. He didn't know anything unless she slipped and gave it away. *Stay cool, Riley,* she warned herself. *Stay cool.* "If you please, Agent Weinard," she said calmly, despite the fear growing within her, "I'm a very busy person."

It seemed to be the right tactic, for his eyes narrowed once more, and he seemed to reconsider her. "When was the last time you saw the man called Shadow?" he asked carefully.

"The day I arrived in New York," she answered readily. "Why do you ask?"

"Your neighbor reported seeing him here last night," he said sharply, ignoring her question altogether.

"My neighbor was mistaken."

"Was he?"

"He was. Do you have any more questions?"

"Just one. Do you have any information, any idea at all, where Shadow might be right now?"

Twenty feet from your beady little eyes. "No. No idea at all."

"I see," the man said. He nodded, then looked at her one last time with his sharp, sharp eyes. "You're lying," he said clearly in the silent hall. "And we both know it."

He turned then, away from her and toward the back of the hall. His hand moved casually inside his jacket, as if to scratch a small itch or tuck in a loose bit of material.

But in that instant, as if it were all in slow motion, Riley saw it, saw it with utter clarity: the hand reaching, finding the gun handle inside the dark recess of the jacket. And she seemed unable to move, simply standing there, her hands coming to her mouth, her mouth opening in a slow, slow scream. The hand pulling the gun out, turning back around, slowly, so slowly.

A moving blur came into view on her left, trying to surge forward, and a scream ripped down the hall, not her own, but another's deep cry of denial.

The gun pointed, focused and fired.

The bang exploded loudly in the silence, jerking her from her shock as Shadow made contact with the stranger's gun arm, the bullet whizzing by her ear. They scuffled, dark blue suit mixing and blurring with tan overcoat until it was impossible to see who had whom. And then there was another shot, one last blast in the silence as the man in the suit sank softly to the floor with unseeing eyes.

Down the hall, a door cracked open, New York–style, and a pair of wide eyes peered cautiously out.

"It's okay," Riley heard herself call out automatically. "Everything's okay."

The door slammed shut, the eyes not wanting to know more, not wanting to acknowledge that violence could come so close, moving in right down the hall.

But Riley saw it, the blue body on the floor, blood seeping into the carpet, red and blue. Blue and red. Shadow stood over the body, his eyes distant and gray as they searched the staring eyes of the dead man.

It seemed to Riley that he was no longer with her at all, but looking far away into the lost times and lost lives of so long ago. It scared her.

"Shadow," she said softly, forcing herself to stay calm when every nerve in her body trembled at the effort and every thought in her mind wanted to be like that pair of eyes down the hall, closing the door, blocking the scene. "Shadow," she called again, this time more urgently.

He turned his head, and she could see the hazy shadows in his eyes as he struggled to bring himself back into focus. At last he blinked a few times, and his eyes snapped clear, looking at her now in regret. "I'm sorry," he told her softly. "I wish it could have ended any other way."

"I know," she said. "I know. Is he really an agent?"

For a reply, Shadow reached inside the man's jacket. Riley tried not to wince as he withdrew the identification card from the dead man's body. He opened it, gazing at it with a critical eye. "It seems to be authentic," he said quietly, his eyes impenetrable as he looked back up.

Riley could only nod jerkily. "What . . . what does that mean?" she finally managed to ask.

"I'm not entirely sure yet," he told her grimly. "But I intend to find out."

Her knees started to shake, and looking at the growing pool of blood, she felt a little faint. "He was going to kill me," she got out. "He was really going to kill me. But why, Shadow? Why me? I'm just a small connection in this case."

Shadow's head shot up and his gaze zeroed in on her pale face. Walking quickly to her, he tilted up her chin with a firm hand. "I know that, Riley," he told her steadily, "but do *they* know that? You're a reporter with the *New York Daily,* and you know about Ko Tan and about my connection with the DEA. In their minds, you're probably a clear threat, someone who will keep digging for the truth and uncover whatever deal they've got going. And I didn't help matters at all coming here at the first sign of trouble. I'm sorry about that, Riley. I truly am."

She nodded, rubbing her arms idly for warmth. "It's okay," she told him, working to regain her equilibrium. "I'm glad you came to me, Shadow. And I'll help you. I want to know who's doing this. And I want to know now, before anybody else gets killed."

He didn't reply right away, but his eyes grew dark and serious. Finally, he shook his head. "It's too dangerous for you," he said abruptly. "I've risked your life far too much already. I want you back out of this, Riley. From now on, I'll work on my own."

She jerked her head from his grasp at the words, her green eyes beginning to flare. "Oh, no, you don't," she whispered vehemently in the hall. "You can't just barge in and out of my life like that, Shadow. I'm part of this now. It doesn't matter if you don't come back. As you said, they still regard me as a threat. Which means I'm not safe until this whole thing is resolved. And if you think I'm going to just hole up like some little rabbit and pray for the danger to pass, you're greatly mistaken. No, Shadow, you can't just walk away now. Besides," she finished almost bitterly, "you still need my computer."

He couldn't deny her words, and she knew he couldn't. That was why she'd chosen them. Words of logic and rationality. Stark truths that were undeniable. No words of emotion, no words of the need that tugged at her heart. She wanted him to stay. She wanted him to turn to her. She needed him to trust her. She wanted to help get rid of the threat to his life. No, she hadn't chosen any words he might deny. She wasn't feeling up to the rejection.

And because she chose such words of logic, he didn't dare reply with any phrases of gratitude. Such as what it meant to him to have someone actually fight for him. What it meant to have a woman like her asking to help him. What it meant to have her in his life. . . .

He didn't say any of those things, though they burned in his throat.

"What do we do now?" she asked finally.

"You'll have to call the police," Shadow said at last, glad for the practical concerns that would no doubt keep them both busy for a while, "and report the shooting."

"What do I tell them," she asked.

"Tell them the truth," he said. "I'm probably already wanted for murder, so one more APB for my arrest can't hurt matters much. Besides, as a reporter, your version of the truth may be more credible. And at least then we can get on record that something is definitely wrong in the DEA's office. Otherwise they wouldn't be shooting at civilians."

She nodded. "And what are you going to be doing meanwhile?"

He shrugged. "I have some things I want to check on" was all he said.

Her eyes narrowed. "Shadow—" she began, but he cut her off.

"I won't tell you, Riley," he warned. "Because when the police ask you where I am now, I don't want you to know. You'll be that much more convincing. Besides, it's probably safer that way."

She glared at him mutinously, wanting to argue but knowing it wouldn't do any good. After a long moment, he relented slightly. "Don't worry," he told her, leaning over to brush his lips over her cheek. "When I'm done, I'll come back. Somehow I'll make it here."

She wanted to say a million more things, but he didn't give her a chance. Instead, he straightened up, and, turning, walked back down the hall. A minute later, he was gone.

Her building manager was a quiet man with bookish eyes and an accountant's demeanor. Not very tall, teddy-bear round, and with a slow, steady walk, it took him ten minutes to get to her floor after she'd summoned him.

There, he looked at the dead body, blinked his eyes several times under his owlish glasses and said, "Oh, my." Then he promptly reached over, patted Riley's hand and again exclaimed, "Oh, my."

But despite his slightly overwhelmed state, Riley found that he made for good company while she waited for the police to come. In her own state of anxiety and fear, she didn't feel much like talking, anyway.

When the elevator finally dinged, door opening, two blue suits racing round the corner, she felt the first squeeze of tension grip her heart. Oh, God, what had happened to her life?

But then there was the shouting, and she collected herself mentally. Showtime. Paramedics wheeled frantically down the hall, only to lean down and pass the verdict she already knew.

From there on it went very fast, with the sharp drill of questions thrown at her over and over again. Given that it involved the DEA, the FBI was called in to grill her, too, and they were definitely pros at it. What was her name? What was her profession? What did the dead man want? What did he ask? What did she answer? Why did she shoot him? Who was Shadow, then? Where was he now? Why did she let him go? When would he be coming back?

And on and on it went, for hours upon hours, as they searched for the tiniest break in her story. Finally, when no discrepancies were forthcoming, one kind gentleman came over, offering her a glass of water from her own kitchen.

They questioned her until nearly three in the morning. Only then did they leave, and that was after warning her they would be watching her closely. As if *she* were the criminal. But by then she was beyond any rage or indignation. Instead she simply crawled into bed and fell immediately into a deep sleep.

Outside, the rain, which had started earlier, continued to fall.

Shadow walked alone in the night, picking his way steadily down the streets, the rain plastering his hair on his head. He seemed not to notice as people scrambled for cover around him.

He didn't try to hide, didn't cower around corners or dodge from doorway to doorway. Instead he kept in the open, walking as a normal, innocent man would. His only concession was to keep his head tilted slightly to one side, obscuring his distinguishing scar in the fading light. Thus he passed by more than one police officer without attracting notice. For, after all, what was there worth noticing?

Night had fallen, bringing shifting shadows with it. Soon he was in Chinatown, and there the mass of glowing lights lit up the streets like daylight. He passed shops with neon dragons and shops with live eels. He passed the brilliantly painted walls of a tattoo parlor and then the sinuous drawings that signified a massage parlor. But he rarely turned his head, for he knew exactly where he was going.

Straight down the block, past the curio shops, the restaurants, the hotels, past exotic bookstores and the scent of burning incense. Around the corner, where the shadows lengthened and the crowds of people thinned down to small groups of young men with strutting walks and the discreet bulge of knives. Around another corner, where the lighting was somewhat better and a sign boasted Rare Chinese Antiques.

He entered, and the proprietor, elegantly dressed in a gray silk suit, was immediately nervous. But he smiled at his customers to cover, talking faster, his Chinese accent becoming thicker. And as subtly as possible, he showed the few shoppers out the door until only Shadow remained.

Even then, the man was tense, moving in a choppy, agitated fashion. The man already knew Shadow, knew him too well for his taste. Found guilty of smuggling opium into the States in Buddhist statues, the store's proprietor had only gotten off by leading the DEA's special task force, Group 41, to a far bigger fish. It had been six years, but he was only now beginning to sleep at night. Shadow's appearance would most certainly bring back the nightmares for weeks.

So the proprietor bustled around, wringing his hands and wondering just who might have seen this man enter his store. But his agitation was useful. He wanted Shadow gone as quickly as possible and Shadow was only too happy to comply—after a few questions, of course.

For this man, with all his underground connections, would have heard of any talk concerning Ko Tan and, most important, the missing bodyguard. It was the one detail about Ko Tan's murder that concerned Shadow at the moment. Ko Tan never went anywhere without his bodyguard. And yet, while Ko Tan had showed up dead, the bodyguard hadn't been found at all. Could he be the missing link in the picture? The person calling the shots, bribing people within the DEA's office? It was a hunch worth following, but unfortunately it was also incorrect.

Wringing his hands all the while, the store owner managed to stutter out that the bodyguard had indeed been found. Not far from the warehouse. Among the garbage cans.

When Shadow left the store with a silent nod, his face was a great deal grimmer but not remarkably surprised. Whoever was orchestrating this deal was certainly playing for keeps. The question was, who?

Who would have the power—the money—to penetrate even the DEA? Who would know Ko Tan's agenda well enough to plan the assassination?

He needed the answers, and he needed them now. His own life, and the life of one particularly beautiful woman, depended on it.

He walked faster, the darkness falling thicker and thicker as he left the glow of Chinatown. For him, the Orient signified the majority of his adult life, the last ten years having been spent with the Group and the DEA. But now he moved away, to darker streets bearing darker memories of darker times.

Soon he was deep into the heart of the mass of alleyways, side streets and dead ends that constituted the underworld of New York. Here sidewalks cracked and heaved, garbage littered the streets, and shadows had a way of appearing and disappearing from toppled doorways. More than once he saw the flash of blades in the darkness.

He'd lived in a world like this for six years when he'd been a child. His mother's death, when he was eight, had left him without a home, and without any family at all. So he'd taken to the streets, skulking through the shadows, learning to survive by learning not to exist. Silent and quick, he'd moved on the outskirts where the darkness proved thickest. Once he hadn't been quite fast enough and even now he could feel his shoulder burn with the memory. Those times were long ago, however, and he preferred not to think about them.

Yet they were a formative part of his life, having taught him the skills to survive. The army and the DEA had finished off the rest, so now he walked the streets, a man with the simple confidence born of trial. It wasn't stupidity that kept him in the open, but understanding. The night was still young, so the criminals were still selective. After one glance at Shadow's steady walk and unwavering gaze, they left him alone for easier prey. As the night grew longer and the desperation grew stronger, the same would not be true.

Soon he came to a rundown block where faint echoes of music could be heard, and the sounds of carousing laughter drifted through the air. He stopped at the beginning of the block, carefully considering the row of crowded nightclubs and bars. Two catered almost entirely to a poorer segment of the population, who took in the badly needed entertainment at the risk of being caught in a firetrap.

But another row down and the bars became catchalls for the downtrodden, miscellaneous ends of society. Shadow headed there.

He started at the first bar and worked his way down. With his ripped jeans, dirty shirt and nondescript overcoat he blended in instantly. He never asked too many questions, never tried to start conversations and never looked around too long. Instead he simply entered, ordered bad beer, smoked a bitter cigarette and kept his shoulders slightly hunched and his mouth shut. Once again, through his very ordinariness, he became invisible. If questioned later, no bartender or patron would be able to identify him. He was merely one of a stream of hunched, broken men that came through each night and tried to ease their troubles with a beer. For them, he was nothing more, nothing less.

Except in the last bar. There, at last, Shadow found the man for whom he had been looking. It had been well over a year and a half since he'd last dealt with the man, but he'd heard rumors just the day before that he was back in business. He was about to find out for sure.

Shadow walked straight over to the table, but the lone seated man with shaggy brown hair and a scuffed-up jacket didn't notice.

"Hello, Mitch," Shadow said softly. The head turned, brown eyes growing huge as they rested upon the man before him. Sweat popped up in little beads on his forehead, and one hand instinctively dropped under the table. "It's been a long time," Shadow continued smoothly. "Mind if I have a seat?"

Mitch's eyes grew rounder and panic bloomed on their edges, but he didn't refuse as Shadow pulled up a chair. "So what've you been up to lately?"

"N-n-not much," the man managed to stutter. Then he gave in to the panic and rushed out, "I'm clean, man. Honestly. I've gone straight. Been straight. Am straight. Honest, man. Honest.''

"I see," said Shadow, nodding gravely. "Congratulations."

Mitch nodded his head furiously.

"So what's your new occupation?"

"Uh, I tend bar here and there. Do odd jobs, you know. Just stuff."

"Sounds a lot like before."

"No! No, no, no. I mean, it's different this time. Honest, man. It is," Mitch insisted furiously, and his face looked so earnest another man probably would have believed him.

"So what's the difference?" Shadow asked casually. "This time you're into knives instead?"

Mitch's eyes popped open, registering pay dirt in the fraction of an instant before Shadow's hand was flashing across the table and whipping out the knife Mitch had been holding on his lap.

"H-h-hey, man," Mitch protested weakly, sweat rolling in one long tear down the side of his face. "It's n-n-not like that at all."

"I don't know," said Shadow smoothly as he flipped the knife easily with one hand. "Looks to me like you're still into weapons."

"A man's got a right to protect himself."

"From whom, Mitch? From whom?"

"Nothin'. Nobody. I already told you, man, I'm not into that stuff." But the sweat was still rolling down, his eyes still circling the room frantically.

"I want information," Shadow said abruptly, all casualness dropping as he leaned intently forward. "I want to know all about what happened to a certain Burmese businessman going by the name of Kaiyi Chu. Who he's been with the last few days, and where."

"Come on, man," Mitch tried to protest. "You can't just show up after a year and a half and ask questions like that."

Shadow leaned back and eyed the man before him for a minute. His eyes narrowed and he toyed with the knife, flipping it over again and again in his hand. He watched Mitch, watched the man sweat, and waited.

After a moment, when Shadow could see the fear building to a fever pitch, he leaned forward again until his voice was just a low whisper in Mitch's ear. "You know what the problem is with this kind of protection?" Shadow said slowly, indicating the knife. "The blade is all wrong." For emphasis, he popped it up, balancing it across the tip of one finger. His voice was friendly as he continued, but with an edge of menace that had the other man paralyzed with terror. "See, the edge is serrated, not smooth at all. Now, if you tried to actually stab someone with it, the blade wouldn't go in very deep at all, the edges giving extra resistance. And that would give your opponent time to come back with a *real* knife. A straight edge that slides in real smooth. And do you know how that feels when it comes out the other side? Do you, Mitch?"

His eyes had never left Mitch's, and now he could see the man squirm, caught fast in the clutches of deep fear. It should have given him some type of satisfaction, for very soon Mitch would be answering away. Yet instead, it filled him with a familiar sense of loathing and disgust. He knew too much about fear, knew too much about how to twist men, how to intimidate them into answering all the questions he desired. It was all too dark, he thought suddenly. All too dark and desperate. He'd spent too long in this corrupt world of the strong using the weak, where only the strong survived. He wanted out, he thought suddenly. So help him God, if he survived this, he wanted out. He wanted to try a real life for a change. A life where he could have a home, a life where maybe at the end of the day, he didn't feel sick to his stomach by all the things he'd done and seen.

A real life. A life... A life like someone might have with Riley.

The thought filled him with almost a deeper despair, and in one crushing instant, he pushed it away. He knew it would never happen. He'd spent too much time in these pits, too much time in darkness. He would never know how to live in a world of sunshine, in a world a woman like Riley deserved. No, he belonged here, threatening weak men, twisting himself a little more, learning to hope a little less. He'd grown up in the darkness, and now he belonged there.

"Wh-wh-what was it you wanted to know?" Mitch was stuttering weakly now, his eyes never leaving the knife still balanced across Shadow's finger. Shadow gave one slow, twisted smile of derision, and felt the despair fill him completely at the sound of the man's fear. But then his eyes hardened, his lips thinned, and for all intents and purposes, he looked like the cold, cruel man he was supposed to be.

"Tell me about Kaiyi Chu."

"Ah, hell, man, you ain't foolin' me. Everyone knows that he was Ko Tan."

"Fine. What kind of deals was he making and with whom?"

"Come on, man. I can't just go around throwin' out names. Hell, I want to live a little longer." A twenty-dollar bill magically appeared on the table next to the knife, but Mitch merely shook his head. "Hey, man. My life's worth more than twenty bucks."

Another twenty appeared, and for emphasis, Shadow twirled the gleaming blade once more in his hand. Mitch glanced around, eyes still laced with panic. Then his hand flashed out and the money vanished from the table.

"He was going to meet with an arms dealer, some high-roller named Thornwall. They had this deal. Big weapons, electrical systems. Expensive stuff. Of course, that's all off now. Left Thornwall in a real situation, after getting his hands on all those weapons, you know."

"Do you know who set up the deal?" Shadow asked. It had actually been himself, but he was curious to see if anyone in the underground had made a connection between Ko Tan's right-hand man and Shadow the DEA agent.

But Mitch was shaking his head. "Naw. No one does. Some guy who worked for Ko Tan showed up eight months ago. But no one knows his name."

"So now, how is it you know Ko Tan's name?" Shadow leaned over, piercing the sweating man with his intense gaze. "What's your source, Mitch?"

"My own eyes. Honest, man, I swear," Mitch babbled out. "I saw them together a few days ago. I didn't know it was Ko Tan then, but I'm not stupid. I heard the news. I can put the pieces together."

Shadow nodded, digesting this bit of news. It appeared then that Ko Tan had personally met with Ray Thornwall. Probably to prepare for the final meeting after Shadow's own abrupt departure from the scene. Still, it was good to know the men had met. He couldn't rule Thornwall out as suspect then, though motive was still shaky.

"So who killed Ko Tan?" Shadow asked bluntly.

"Oh hell, man. You oughtta know that better than the rest of us."

"What do you mean by that, Mitch?" Shadow asked sharply.

"Oh, man." The panic in Mitch's eyes finally blossomed into full-fledged terror. "I don't know nothin', okay? I don't know, and I don't wanna know. Just leave me outta this."

Shadow looked at the man for a long time, registering his wide eyes and the still pouring sweat. Then, slowly and carefully, he took out a hundred-dollar bill and placed it on the table. "Just out of curiosity, Mitch, if you had hypothetically heard or seen anything, what would it have been?"

"Hypothetically?"

"Hypothetically."

The hand flashed back out, and the bill disappeared.

"Hypothetically," Mitch said slowly, his eyes darting once more around the dark, crowded bar, then returning to the silver blade resting in Shadow's hand, "hypothetically, I'd say it stinks."

"Explain."

Mitch leaned nearer, keeping his voice low as his eyes continued circling the room. "Well, man, this whole thing kinda reminds me of Dong. You know, the Chinese dealer from a coupla years back. He came to the States, too, you know, first time in four years. Everyone suspects a DEA trap, right? He's a big-time player and here he suddenly is in New York. People are talking, expecting a bust. But then—bam—three days later the guy's dead. *Dead.* Sound familiar?"

"But that was two years ago," Shadow observed lazily, his mind already turning over possibilities.

"Yeah, man. I know, I know. But still, man, it takes powerful people to knock off powerful people."

"And powerful people also have powerful enemies."

"Sure, man. Sure. But if an *enemy* had gotten Dong," Mitch said slowly, and for the first time his eyes revealed the small glint of suspicious intelligence that had kept him alive thus far, "then why doesn't anyone know who it was by now?"

Shadow leaned back, eyeing Mitch carefully. It was a very good point. Powerful people had a way of eventually bragging about their powerful deeds. If a rival had killed Dong, he would have had plenty of time by now to consolidate his own position and do a bit of crowing. Killing a man like Dong would certainly elevate the new rival to the status of a major player. So it wasn't something to keep quiet about. And yet two years, and not a peep. Not one word.

Group 41 had even been involved in that case, though they hadn't been setting up a bust as Mitch had suspected. While Shadow hadn't personally worked on the case, if he remembered correctly, the Group had merely gotten last-minute news of Dong's plans to come to the States. Of course, the Group had wanted to move on him while he was here, but they'd still been trying to put together a plan when he'd showed up dead. A few agents had looked into the matter, but never discovered anything. In the end, Shadow's boss had shut the file with a shrug. One less dealer to bust, they'd all finally agreed.

And that had been the end of the matter.

Until now, two years later, and nearly the same thing had happened again, except this time with Ko Tan. And this time there was a suspect. Shadow.

What the hell was going on?

But then again, he was half-afraid he knew all too well the answer to that question. It was going to be a long night.

He pushed back his chair and rose from the table. "Always nice seeing you, Mitch," he said, casually flipping the knife back to the other man. "But if I were you, I would definitely find a new occupation. Arms deals are kind of dangerous, know what I mean?"

Mitch nodded furiously, the relief at Shadow's impending departure only too evident on his face. "Sure thing, man. Sure thing."

With another short nod, Shadow turned to leave, but not before he saw the calculated narrowing of Mitch's eyes. Shadow didn't turn back around, though. Instead he took a steady step forward, all his concentration turning abruptly inward, consolidating, waiting.

On the third step, the tingling ripped up the back of his neck, and he threw himself sideways to feel the whisper of wind as the knife sailed by his right ear. The blade lodged in a board next to the door, and while the three burly men next to it stopped to give it a cursory glance, the rest of the bar hardly noticed.

Even those three men quickly averted their gazes as Shadow calmly stepped forward and pulled the knife from the wall. He turned around, but Mitch had already vanished, no doubt running for some back exit as fast as he could.

With a slight nod, more to himself than anyone present, Shadow pocketed the knife and left the bar.

He knew what he needed to know. Now it was time to go back to Riley.

Chapter 12

Riley awoke with a start to find Shadow standing at the foot of her bed. Shrouded in darkness, streaked with two thin rays of dim moonlight, he looked like a specter of a man, stepping out of her dreams and into her bedroom.

She tried to speak, but he motioned her silent with a short movement of his hand. Without making a sound, he came forward until he stood beside her, gazing down with deep, dark eyes.

He simply looked at her for the longest time, taking in her shiny red hair tousled on the pillow, the pale satin of her skin, glowing in the night. He opened his mouth once, and she thought he would say something, but then he closed his lips again, leaving her with a curious sense of loss.

Shadow looked at the woman in front of him and felt something burst inside him. He wanted her, wanted her right now, with an intensity that scared him. The night had been filled with such ugliness, he could almost feel it deep down in his soul. He was a stained man, a man whose living was based on fear and corruption and death. Sometimes he thought he would never escape. Sometimes he was certain that he would die in the very darkness that had been his life, alone in some dark alley, most likely on some mission that had finally gone wrong.

He needed to see light. He needed something pure, something warm, something good.

He needed Riley.

And that scared him.

But he couldn't deny it. It had torn at him, drawing him to her apartment even when he'd known that it wasn't safe, even when he'd known that he should go somewhere else. But he wanted to hold her. He wanted to touch the white satin of her skin, see the clear green of her eyes. And he wanted *her* to hold *him.* Then maybe, for a minute, the darkness would leave. Maybe, for a minute, he could lose himself in the pure wonder of her touch.

Maybe for a minute...

His throat worked once more until finally the words were torn from him. He spoke quietly, hoarsely, into the night. "I need you."

She nodded from the bed, mesmerized by the darkness of his eyes. "How did you get in?" she whispered.

"The window," he said simply.

"But how did you get up?" she persisted.

"The fire escape, and a bit of luck."

"The police?"

"Maybe next time they'll learn to watch the windows."

"It's not safe—"

"Shh. It's all right for now. They're looking for me outside, not in here. We have a little time. Riley..."

She smiled softly in the dark then, gesturing to the space beside her. "Yes, Shadow," she told him. "Yes."

It was the only word he needed to hear. With a sigh, his lips came down, seeking her. In the dark of the night, his hands found the satin of her gown and lifted it up and off with a whisper. In the dark of the night, he searched for the one woman who could possibly save his soul. In the dark of the night, he permitted himself this one moment of hope, this one moment of love.

In the dark of the night. Always in the dark.

His lips were on hers once more, kissing her with an aching tenderness, asking more than taking. She could feel a strain of sadness running through the kiss, a thread of haunting pain she couldn't fully comprehend. He needed her. Tonight he really needed her. She wouldn't deny him.

Her hands found the buttons of his shirt, popping them open one by one, then sliding the shirt smoothly from his shoulders. She found the raised satin of his external scars, and whispered over them with her lips, kissing away pains from years and years ago. Then she returned to soothe his lips with her own, kissing him with exquisite tenderness and gentle need. She kissed the corner of his eyes, tasting the salt that had gathered there. And she kissed the corner of his mouth, the hollow of his throat, the curve of his ear.

She could feel the need building in him, feel him pulling her closer, silently asking for the final reprieve only she could grant him. In answer, her hands drifted to the waistband of his jeans, unbuttoning them and pulling them slowly down until he was as naked as she.

But she didn't give in immediately. Instead, she pulled him down to the bed, until she could feel his entire muscled length, hard and strong against her own softness. Then, starting at his ankles, she worked her way up his legs with teasing little kisses, until at last she reached the top of his muscled thighs. She paused, raising her head until she could see his eyes, burning and needy in the night. She gave him a smile, a sweet, tender smile that revealed all she felt for him. Then she lowered her head and slowly, exquisitely, showed him her love with her lips.

She heard the sharp intake of his breath in the darkness, felt his hips surge forward in helpless desire. But she didn't stop. Her hair spread across his stomach and thighs like a satin sheet, she loved him tenderly until she knew he could take no more. Then she rose and, in one fluid motion, she took him inside her, feeling his hard length penetrate in one long, burning thrust.

She gasped at the impact, reveling in the thrill of having him so close, buried deep inside her, joining them as one. Her own desire took over and, moving her hips against his, she leaned forward, burying her face in his neck as passion swept over her. His hands found her hips, guiding her as the fires blazed hotter and hotter. Guiding her until, with one blinding explosion, they swept over the edge, plummeting back to earth with each other's name on their lips.

Afterward, she lay quietly with her head on his shoulder, his hand gently stroking the silk of her hair. Neither said a word for a long while, just savoring the touch and comfort of the other.

Her own fingers were spread out on the smooth expanse of his chest, feeling the rhythm of his heart against her palm. Then they slowly moved up to cup the shadowed beard on his cheek, turning his head slightly until she could gently touch his lips with her own. In answer he curved her closer, resting his head against her.

Finally, she spoke.

"Are you okay?" she asked softly.

He didn't speak, but nodded his head.

There was silence again, broken only by the sound of their breathing and the gentle pitter-patter of the rain. From where she lay, Riley could see the red numbers of the digital clock glowing 5:00 a.m. in the darkness.

"Did you find anything out?" she asked finally.

He nodded his head, his hand absently beginning to stroke her hip. "The bodyguard's dead," he said finally.

She stilled for a second, then sighed next to him. "Whoever it is, they're certainly efficient."

Shadow simply nodded against the pillow. "How did things go with the police?" he asked quietly.

She shrugged against him. "They asked me a lot of questions, and I answered them truthfully, like you said. They really want to get their hands on you, Shadow. You're definitely the number-one suspect."

"It's to be expected," he said.

"Did you get any leads?" Riley prodded after a bit.

"Only more questions," he told her bitterly. "Only lots more questions."

She opened her mouth to ask more, but he silenced her with a finger on her lips.

"In the morning," he said quietly. "Ask me in the morning."

She nodded, even though she really did want to know more now. But he was tired; she could feel the weariness in his body. They could both use the sleep. With a sigh, she wrapped herself more tightly against him and closed her eyes. Minutes later, she was asleep.

In time, he joined her.

When she awoke again, gray light was streaming dimly
through the cracks in the blind, and the space next to her was
empty. For a moment she felt cold panic squeeze her heart. He
had left her again. He'd come and then simply left without so
much as a goodbye. But then she heard the telltale clickety-
clack of computer keys from the living room. He must be
working.

Getting up, she wrapped her dark jade robe around her and
padded out to the living room. There, sure enough, she found
him in jeans and an unbuttoned shirt, hunched over her small
computer. He looked tired and grim, not even glancing up as
she entered.

"How's it going?" she asked casually, examining the screen
from over his shoulder.

"Slow," he answered curtly.

She nodded, trying to understand what she was seeing. It
appeared that he had accessed financial records somehow.
"Bank statements?" she asked after a bit.

He nodded in confirmation, drawing up a new screen. At top
was the name Robert Hartwood, but it meant nothing to her.
"Who is he?" she asked.

"DEA," Shadow replied flatly. He was scanning up and
down the information, looking at each entry. So far he couldn't
find a record of any large withdrawals or deposits. Nor had he
for any of the other DEA men except for Scott Weinard, the
agent who had tried to kill Riley. Weinard's account recorded
two irregular lump-sum deposits in the last year. Apparently he
was being bought off. But by whom?

He needed to know.

"What about the arms dealer?" Riley was asking.

Shadow nodded, exiting from his connection with the bank's
data base. Using the codes he knew, he shortly accessed the
federal files.

"'Ray Thornwall,'" she read over his shoulder. "That's the
man you contacted for Ko Tan?"

Shadow nodded. "He has a legitimate high-tech electronics
company where he sells everything from home security systems to electric training systems. About two years ago he be-

gan dabbling in weapons on the side. We first became aware of him then, and given how rapidly he built business, we started to pay attention. Getting him, along with Ko Tan, during the bust would have been a huge bonus.''

"And now?"

Shadow shrugged. "According to his file, he's still under investigation. I looked at his bank records earlier, but nothing comes from them. I would imagine he has a Swiss bank account for his illegal dealings.'' Shadow pushed a few keys, and a new screen bearing the name Sly Sleid appeared.

"Who's he?" Riley asked.

"Thornwall's errand boy," Shadow said. "Look at this." He pointed to the rap sheet now appearing on the screen. "Petty theft, possession of illegal weapons, extortion. All small-time crimes, but enough of them to keep a man busy. The question is, has he graduated to murder?"

Riley looked at him sharply. "Do you think so?"

Shadow shook his head. "I think he's too small-time. He takes orders—he doesn't give them. I can't be sure, though, since he doesn't seem to have a bank account for me to check."

With a sigh, Shadow reached behind and turned the computer off. Uttering a small blip, the screen went blank. "That's about it," he said, pushing back the chair to stretch.

Riley watched him silently. "What now?" she asked.

He didn't look at her right away, staring at the wall instead. "I have to go," he said shortly. "It's not safe to stay here anymore. They might come back to ask you a few more questions."

"But where will you go?" Riley argued.

"Don't worry about it," he said abruptly.

She stared at him suspiciously. "You know something, don't you?" she accused.

He didn't deny or agree with the statement. Instead he began buttoning his shirt.

Her eyes narrowed, and her jaw tightened. "What did you learn, Shadow?" she demanded to know. "Tell me what's going on."

His hand paused for a minute, then quietly resumed its task. "Nothing's going on, Riley," he said levelly.

But she shook her head. "I don't believe you," she said boldly. "I think you *did* learn something, but you're not going to tell me. Why, Shadow? I'm here to help you, dammit. If you'd just let me—"

His hands reached the last button as he cut her off. "It's for your own good. Just trust me, Riley."

Abruptly her anger exploded. He'd left her in the dark once too often, danced around her questions too many times. Just hours ago he'd said he needed her. Now he wouldn't even talk to her. She just couldn't take it anymore.

"Damn you," she told him, fists clenching and eyes darkening with frustration. "Damn you, damn you. Who are you to talk to me about trust? You haven't trusted me since the day we met. Always harboring your secrets, always keeping your thoughts and discoveries to yourself. Well, it's not right, Shadow," she said urgently, "things can't work like this. I need you to talk to me. I need you to let me in."

"I can't," he said simply. "For your own sake, I can't tell you anything—"

"No." This time she cut *him* off. Fiercely, she continued, "Don't shut me out and then tell me it's for my own good. I'm not a child and you're not my parent in charge of protecting me. I'm a grown woman who knows the risks involved here and has the right to take them. You think I don't understand the kind of danger staring us in the face? For God's sake, Shadow, a man just tried to kill me yesterday. I'm not an idiot. I understand the implications of that."

"Then you can understand why I need to protect you."

"But I don't want you to," she protested. "Don't you understand that yet? I have never asked for your protection, nor do I want it. We are in this together. I accept that. Why don't you?"

"It doesn't matter," he said abruptly, and she could see the anger beginning to build in the depths of his eyes. "I won't put you into any more danger, Riley. I won't risk you. It's final."

At the words, Riley spun around in frustration. Then, her eyes growing darker, she turned back around and placed her fists on the front of Shadow's just-buttoned shirt. With one smooth motion, she ripped it open.

"Fine," she retorted angrily. "If you refuse to let me in on that subject, then let me in on this." Her hand came to the round scar on his shoulder. "How did you get this?" she demanded. "Tell me, Shadow."

"You know I don't talk about such things," he warned softly. "So why demand it of me?"

"Because I want to know," she cried. "Because I need to understand this person I'm with. Because I need to know that you trust me enough to talk to me."

"It's not a matter of trust."

"What then? Are you afraid? Are you afraid to open up and let me in because you'll lose me? Because losing me will hurt, like losing Nemo, like losing Johnny?"

"Don't," he told her. "Just don't."

"Why not?" she demanded intensely. "Come on, Shadow. You've spent all this time shutting me out, and frankly, I'm tired of it. I'm tired of wondering who the real Shadow is. I'm tired of trying to guess who it is that I'm sleeping with. I won't bite, Shadow. And I won't just walk away, either. So please, open up. Stop living on the edge of life, watching everything go by. Demand a slice of life for yourself. Open up and live, Shadow. *Live.*"

"Do you think it's so simple?" he said, and all of a sudden there was a wealth of bitterness in his voice. "I am who I am, Riley. That's just the way it is."

"But *who* are you?" she asked, desperation now edging her voice. "Do you realize that after all this time, I don't even know your name?"

"You know as much as I know," he informed her curtly.

"What is that supposed to mean?" she said in frustration again. "I'm sorry, but I simply don't understand all of your riddles."

"It means," he explained sharply, "that you know as much as I know. You know my name is Shadow, that's all you know. And that's all *I* know."

"But you couldn't have been born with that name," she insisted. "No one is born with a name like Shadow. Besides, the military would never go for it."

"While the government insisted on assigning me a last name in order to issue a social security number, they kept Shadow as my first name. If I ever had another name, I don't remember," he said flatly. "Whatever I was called before, I don't remember."

The answer silenced her, reining in her anger abruptly as she looked at the man before her. His eyes were angry now, but they were also clear and honest.

"What about your parents?" she asked. "Don't you have a family?"

"No."

Her eyes widened, and she couldn't stop the rush of confusion and sadness. But instead of welcoming it, he turned away coldly. "Don't," he told her in a tight voice. "Don't look at me with pity. I've never wanted that."

"I'm sorry," she said immediately, reaching out and resting a hand on his shoulder. "I didn't mean to do that. It's just . . . It's just a lot to absorb at once. Were you in an orphanage?"

He shook his head. "My mother was alive for a while," he said, his voice sounding distant now. "I lived with her then."

"How old were you when she died?"

"Eight."

"What was she like?" Riley prodded softly. She moved, walking around him until she could see his eyes again. They were a soft gray, gray and distant. "Do you remember her at all?" Riley whispered.

"A little." His eyes focused inward, peering into the past that hovered on the edge of memory. "She smelled of lilacs," he whispered, almost against his will. "She had soft gray eyes, and she smelled of lilacs."

"You loved her. You loved her a lot," Riley said, a peculiar catch in her throat.

He smiled, but it was a bitter smile. "Yes, I loved her a lot. A thin, frail woman who died all alone one day while I was at school. I loved her, Riley, but it wasn't enough."

"What did you do when she died?"

"I ran away. I knew they would put me in a home if I stayed, so I ran away."

Riley frowned, searching his eyes once more, but it appeared he was telling the truth. "Where did you live?" she insisted, not understanding. "Where did you go?"

"I lived on the streets."

"But you were only eight!"

He looked at her with his dark eyes. "Yes, I was. I went from Seattle to Portland. There someone started calling me Shadow, and it stuck."

"Why 'Shadow'?"

He gave a grim smile. "I was small, silent and gray, and I knew how to disappear."

She could only nod, not quite able to imagine such a life. Her childhood, difficult as it had been, suddenly seemed like a cakewalk. Her heart aching for the lost little boy he'd been, she asked, "Did you get these scars then?" Sketching the various lines across his chest with her fingertips, she added, "Or were they from working with the DEA?"

"Both."

"And this one?" she asked, her hand moving to the large round scar on his shoulder. "Where did you get this one?"

"I was on the streets then," he told her. "Some man was drunk, waving a gun around. He was roaring a lot of questions. When I didn't answer, he started firing. I didn't run quite fast enough."

"Why didn't you answer his questions?" she prodded gently. "Were you undercover?"

"No. I was nine at the time, and from the day my mother died until the age of fifteen, I didn't say a word."

She was shocked once more. "Not at all? Not one?"

"No."

"Why?"

"Because there simply weren't any words for what I felt."

The statement silenced her, tightening her throat and burning her eyelids with emotion. *There simply weren't any words for what I felt.* He had been only nine, but already so alone, already so sad. And already bottling everything up and tucking it way down deep. Even at nine he must have had ancient eyes. Even at nine.

"But you learned," she said softly. "Eventually you learned."

"When I was fourteen, I met a woman named Sabrina Duncan. She ran a shelter for children like myself. Eventually, I stayed."

"But then you left again." It wasn't a question. Somehow she knew that he wouldn't stay long anywhere. Just as he wouldn't now.

"Yes."

"Why? Why leave Oregon? Why leave the person who helped you?"

"Because when I first met her, Sabrina needed me a little. We helped each other. She'd witnessed a murder, and the murderer found her. At the time she also met a cop named Thomas and fell in love. I wanted to help protect her, to repay her for her help."

"Did you love Sabrina?" she asked softly.

"I was only a boy, Riley."

"But you still cared," she insisted. "Is that why you left? Because she fell in love with this man, and you were left out?"

"Thomas was—*is*—a good man," Shadow said abruptly, his voice cold. "I knew he would take care of her."

"So you left. Have you spoken to them since?"

He shook his head. "No. But I think she understands. She's very special that way."

For a moment, Riley was surprised by the pang of jealousy that shot through her. Suddenly, fiercely, she threw her arms around Shadow and hugged him tightly. "Thank you," she told him. "Thank you for talking to me."

For a moment, he remained tense against her, defensive against all the words she had forced out of him. But then, with a long sigh, he wrapped his arms around her and buried his face in her neck.

All those things had happened so long ago, and even now, sometimes, they still had the power to hurt. It was why he didn't like to remember, why he didn't like to talk. But this woman had a way of wringing things from him . . . and she had a way of touching him, making him believe that maybe things really could be all right, if only for a minute.

If only for a minute.

He forced himself to pull away. "I need to go now," he told her quietly.

"You still won't tell me where, will you?" she said.

He nodded. "It's just not safe, Riley. This is far more dangerous than either of us imagined. I want you to stay here and lay low. Don't do anything foolish."

Her chin went up a notch. "I won't promise any such thing," she informed him stubbornly. "You do what you have to do, and I have the same right."

"Riley—" he began firmly.

But she cut him off. "No deal, Shadow. You want to be a vigilante. Well, I can do the same."

His eyes darkened to an ominous shade of pewter. "I have training, Riley. You don't. Now, promise me you won't do anything stupid."

His voice was firm enough to make her waver just a little. "I promise I'll be careful," she said finally.

He wasn't convinced, but after a long moment, he was also forced to compromise. Nodding curtly, he walked over to the couch and retrieved his coat. "I'll try to get word to you," he said.

She nodded, though it wasn't the reassurance she needed. She didn't want him to go. She didn't want him to disappear once more from her apartment into the murky darkness of the world. What if things didn't work out? What if the next time she saw him was in a body bag? Shivering slightly, she wrapped her arms around herself.

She'd just met Shadow. Had just started to really discover who he was. Had just started to fall in love.

And it could be gone in an instant. There was nothing she could do.

He stood there a moment longer, not quite sure what to say. Looking at her one last time, he took in her flaming hair, her brilliant eyes. And for one crushing instant he let all the doubt and uncertainty crash down upon him. He didn't know if he would see those eyes again, didn't know if he would ever touch her hair. There was a good chance he would wind up dead. Slowly and surely the pieces of the puzzle were beginning to fit together, but now he was discovering that he was in far more danger than he'd ever imagined. It seemed he had left the jungles of Myanmar only to become involved in a bigger puzzle here.

And for what? After all this time, really, for what?

He felt the regret, stinging and harsh. And even as he pictured Johnny in his mind—Johnny with his laughing eyes, Johnny with his winning ways—Shadow wondered for the first time if the price might indeed be too high. In the beginning he'd understood that this venture might cost him his life. Now he realized it might also cost him his only chance at love.

He reached out, touching her cheek one last time. If only they had met before. If only...

He turned, exiting by the fire escape without uttering a word. He had been right before—there were no words for what he felt.

Riley stood there for a long time afterward, looking at the empty window where he'd disappeared, the tears streaming silently down her face.

Chapter 13

The days grew long and frustrating. The police still hovered outside her apartment, still hounded her with endless questions. And she still had nothing to tell them, for she knew nothing at all.

He'd climbed out of her window seven days ago.

And disappeared without a trace.

Sometimes she wasn't so sure the entire night hadn't just been the creation of an overworked imagination. Sometimes, lying in bed late at night, she wondered if it hadn't all been a dream. But then she would catch the faint scent of him, still lingering in the covers, and know that he'd been there once, even if she didn't know when he'd be there again.

She worried. She worried a lot. In the beginning, she'd tried to tell herself she shouldn't care, but she knew better now. Once he'd been a mystery to her. Once he'd been a mercenary and a stranger. But now she knew this man. She knew the tight control of his jaw, the endless age of his gray eyes. She knew what it was like to touch him, what it was like to curl up and sleep in his arms.

He was an unemotional man, but she understood it better now. His life had been filled with such tragedy, more than she could possibly imagine. From what she'd seen, everyone he'd been close to had left in the end. His mother had died. Johnny had died. Sabrina and Nemo he'd pushed away, as he'd tried to push her away. Closeness scared this solitary man. It reminded him what else was out there, and of all the things he'd already lost.

Just thinking about it made her grow sad, until she was desperate to see him again. She wanted to wrap her arms around him. She wanted to tell him he couldn't push her away this time. This time he was stuck. Because somewhere along the way, she'd fallen in love.

She'd fallen in love.

It had taken her a few days to become comfortable with the idea. First, because she'd never really thought she'd do such a thing. Second, because she wasn't sure she could handle the fear. She loved this man, and she didn't even know where he was. What if he was in danger? What if the next time she saw him was in some city morgue? He'd told her he'd try to be in touch. So why hadn't he called? Why hadn't he done anything at all?

The days remained silent, and it was killing her.

She tried to keep busy on her own, tried to sidetrack herself. She wrote up the ensuing investigation into Ko Tan's death for her paper. Her editor was pleased, and once again it was featured in the front news section. She also tried to find some leads of her own. She started with the warehouse owner, wondering if she could find any ties between him and either Ray Thornwall or the DEA. But it turned out that Arthur Conner was simply a businessman whose business had gone belly-up the year before. He claimed that he'd been unable to sell the warehouse, then bemoaned how he would never be able to sell it now.

He was a rather pathetic person all around, and Riley couldn't see how he fit into the picture at all. Which left her with one more avenue to pursue: Sly Sleid.

As Shadow had said, Sleid was really just Ray's errand boy in New York. But errand boys, especially observant ones, had access to a great deal of information. Shadow hadn't believed Sleid would have *committed* the crime on his own, but Riley wasn't ruling out the possibility that he knew who had. After

all, Sleid had known Ko Tan, Ray Thornwall and Shadow.
Perhaps he'd seen or heard something that might be of assistance.

It was at least worth a try. After all, she didn't have any other
hot leads to follow.

In her years in the city, she'd made a contact or two. From
her early days following the police beat to reporting simple news
briefs, she knew a few prostitutes who had volunteered information from time to time. Now she went back to the streets,
trying to utilize their special knowledge of the underground to
help her track down Sleid.

Armed with his picture from the police file, she even spent
one night going from one bar to the next, hoping to elicit comment. Often as not, it was what wasn't said that told her more.
But even the one bartender who'd become aggravated upon
seeing the photo hadn't panned out. She'd gone by the place for
the last four nights without avail.

The streets remained silent. And the phone refused to ring.

Somewhere out there was the man she'd given her heart to.
And she had no idea where.

The man detached himself from the dark shadows with deceptive silence. Moving smoothly, he edged along the outside
wall until he came to the window. Extracting a small glass cutter from his pocket, he quietly cut a circle in the glass, detaching it completely with a suction cup. Then, with one last glance
at the surroundings, the man reached in, unlocked the window
and slowly raised it up. With a small heave, he pushed himself
through the opening and closed the window behind him.

Then he selected one of the fine leather chairs and sat, waiting.

He didn't have to wait long.

Just five minutes later, the front door opened, and Bob
Hartwood entered his apartment. With a small click, Shadow
reached up and turned on the light. "Hello, Bob," he said quietly.

Hartwood paused in the doorway, surprised by the sudden
appearance of the man before him. But then, recovering himself, he shut the door behind him, sliding the bolt lock se-

curely in place. "Shadow," Hartwood acknowledged as he hung up his coat. "I didn't expect to see you here."

"Where did you expect to see me?" Shadow quizzed casually. "In jail?"

The older man frowned, stepping forward into the living room. "You know we'll do everything to help you," he stated firmly, but Shadow only shook his head.

"It took me a week to put it all together," Shadow told him quietly. "I'll give you credit for that. But in the end, even you left a trail. It's funny, Bob. I spent a year and a half in the jungle with a murderer. The last place I ever thought I'd confront such ugliness was here, with my own boss."

Hartwood frowned again, doing his best to look confused, although his step faltered. "Now, Shadow—" he began.

But Shadow cut him off with one short motion of his hand. "Forget it. I don't want any more lies. Too much of my life has been lies, and I'm tired of it. I want the truth, Bob. I want all the cards on the table. You orchestrated it. It had to be you. I want to know why."

"I don't know what you're talking about—"

"Cut the crap, Bob. I know it was you. Actually Mitch tipped me off to it. He brought up the matter of Dong. You remember Dong, don't you? Another prominent drug lord who just *happened* to suddenly come to the States and just *happened* to wind up dead. A lot like Ko Tan. And, just like Ko Tan, the Group was involved. I wondered about that for a while, Bob. Who would be in a position to know about Dong, who was also in a position to know about Ko Tan? You, of course. And who knew about my undercover mission with Ko Tan? You, of course. And who knew about Riley? You, of course. Always you."

Hartwood shifted his weight from side to side, looking very uncomfortable. "Shadow—" he tried again.

But once more Shadow cut him off. "Just tell me why, Bob. That's what I haven't been able to figure out, yet. The motive. Originally I was thinking someone in the DEA had been bought, but I couldn't find any record of large deposits in your account. Do you use a Swiss account?"

Hartwood stiffened slightly. "I'm not a dirty agent," he uttered coldly.

"Oh?" Shadow asked sarcastically. "Then what do you call it these days? For God's sake, Bob, you tried to kill an innocent bystander. A young female reporter."

For the first time, Hartwood's shoulders slumped forward. His features fell, the accusation seeming to overwhelm him. "Things got out of hand," he whispered finally. "Everything just got out of hand."

Shadow nodded, but his face was still cold. "Start talking, Bob. Start talking *now.*"

The older man sighed, the fight leaving him completely. He walked forward and collapsed onto the couch in front of Shadow.

"There's just four of us," Hartwood said slowly. "We've been around for a while. Working a hard job, you know how it is. And yet, no matter how hard we worked, the bad guys just kept getting away. The justice system doesn't work anymore, Shadow, you know that. Half the time we finally arrest these guys and they pay for some bigwig attorney who gets them off on some damn technicality or another. It doesn't matter how hard we try, how many good men are killed. Do you remember Johnny, Shadow? Do you remember what it was like to see him shot down and know Ko Tan was still out there, unreachable, untouchable?

"Well, we solved the problem, Shadow. They play for keeps, so we started to, as well. When Dong arrived, we thought about just busting him. But there were so many things that could go wrong, so many men whose lives might be lost. Like Johnny, Shadow. Just like Johnny. So we came up with a different idea. Something neater, cleaner. Assassination."

"So you killed Dong," Shadow finished for him, getting to the bottom line.

"We paid a man to," Hartwood admitted. "Nice thing about this business. You get to hear who's for sale."

"And Ko Tan?"

"The same. Well, at least it was supposed to be the same."

"What? You panicked, thought you needed someone to hide behind, so you turned me into the patsy?" Shadow demanded to know.

But Hartwood shook his head. "We didn't panic. Shadow, we never intended to frame you. Please believe that. We were

looking to help agents, not hurt them. No, the hired gun panicked. He thought he'd been spotted, and he was looking for a
diversion. Knowing about you, he thought to throw suspicion
your way. Afterward, we couldn't very well undo it.

"And then Weinard got out of control. He'd been nervous
all along, and you getting the blame seemed the perfect out. But
then you started looking into things, and Weinard found out
about Riley and her journalist background. I think it scared
him, I don't know. I never knew what he intended. If I'd
known, Shadow, I would have stopped him, I swear it."

"Not good enough," Shadow informed him coldly. "You
took an oath, Bob. We all took oaths. We're supposed to defend the damn laws, not break them. And don't tell me about
Johnny. I was there—*I* held his head, *I* watched the blood soak
into my clothes. And if he could see what you've done now, he
would be sick. So don't tell me about him. You crossed the line.
You became the evil you were supposed to fight. There's no
excuse for it. None at all."

His voice was strong with the conviction of hard-earned
knowledge. He'd lived his life in the darkness, had despaired of
ever escaping it. But he *had* held out. He hadn't plunged over
the edge completely. He knew that for sure because of Riley. He
knew because, when he saw her, he could see the light again.
And he could touch her, he could feel her beauty, and know it
wasn't all lost yet. She was everything good and pure. She was
everything he'd vowed to defend in both the army and the
DEA. And seeing her, being with her, let him know it was
worth it. Somewhere out there, the light still burned. Which
made his boss's actions and logic all the more twisted and evil.

Now he stood up, strong and cold before the man who had
once been his mentor. "It's over now," he told Bob curtly.
"You have to turn yourself in. It's the only way, Bob. It will all
just keep going downhill from here. You know that."

But Bob was shaking his head. "I can't do that," he told
Shadow. "This is my life. I can't just give up."

"No—" Shadow began.

But all of a sudden a small chrome gun was pointed at him.
Hartwood's eyes were wilder now, but his grip on the gun was
steady. "I won't give myself up," he told Shadow desperately.

"Things may have gotten out of control now, but if we can just get through this, I won't do it again. I swear."

Shadow looked at him, long and hard. He could feel a small trickle of sweat whisper down his back, but none of it showed on his face. The situation demanded complete control, and this was what he excelled at. "And how are you going to do that, Bob?" he asked quietly. "Are you going to shoot me? Are you really willing to kill your own agent in cold blood?"

The gun wavered.

"Come on, Bob," Shadow prodded, pushing his advantage. "Either shoot me, or put the gun away. And you'll have to shoot me, boss, because I won't just let things go. You know me well enough to know that by now. So, what do you say? Are you going to kill me after all these years?"

The gun wavered one last time. Then, with a small choking sob, Hartwood sank slowly to the floor, letting the gun drop, and burying his head in his hands. Shadow watched him for a long while, the control still tight on his face. All these years he'd known this man. All these years he'd trusted him. And Hartwood was dirty. In actuality, Shadow would have been here days ago, except that he'd had a hard time getting himself to believe the final facts. This man had been his superior. Shadow had respected him, looked up to him.

But Hartwood had spent too long in the darkness, and in the end, it had won.

Grimly, Shadow squared his shoulders. In the last few days, he'd done a lot of thinking. And most of it had involved one certain, beautiful, red-haired woman. He'd told himself, if he could get them both out of this, survive this one last case, then he would give up this life. He was going to walk away from the darkness after all these years. And maybe, just maybe, he could build a future with her instead. He'd promised himself he would try, if he just made it out.

And now he had. Now it was time to go home.

Bending down, he touched Hartwood's shoulder. "Tell me who you hired," he asked quietly.

The phone rang a little after ten, making Riley jump at the computer. It was one of her informants. Sleid had just arrived at the bar. Riley thanked her and hung up, then took a deep breath. Game time.

She still wasn't completely convinced of her plan, but it was the best she could do. Originally she'd contemplated approaching Sleid as a reporter. But given his line of work, she figured he would probably just clam up. After all, errand boys who talked to reporters probably had a hard time getting a job, or staying alive for that matter.

That was when she'd hit on option B. How would the infamous Sleid respond to a beautiful woman instead? As the answer to this question wasn't exactly clear, her plan wasn't foolproof, but Riley had done a bit of acting in high school and college, so she figured she could play the femme fatale for an evening. With a bit of simpering, and hopefully a great deal of booze, perhaps she could get Mr. Sleid to do a bit of bragging.

Accordingly, she put together a rather shocking outfit consisting of a tight black leather skirt, a deep purple off-the-shoulder blouse, fishnet stockings and three-inch heels. It certainly looked overt enough, and she complemented it with teased hair and a solid layer of makeup. Popping a piece of bubble gum into her mouth, she completed the picture with a long, swinging stride.

She was ready.

Dimly, she remembered Shadow's warning to lay low. But she ignored it. "Laying low" wouldn't do any good. And she wasn't a waiting kind of woman. Especially when it involved the man she loved.

With another deep breath, she peered down the hallway. No cops were in the immediate area, so she ran for it, praying her ankles would hold out. Minutes later she was out on the street, flagging down a cab. Fifteen minutes after that, she was there.

Having gone to Ernie's before, she was already prepared for the neighborhood. Even so, her stomach rolled as she stepped forward and her heel clicked against a discarded hypodermic needle. But there was no going back. So, with a determined shake of her fiery hair, she stuck up her chin, practiced her shimmy, and entered the bar with a seductive flourish.

She saw Sly Sleid right off, sitting on a bar stool where, judging by the number of empty bottles before him, he looked to be on this third beer. He was younger than she'd expected, not any older than herself. And from the entrance, he seemed almost a sad figure to her, hunched over his beer with sagging shoulders. His hair was a nondescript brown, his cheeks sported a shadowy beard, and he wore a bright purple sports coat that simply added to his image of apathy.

She didn't go over to him immediately. Instead she sashayed up to the rundown bar, took the stool right across from Sleid and then proceeded to cross her legs in a display that instantly earned her four companions.

With a practiced throaty laugh she dismissed them all and ordered a beer. Then, with a slow smile, she sat and waited. It didn't take long. The minute he glanced over he saw her, and he would have had to be blind not to get the message she silently sent with her heavily mascaraed eyes. Playing along, she flashed him a wink, then blew a bubble with her gum before coyly turning away to admire some beer poster.

She almost toyed with a strand of her hair, but then decided that would be overdoing it. After a long moment, she risked another glance to find that Sleid was once again staring morosely at his beer. With a sigh, she realized she was going to have to make all the moves herself.

She waited another five minutes, then slowly slid from the bar stool and sauntered closer. "Hi," she said, and cracked her gum loudly as she gave him a blatant once-over.

"W-w-what?" Sleid stuttered.

"Hi," she tried again. "Mind if I sit down?"

He looked around at the empty bar stools, then stared back at her. "Yeah. I guess. I mean, no one sitting there or anything. So sure. Yeah. Of course."

She was beginning to wonder if this man had ever seen a woman before. "Thanks," she said with another crack of her gum, then sat down in a leggy display that was sure to keep his attention. "So what's your name, sugar?"

"Mine?"

She managed to giggle, and was enormously pleased with the results as he blushed uncontrollably. "You're kinda cute," she said and giggled again. God, this role was sickening. "Wanna buy me a drink?"

He certainly did, and in the process decided to buy himself another, as well. Riley was careful to sip slowly, but under her calculated maneuverings, she soon had the man downing beers like water. It was a simple equation, really. The more she flirted, the more he drank. And the more he drank, the better he thought the whole deal was.

Soon, Sleid was an enormously happy man. As he downed his tenth beer, his shoulders were back, his chest puffed out and his arm was hanging around the hottest girl in the whole damn bar. And she was with *him*.

"So, what do you do, sugar?" Riley cracked and giggled. It was time to start getting some information here. Her feet were beginning to ache and her jaw was tired.

"Oh, I'm important," he assured her and took another sip of his beer. "Very important."

"Wow," she giggled again. "I like important people." For emphasis, she ran one long painted nail down the front of his sports jacket, and Sleid wound up downing the entire beer in one gulp.

"Then I'm 'specially important," he declared with a slight slur. "Def'nitely, def'nitely important."

"Ooh. Tell me more." Her own display was starting to disgust her, but, boy, was it effective.

"I do important stuff," he declared grandly. "I take care of things."

"Wow," she said breathlessly, leaning slightly forward. "Tell me," Riley whispered in his ear. "Is it dangerous stuff?"

"Oh yeah. Def'nitely. Very dangerous."

"Wow. Have…have you ever…well…you know… Have you ever killed a man?"

"No," he said with a slight hiccup, then saw how she deflated visibly, pulling away an entire foot. "But," he amended quickly, "I know someone who did."

She perked up again. "Really? Did you see it?"

He looked a bit uncomfortable now, but then he puffed his chest back up. "Yep, I did."

"Who did it?" she breathed out with wide eyes.

"Oh, no," he said with a wave of his hand. "I can't tell you that. That would be dangerous."

Once again, she appeared deflated. "Oh," she said quietly. "Oh, I guess I understand." But her voice didn't sound very convinced.

"Well, well, I can't," he tried again, but she just looked at him with big, sad eyes. "No, no... well..."

He didn't get any further. Before Riley's very eyes, a huge man rose out of the booth behind them, his meaty fist landing on Sleid's shoulder. She saw Sleid's eyes widen, saw the fear chase the alcohol from his blood before the switchblade even popped open with its subtle click.

"You were saying?" the man growled.

"Oh, hell," Sleid said frantically, the sweat popping onto his brow as his muddled system frantically searched for a way out. "Luke, I haven't said anything. Anything at all. I swear, man. Honest. I've said nothing. Nothing."

The rest happened in a blur Riley couldn't for the life of her complete later. What she *did* remember was how the blade came forward and, without thinking, she gave the numbed Sleid a heaving push out of the way even before two men sprang off their bar stools with pointed guns.

A voice yelled, "Freeze!" But the man with the knife sprang forward, anyway, only to be tackled by two waiting men. Within minutes, the police were leading Luke and Sleid away. And while Riley simply sat there, staring at it all in stunned amazement, Shadow seemed to simply materialize before her.

His face was grim as he raked her scantily clad form with steel gray eyes. "I thought I told you to lay low," he said tightly. His entire life had passed before his eyes when he'd looked over and realized that Sleid's companion was actually Riley. Once more his eyes raked over her wild outfit. His jaw clenched even tighter. When Luke had pulled out the knife... The whole world had gone red.

Riley sat up a little straighter at the edge in his voice. Self-consciously, her hands sought to pull her mini down to a more decent level. It didn't work. "I was trying to help you," she said defensively.

"And I was trying to keep you safe," he retaliated sharply.

"Safe?" she quizzed. "*Safe?* Shadow, for the past seven days, I've been going out of my mind with worry. I had no idea what had happened with you and it was driving me crazy. Trust me, I'd rather be doing anything than be 'safe.' "

He wasn't completely mollified. The vision of Luke's knife coming at her was still too strong. "Next time," he found himself saying huskily, "at least wear more clothes."

Her lips tightened, but she bit back the retort that rose to her tongue. Instead, she launched an offensive of her own. "How did you get here?" she demanded.

"Bob Hartwood," Shadow replied curtly. "He was the one who engineered this whole thing. He and a few others paid Luke to get Ko Tan, so we came to get Luke here."

"Bob Hartwood?" Riley quizzed. Then her eyes opened wide. "You mean your boss?" Shadow only nodded, his eyes deep, unreadable pools. But Riley understood. She didn't need words this time, for she'd come to recognize that look on his face. In a burst of compassion, she reached out, placing her hand on his shoulder. "I'm sorry, Shadow," she whispered softly. "I'm sorry."

He nodded once more, unable to speak or think. He could feel the brilliant heat of her small white hand on his shoulder. All of a sudden he wanted to clutch that hand. With the desperation of a drowning man, he wanted to bring it to his cheek and hold it. How many times in the last seven days had he despaired of seeing her? How many times had he remembered the beauty of her face, the brilliance of her eyes, and wondered if a future with her could ever be? He'd told himself that if he could just make it through, he would quit everything to be with her. But now, confronted once more by all the dazzling, wonderful softness that was Riley's, he felt the uncertainties rear up again, hard.

He was just a dark shadow of a man. He may not have gone over the edge like Hartwood, but he walked it every day. He'd never had a normal life; he'd never tried to be just a man. He probably wasn't any good at it. And Riley deserved someone who was. She deserved someone who could talk to her, someone who knew how to laugh and smile. She deserved the best, and he knew he wasn't that.

He was a person of solitude. He didn't know any other way.

Abruptly, he turned his head. "It's over now," he said quietly.

She nodded. Then, for the first time, the full impact of that hit. Yes, it was over once more, like the time when they'd first arrived back in the States. Except now it was *really* over, no more loose ends. In Myanmar, she'd needed him. Here, he'd needed her. And now there wasn't any need anymore. It was truly over.

There was no more reason for him to stay with her. None at all.

For the first time her own eyes faltered, and she, too, looked away. "Will everything be all right now?" she asked finally.

Shadow nodded. "Hartwood confessed to the police, so my name's cleared, and my real records as part of the Group will be reinstated. All that was left was to round up Luke, which is why we came here to his favorite watering hole. And now that's been taken care of, as well."

"What will you do?" Riley asked, fighting to keep her voice emotionless.

He shrugged. "I don't know," he told her finally. "It's been quite a while since I've had to think of such things. I think I'll take some time off, maybe go on a vacation. I'll sort things out from there. And yourself?"

"Write," she said. "My editor really liked my stories for this. I can probably write up the concluding article—maybe I'll even get boosted up to writing feature news stories. You never know."

Shadow nodded. "You'll do well, Riley," he said quietly. "I know you'll do well."

The words sounded final to her. Like those of a stranger seeking some solid closing line. Abruptly she felt the sharp sting of tears in the back of her eyes. She'd missed him so much this past week, despaired of ever seeing him again. Now he was here, and she didn't want him to go. She didn't want this to be the airport scene all over again. She wanted him to stay. She wanted to fling her arms around him and bury her face in the protective warmth of his neck. She wanted to hold him forever.

She loved him.

But somehow she didn't quite know what to say.

"I need to go down to the station," Shadow said abruptly. He couldn't bring himself to look at her anymore. He was afraid one more look at her sweet face would bring him to his knees. He never should have gotten involved, he should have let her be, all those weeks ago in Myanmar. He'd known even then this wasn't the kind of woman you could walk away from. He'd known even then. . . .

Still, the time they'd spent together would be precious memories for him in the long, lonely years to come. Memories of light, memories of hope. Memories of love.

He turned completely away. It was time to go.

"I have to be leaving now," he said in a low voice, his throat suddenly much too tight. "If you need anything, give me a call."

She nodded at his back, feeling her world shatter into a million bitter pieces. *Call him back, Riley,* her mind commanded. *Call him back now, before it's too late.*

But the words stuck in her throat.

Shadow began walking, the door looming ever closer. One step, two steps, three—

"Wait!" she cried suddenly, causing heads to turn. "Shadow, wait." He froze immediately, his heart leaping in his chest as he turned to see Riley jump off the stool and run toward him. "Don't go," she told him earnestly with huge, shining eyes. "Shadow, I don't want you to go."

The sight was almost too much for him, but he forced himself to remain strong. "Don't be silly," he told her curtly. "You're doing just fine, Riley. You have a great career, you're young, you have your whole life in front of you. You don't need me anymore, Riley. And you're much better off without a man like me. You'll be happier, much happier in the long run."

"No," she cried, the tears spilling out uncontrollably and racing down her cheeks. "Don't you see, Shadow? All my life I've been searching. All my life I've run from place to place and story to story. All my life I thought that if I was just successful enough, then this time I would be happy, then this time the restlessness would leave me alone. But it was never my job, Shadow. It was never some prize, some grand scoop I was looking for. All my life, Shadow, all of my life, I've been searching for *you.* You, Shadow. Just you."

"Stop," he tried to tell her, but the sight of her tears was breaking him apart, ripping down his defenses. "It just wouldn't work," he began almost desperately. "I'm not the right man for you. I don't even know how to exist in the real world. I'm all darkness, Riley. I'm all emptiness. I'm...nothing at all," he finished brokenly. "Just a shadow, passing through."

"No," she told him defiantly. "That's not true. That's not true at all. You're not the wrong man for me—you're the *only* man for me. I love you, Shadow. So help me God, I love you." And the minute she said the words, she felt a huge weight lift off her shoulders. Those were the words to say. Those were the words that needed to be said. "I love you," she said again and kissed him through her tears. "I love you, I love you, I love you."

He wanted to tell her not to, wanted to tell her she couldn't possibly love a man like him. But he just couldn't find the words to deny her. He couldn't find the words to deny himself. So he stood there, helpless before the torrent of love and kisses and pain and tears.

"Say it," she demanded from him as she kissed him once more. "Please tell me you love me, too." There was a trace of uncertainty, a desperate edge to the words. Maybe he wouldn't. Maybe he didn't....

"I can't," he whispered hoarsely, feeling himself suddenly drown under the dark onslaught of fear and pain and confusion. "I just...can't."

The animation drained out of her face, her eyes widening, her arms falling from his neck as the words hammered home. He didn't love her. He didn't love her. He didn't, he didn't—

"Oh," she whispered softly. She began drying her cheeks with the back of her hands, struggling for composure. "I'm sorry," she said at last, sniffing valiantly. "I didn't mean to make a big scene like that." She tried smiling brilliantly once more, but her equilibrium was too shattered to pull it off. Starting to feel incredibly numb, she switched to autopilot. "I think I'll go now," she said mechanically.

He just nodded, his dark eyes once more unreadable. She took one more uncertain look, then she turned sharply away. Taking a deep breath, she headed straight out the doors and into the cold night. He watched her go, feeling his heart heave and explode in his chest. He opened his mouth, only to close it, trying to say the words she wanted to hear.

But all that came out was silence.

He'd been alone too long, he thought frantically. All his life, the lone boy without a mother, without a home. Passing through, wandering on, learning to survive in places where more powerful people failed. Learning not to care, learning not to hope. Learning that in the end, he would always be alone.

And now...

His whole life stretched out before him in one long, gray blur. Waking up in the late hours, dreaming of a certain red-haired nymph, reaching out for her soft form. And finding himself alone.

Always alone.

Until what? Until he finally did manage to kill himself, until this time the bullets did hit home? Until it was finally over, and he even died alone.

His mouth opened again, wanting so badly to say the words, wanting to call her back even as she vanished from his sight. She was his only shot at real hope in his entire adult life. His only chance at perhaps becoming something more than a dark and lonely man.

His only hope for love.

He needed her. *He needed her.*

He didn't know when his feet started moving, but the next thing he knew, he was running out the door, running through the night. There, up ahead, she walked, a brilliant blur in the darkness. He headed straight for her. She was still far away, but his voice was loud. Now, after all these years, he finally freed himself from the last of the silence. "I love you," he yelled for the entire night to hear. "Hey, Riley McDouglas, I love you!"

He didn't wait for her reaction. Having finally said the words, it seemed to him suddenly that he'd already waited far too long for this moment. Far too long. Even before she turned around, he was scooping her up into his arms. "I love you, Riley," he whispered fiercely. "So help me God, I love you!"

In reply, she buried her face in his neck. "What took you so long!" she cried. "You've made me miserable!"

"I know, I know," he breathed. "But it's okay. Now we have forever to make it up."

She raised her head, looking at him with luminous eyes. "Forever?"

"Forever," he told her. "I don't want to work for the DEA anymore. I want to resign and build a real life. Maybe out in the country, and you can commute in or fax your work. We'll work it out. I just want to be with you, Riley. I want to spend forever with you."

She nodded, her face lighting up into a brilliant smile. "I love you, too, Shadow," she whispered. Reaching up, she captured the back of his head and dragged it down for a passionate kiss. "Come on," she said finally, breathing harder now. "Let's go home."

He nodded, marching forward with her still secure in his arms. Yeah, let's go home. After all these years, finally a home.

Epilogue

The gray-eyed man looked up immediately at the sound of the child's laughter. Sure enough, the toddling two-year-old was running as fast as her chubby legs could carry her, red hair glowing brightly in the midafternoon sun. Her considerably more graceful mother followed close behind in hot pursuit. One minute later, Riley caught up with the mischievous little Ripley, swinging the girl into the air while she shrieked in two-year-old delight.

Watching the pair, the man could do nothing but smile. Sometimes, it was hard to believe that all this was now his. The small, but cute suburban house outside of New York, the big, mangy dog lying at his feet. But most of all, it was the glowing, pure smile of his wife that still dazzled him, even after three years. Not to mention the clear, trusting eyes of their little girl.

Who would have thought that the street kid from Oregon would one day manage all this? Who would have thought he would finally find love?

The darkness of his past was long gone, the last of the ghosts finally exorcised. The corrupt DEA men, including Bob Hartwood, had all been sentenced to jail for taking the law into their own hands, while Luke was now serving a life sentence for the murder of Ko Tan. Shadow had left field work with the DEA. He was more of an independent consultant now, coming in from time to time to help out with those special assignments where his past knowledge of people, and his contacts, were needed. For a while, he'd even continued advising on the situation in Myanmar, as Ko Tan's death had opened a power vacuum in the Asian drug triangle, and his well-trained guerrillas had disintegrated into fighting factions, Ko Tan never having designated a successor. However, after six months of infighting, one of the corporals had emerged victorious. After killing off the rest of his competitors, the new man had once more solidified control over the poppy fields in Myanmar. Such was life in the drug world.

Though he found it very discouraging, Shadow kept doing his part the best he could, offering expert analysis and a wealth of understanding of the underworld. Slowly but surely, progress would be made in the war on drugs.

These days, Shadow had more important priorities—such as his beautiful family. Riley's career was going strong. She'd left the grind of newspaper life just last year to pursue feature stories for magazines. The free-lance work allowed her to spend more time at home, and considering her talents, was also highly lucrative. They'd built a nice life here. Just watching his family now, his loving wife and adorable child, he felt the contentment like a warm glow through his blood.

All those years of hell, and now here was heaven.

It had been hard in the beginning. A lifetime of silence didn't end overnight. After the case had been officially closed, Riley had spent many afternoons in persistent anger, forcing him to open up. But slowly Shadow had come to leave his solitary ways behind for good. He had learned the wonder of trust, the joy of sharing completely. He had learned that he was no longer alone.

He'd even sat down one night, and written a long letter to Sabrina and Thomas. It had been hard to get the words out, hard to know what to say after all these years. But Riley had helped him, supporting him all the way. And just one week after mailing the letter, he'd received a late-night call from Sabrina. She'd been ecstatic to hear from him, and just hearing her warm voice, he'd been ashamed of himself for cutting such a wonderful woman out of his life the way that he had. She had gotten him off the streets. She'd given him this shot at his future. Without her, he would never have met Riley.

Barely three months after that phone call, Sabrina and Thomas had flown in for Shadow and Riley's wedding. It had been emotional to see them, and even Riley had had tears in her eyes. And after all these years, Sabrina and Thomas had still looked as in love as ever. Thomas had quit his job at the police force five years back, and now both worked full-time running a shelter for children in a converted warehouse. They looked happy; they seemed content. And just watching them, Shadow had known that this was what life with Riley had in store for him.

A lifetime of love. A lifetime of trust, of sharing, of growing old side by side.

Smiling to himself now, he rose from his chair. The old mutt stirred, and Shadow paused long enough to pat the dog's head. Then he straightened, and walked down off the porch.

He joined his redheaded wife and shrieking child in the midday sun.

*   *   *   *   *

HE'S AN

AMERICAN HERO

January 1994 rings in the New Year—and a new lineup of sensational American Heroes. You can't seem to get enough of these men, and we're proud to feature one each month, created by some of your favorite authors.

January: CUTS BOTH WAYS by Dee Holmes: Erin Kenyon hired old acquaintance Ashe Seager to investigate the crash that claimed her husband's life, only to learn old memories never die.

February: A WANTED MAN by Kathleen Creighton: Mike Lanagan's exposé on corruption earned him accolades...and the threat of death. Running for his life, he found sanctuary in the arms of Lucy Brown—but for how long?

March: COOPER by Linda Turner: Cooper Rawlings wanted nothing to do with the daughter of the man who'd shot his brother. But when someone threatened Susannah Patterson's life, he found himself riding to the rescue....

AMERICAN HEROES: Men who give all they've got for their country, their work—the women they love.

Only from

He staked his claim…

HONOR BOUND

by
New York Times
Bestselling Author

Sandra Brown

previously published under the pseudonym Erin St. Claire

As Aislinn Andrews opened her mouth to scream, a hard hand clamped over her face and she found herself face-to-face with Lucas Greywolf, a lean, lethal-looking Navajo and escaped convict who swore he wouldn't hurt her— *if* she helped him.

Look for HONOR BOUND at your favorite retail outlet this January.

Only from…

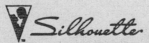

Silhouette

where passion lives.   SBHB